Beyond the Gate

Also by Cristy Fossum
Sunday by Sunday, the Series

BEYOND THE GATE

Cristy Fossum

To Dinah and John ~
   With gratitude for friendship
and for your help with this
project. There are changes but
I reckon it will seem familiar...

Create in Me *Cristy*

BEYOND THE GATE. Copyright ©2020 by Cristy Fossum

Cover art/design by Sara Boggs Rowell
Cover font: Skinny Me by Mike Evans:
https://www.dafont.com/skinny-me.font

Interior design/formatting by Rich Erwin

Author photo by Brad Smith

Printed in the United States of America.
Library of Congress CIP data applied for.

ISBN: 978-0-9820207-4-6 – Paperback
978-0-9820207-3-9 – E-book

Dedicated to my sister Robin

who has flown away to the next world

and who also loved writing stories

Beyond the Gate

1

Aunt Barb had said, "We're calling you a specialist in infestations because you are, Jessie, and we're saying fifteen bucks an hour. When rich people get infested they're desperate; they'll pay." And it had worked, at least maybe.

This was it. Twenty-six thirteen South Harvard Drive. Jessie panted up to the large two-story house five minutes late. A black wrought iron fence surrounded it. She stood at the gate breathing, trying to make her hand reach for the latch. Her head turned to watch a car pull into the wide expanse of concrete driveway and a woman emerge who contrasted to her in every way: large-framed and tall, dark-skinned, professionally dressed and made-up, comfortable-looking in stiletto boots. She hurried to Jessie and offered her hand. Jessie's aim was off returning the gesture—this was her second or third handshake ever—and she wanted to sink into the ground, but the woman easily adjusted and shook firmly.

"Hi, Ms Stewart. Jessica, right? I'm Lauren McCoy. Thanks for coming. This is my uncle's house. He's really let things go since my aunt died a few years ago," she said, opening the gate. "And now we've got problems."

They walked a stone sidewalk through neglected flower beds on each side of the ornate wooden front doors. Lauren McCoy turned her key in the lock, and they entered a foyer at the foot of a wide staircase. Jessie could smell the roaches, like rotten brown sugar.

"Let me tell him we're here," the niece said, and turned right to the end of the hallway and right again down some steps. While she waited, Jessie took in a fancy side table under a fancy mirror. It held a nice lamp but was covered with disheveled mounds of mail. An expensive looking rug littered with yellow cat hair and assorted bits of debris led to light blue-gray carpet on the steps, a dark and dirty path up the middle. Thick cobwebs hung from the brass chandelier. Jessie's nose twitched at the smell of cat pee, a smell she detested.

"He's really let it go," the niece repeated upon her

2

return. "I had no idea," she said, shaking her head and leading Jessie left through the hallway, a string of shipping boxes, opened and unopened, making it tricky to navigate. They passed a small sitting room on the left and a living room and formal dining room on the right, both dusty and cluttered, into a large, sunny kitchen with a bay window breakfast area. *This place is way worse than Aunt Barb's*, Jessie thought, her eyes flashing around. She moved toward the stove where small brown bugs skittered in and out of the burner wells, pausing over crumbs and spills. *That's where I'll start.*

"The exterminator should be here soon. I only discovered a couple days ago that it was this bad."

Jessie nodded and turned slowly around to see dead plants, boxes and bags of trash, an island counter and sink piled high with food cartons, and a sticky, dirty floor. *At least two weeks, maybe more, for the kitchen.*

"What do you think, Jessica, if I may call you that."

"I can do it. I charge fifteen dollars an hour."

"Yes, that's agreeable," Lauren said, but with hesitation. "Now, Jessica, are you sure you can handle this? You seem so—young. How old are you, if I may ask?"

"Nineteen," she said, tucking her gum into her cheek. "I

3

can do it."

"Are you bonded?"

She didn't know what that meant but was pretty sure she wasn't and shook her head.

"Well, I'm having my doubts here. This is a major project. It's a terrible mess, I have to say. I don't want you to be in over your head, and my uncle..." She paused. "He's a good man, but..." She paused again, looked away. "He's had some upsets. His wife and dog died on the same day, for mercy's sake, and, well, he can be very particular—although he's been resigned lately to—or depressed, I don't know—it's like he's lost himself—and I stopped coming over a while back and—oh, gosh," she said, shaking her head like a wet dog and looking back at Jessie, "Anyway, you're very young and..."

"I can do it. Those are German roaches. My aunt had them and I got rid of hers. And I've done three other houses too," she lied for emphasis.

Lauren gazed down on her. "Alright then," letting out a big breath. "Let's try it."

I feel like I'm in a car half off and half on a cliff. It's great it didn't go over, but what now? My next move could tip it. I don't know if I can do this job. It will probably be a disaster. Walking home in the middle of Friday afternoon traffic with its congestion and blasting horns, Jessie's stomach filled with knots of anxiety that tightened and tumbled when she passed by her alma mater, Fremd High School.

She tried not to think at all. That used to be easier, but not now, with everything that had happened. Jessie had lost her father, mother, husband, child and aunt one right after the other. She didn't miss any of them particularly. Maybe Aunt Barb, and not just because she had owed Jessie money when she died. That was causing a problem though, with rent due. *So much,* she sighed, half-stumbling along, her mind ablaze with unbidden, unwanted questions and memories whirling around like sparks from a campfire rising into darkness.

What did my father die of? Where did he live? Why does it even matter? I mean, who cares? Her face in a deep grimace, she walked right into the path of a car turning right from a side street and jumped at the honk. *What happened between my mother and Aunt Barb? What was wrong with my mother? It seemed normal how she came home from work every day and went upstairs and shut herself in her room, but Doug showed me it wasn't. But why did she?*

5

Focusing on the ground, she barely smelled the pizza restaurant or the pungent aroma of the mum beds at the park entrance or even the frightful stink of a duck carcass rotting on the bank of the Salt Creek. Paying no mind to the mechanical growl of the municipal digger filling potholes or the dad pushing his kid in a plastic car stroller who had to swerve out of her way, she walked on, her small body an engine of determination.

She turned into the narrow driveway of her apartment building, worn out by her busy brain, and stepped on a stone, lurching forward three awful times before catching herself. *Okay, okay, I'm okay. In a minute, I'll be safe in my apartment.* She took a left around the building, feeling the sharp gravel through her worn sneakers at the same time a home-sweet-home feeling began to glow inside. But there was Doug's car, and there was Doug, sitting on the rickety picnic table in the small patch of weedy grass.

"How's it going, Jessica?"

"With Aunt Barb dying, I can't pay my rent this month. Can you help me one more time? I'll pay you back."

"Hey, remember? As long as you're my wife, I won't let you be homeless. And you know you don't have to pay me back. How much?"

"Three hundred."

He pulled some bills out of his wallet and handed them to her. "But I can't keep paying two rents, and pretty soon you won't be my wife anymore. You need to get a job."

"I have a job," she told him. "This should be the last time I need anything from you."

"You have a job? What is it?"

"Housecleaning again. Fifteen dollars an hour."

"That's great. I'm proud of you."

She winced. She didn't want him to be proud of her. She only wanted him to go away. But he stood there, looking at her with that look she hated, love or whatever it was.

"We could have made it, Jessica, if you hadn't..." His voice broke, and she started by him, desperate to get inside and lock her door.

"Don't you want to see Fiona?"

She froze, then went to the car, trying to swallow the panic in her throat, and peered in at her sleeping baby.

2

---⚬⚬⚬---

Today was Halloween, the end of Jessie's second week at her new job. She loved the work so much she wanted to smile at times. Roderick McCoy was like a ghost in the basement, so this kitchen was her world to fix. But after writing, "Please cover food with paper towel while heating," and taping it to the freshly cleaned microwave, and finding it the next morning with "No notes!" scrawled across it, she remembered it wasn't hers at all.

From eight to five each day, she stomped roaches on the floor, slapped them off the walls and counter tops, and ground them in the garbage disposal. The pesky bugs didn't bother her as much as the cat. "You are an obnoxious, long-haired bag of bones," she muttered at it, prancing all over the table and furniture as it pleased, haughty and cat-like, throwing up on the carpet leaving faint reddish stains. Worst of all, when she'd be down on all fours scrubbing the floor or wiping the grime off woodwork, it would rub up against her, nudging her arm with its slimy nose. "You are so gross!" she growled, jerking away.

Pulling the refrigerator out for the daily cleaning behind and underneath, Jessie watched the bugs scurry, some of them racing back up into the appliance before she could suck them into the vacuum. Patience and gradual progress kept her satisfied with the job, but her heart hit bottom when she told Lauren she needed another Bag o' Rags.

"Jessica, I don't have time for this," she'd said. "I'll tell you what. I'll open an account at Zimmer Hardware by the town park, and you can go in there and get whatever you need. And here's a key. Have a duplicate made for yourself and leave this one on the counter."

Thinking about it is worse than doing it, she told herself after a couple false starts—walking down the block and back, jittering on a park bench. *People shop every day—it can't be that hard—and it's not my fault my mother and Doug never took me shopping. Okay, maybe it is because I never wanted to go.* She finally entered the old store. There were no other customers, and the man duplicated the key and checked out her purchases with hardly a word. She'd found a fresh supply of Doublemint in a rack by the checkout and added it to the rags, scouring pads, rubber gloves and the new key. *Wow, gum and my own key.* She slipped it into her pocket and walked back to Harvard Drive, lighter and brighter.

Ooh, I love this recycling center! Jessie sorted each item into its proper place simultaneously picturing the orderly spaces left in the garage. Putting her little corner of the world right, along with her painting, had always been her way of handling life.

Struggling to push the last flattened box through the slot at the top of the dumpster, she startled when someone took it out of her hands from behind and pushed it through. She swung around into a young man who stepped awkwardly back. They stared at each other, and then he spoke.

"Um, thank you for recycling. People like you may yet save our planet."

She looked at the ground, wanting only to be back in the truck, driving away.

"Am I freaking you out?" he asked, ducking to look

into her face.

She nodded.

"Oh, no," he groaned. "Okay, I'll go away," but he kept talking. "I thought you were a child, I thought you needed help, but now I see you're a full-grown woman."

Jessie glanced up, eyes magnified through her thick lenses, then stepped around him.

"Thank you again," he said to her back as she walked away. "I admire you," he called as she climbed into the truck.

Stiff as a rod, Jessie leaned slightly to her right to look at him out of the corner of her eye in the side mirror as Kelly eased the truck away. Medium height and blond with an expression on his face both eager and worried. She didn't calm down until they were back in Palatine, driving through darkening streets alive with football players, Dementors, super heroes, and Dorothy in ruby slippers.

"Cousin, how long had you been cleaning for Ma before she died?"

"Four months. She asked me at my mother's funeral. I remember exactly what she said: 'Jessie, I got roaches, baby. How about gettin' your butt over to my house and helpin' me out? Ten bucks an hour.' Except she didn't say butt."

"Yup, that's her," Kelly nodded and blew a trail of cigarette smoke out her window. "You know, you're practically a businesswoman, Jessie, hiring me like this. Make sure my pay covers fifty cents a mile on top of my time, okay? And maybe a happy meal, now you can write it off on your taxes," she teased.

I don't mind paying, but I'd never have gotten in touch with you if I knew anybody else with a truck, Jessie thought, looking out her window. *Gosh, I didn't even see her for ten or twelve years until her mother died. I hardly remembered her. I think she wants to be friends,* and she cast a sideways glance at Kelly. *I don't think she was very nice to me when I was little. Besides all that, who needs green hair? What was it Aunt Barb would call her?* Jessie pondered. *Oh yeah. Ungrateful, disrespectful spitfire.*

"So who's this guy you're cleaning for?" Kelly asked as they drove along.

"Roderick McCoy."

"Well, is he okay?"

"I guess."

"Look out. He could be anybody. He could attack you or accuse you of stealing. He could go paranoid on you at any time. I knew this guy once, he painted the whole inside of this lady's house, bought the paint and everything.

When he got done, she charged sloppiness and said she didn't like the colors. He never got a cent. I'm tellin' ya, look out, girl. You could wind up on CSI."

Whatever CSI is. Probably a TV show. Just drive me home.

After a while, Kelly said, "Hey, Jessie, wanna go see Get Out, that new horror flick? It'd be perfect for Halloween night."

"No." *I want to go home and count my money.*

"Wow, I see you still don't know how to have fun. You were dull as a kid, and it looks like you haven't..."

"But could you stop at Jewel-Osco?" Jessie said, a sudden craving for something yummy overcoming her dread of going into the busy store.

"Oh, yeah, for some Friday night treats? Great idea."

They did their shopping and got back in the truck.

"What'd you get? I got Cheetos, French Onion Dip, a bottle of Merlot, and Almond Joys."

"Coleslaw and gum," Jessie said.

"Wow again. Way to live it up."

I am living it up, with enough money to pay my bills and some left over. All alone in my very own place. A whole quart of coleslaw. That's all I need.

Kelly drove through her driveway and turned left into

the small parking lot. "Hey, when's your divorce hearing?" she asked as Jessie slipped down and out.

"Tuesday."

"Good luck with that. I hope you come out better than my friend Heather. She'll have a hard time getting back to point zero," she said, shaking her head. "Devante, that's her ex, emptied their bank account, and then he..."

"I don't want to hear," Jessie said.

"Oh. Sorry," Kelly said, surprised. "But listen, I'm all ears if you need to vent. Want me to come in?"

Jessie shook her head and pushed the door shut. As soon as she'd locked herself inside, right there by the washing machine, she stripped and put all her clothes in a hot, sudsy wash, a daily routine to kill any roach eggs that might have attached. She put the slaw in the refrigerator, took a hot shower, got into her pajamas and lay down on her bed. Maybe tonight she would start hanging her pictures. They were all safe in her utility room now, all seven boxes of them, the biggest gift her mother had ever given her—not throwing them out. When they first got married, Doug had said they didn't have room for them, but when they'd cleaned out her mother's apartment after the accident, the paintings had come back to her.

Two minutes later, someone rapped on the door. She crept through the utility/entry room and peeped out through the blinds. Doug, with Fiona in an elephant costume. She opened the door, and he thrust the furry ball into her arms. The trunk hung over the baby's head and bopped Jessie in the face. Through the circle in the gray plush, Fiona peered up at her

"I'm going to get a haircut. You two have fun," Doug said, and she was alone with her daughter, who watched intently as her daddy got in his car and left. Then, she looked Jessie straight in the eyes and, after a moment's consideration, let out raucous cries. If she knew how, Jessie would have joined in.

3

On her eleventh day of cleaning Roderick McCoy's house, Jessie unlocked the front door and went straight down the stairs to his den for the first time. He and Lauren were at a doctor appointment. For once, the TV was not blaring, but she stopped on the bottom step anyway and peered around the corner through the shadows before entering.

She marveled at the mess, moving slowly from one area to the next. The smell of old beer mingled with urine odor from the half bath made her cough. Wide-eyed, mouth hanging open, she stole around this wonderland of grimy disorder, pausing at his recliner where bits of food made a greasy layer on the chair and the shag carpet around it.

If I ever get down here to clean, the first thing will be to collect the beer cans. That alone will make a big difference. I'll tidy up those bottles of spilled pills and get a basket or something for that pile of snacks.

A velvety coat of dust covered the whirling blades of the overhead fan, mimicking the purr of the cat asleep in the recliner. The fan had flung years of dust up and around, forming a dark circle on the textured ceiling, like a storm cloud brewing. The window and door frames and bookshelves hung with cobwebs of the same gray filth. The laziness of the cat contrasted sharply to the exhilaration for cleaning this place up that quickened Jessie's pulse. But she also felt wrong being there, afraid she might get caught, and soon hurried up to her own territory.

She was cleaning the inside of the refrigerator when they came in the front door several hours later. "Come into the kitchen and meet Jessica," she heard Lauren urge and then his grunt as he went in the opposite direction. Lauren came in the kitchen but hadn't yet spoken when they heard him fall down the steps. Jessie ran down the hall behind Lauren, and in a flash, Lauren was climbing over her fallen uncle, the two of them cursing, a chaotic jumble of her trying to sit him up and him pushing her away, Jessie watching from above.

"I'm okay, leave me alone!" he yelled.

"You might be okay, you might not, you stubborn old codger. Now let me..."

He struck her hard, and she flew backward. He jumped up in defensive stance, looking down at her, fists in the air.

"Uncle Roderick! It's me, it's Lauren," she screamed.

A long silence followed except for his heavy, horrified breaths. When Lauren spoke again and rose to lead her uncle gently down the last steps, Jessie retreated to the kitchen and resumed her task. *Maybe I should get my coat and get out of here right now. But so much money—and I love this work—and how would I find another job?*

"Sorry," Lauren said when she returned to the kitchen. "He's been having some strange bouts lately. The V.A. doctors think it's PTSD starting up, after forty-five years. I didn't know that could happen. And his arthritic knees are killing him and..."

And he's drinking too much beer and taking too many pills.

Leaning her forehead on her hand, Lauren spoke from a faraway place. "I'm not sure how much longer I can put up with this."

Jessie had her head in the refrigerator and kept it there.

18

Roderick's doorbell rang. *Whoever that is has nothing to do with me, thank heaven,* and Jessie kept mopping the kitchen floor. It rang again, and then, after a minute, somebody banged on the side window of the kitchen yelling, "It's you!"

Her head jerked up in shock and she choked on her gum and dumped the mop bucket. *What in the world? Oh, my gosh. It's that guy from the recycling center! Why would he be here?*

The grin on his face quickly disappeared, and his expression copied hers. He took off. She ran to the window and closed the blinds and then all the blinds in the kitchen and cleaned up the mop water. *Is he still out there? Probably not. He looked more scared than me.* Her heartbeat slowed as she worked, and by the time she started home hours later she'd forgotten the guy at the window. She had more important things on her mind.

She liked the morning and evening walk to Roderick's house except for having to walk by the high school. Afternoons around five-thirty were quiet, and every single time she passed, relief settled over her that she didn't have to go there anymore. Mornings were different, with throngs of students and their incoherent shouts conjuring up

19

memories. One day she had heard what sounded like "pretty" rise shrilly above the chatter and remembered when she and Pam, the only friend she'd ever had, were walking along and a girl in a group of girls approaching said, "Those are pretty glasses, Jessica." She was surprised the girl knew her name, and when Pam said, "She's making fun of you," the laughter behind them made her realize Pam was right.

Pam looked more normal than Jessie, but bullies got on her because she was so thin. "Walking Stick" and "Skeleton Girl" were some of the nicer names Jessie heard. She and Pam ate together in the cafeteria a few times, but they were both absent so much they didn't spend much time together. And then Pam died from anorexia. Jessie wouldn't have known but for whispers in the library.

But today, she didn't even notice the school. *I'm going to organize my life like never before. And I've never had so much to organize!*

She stepped down her three steps and unlocked her back door. She was seeing only a few bugs once in a while at Roderick's house now, so didn't bother to shower immediately. She glanced at the seven boxes of her paintings, stacked against the wall to the right, and passed into the kitchen, grabbing the magnetized list and pen set she'd found at Jewel-Osco and liked so much. Over an egg and cheese sandwich and carrots and celery, she started her list.

#1. Go to bank – She was eager to have a checking account now that she had money. *I'm going to balance my statement like Doug does. That will be fun. But—oh, gosh—I have no idea how to open a bank account. But I'll worry about that when I get there,* she told herself, legs jiggling.

#2. Get file box – For the bank statements that would be coming as well as her divorce papers and time sheets. *What sort of store has file boxes?*

Doug had done all the shopping and public jobs while she took care of the apartment. She'd hardly ever gone out except to church functions with him. Before Doug, her mother had done everything, including buying her clothes, basically a uniform of khakis, T-shirts and sneakers. After these months on her own, buying groceries was getting to be pretty okay, walking across the street and down the block to the store first thing Saturday morning, the place practically empty and the cashiers not awake enough to be talkative. *And I'm not as nervous in Zimmer's, so I guess I can step out a little more.*

21

#3. Get step stool –*I love the one at Roderick's, and I'm going to need one to hang my pictures.*

#4. Fiona. *I didn't mean to write that down. I just can't stop thinking about her.*

"You're her mother, Jessica, even after what you did," Doug had said the day he'd helped her move. "I'm looking for another wife, but at least until God guides me to the right woman, she needs you."

No, Fiona definitely does not need me. I'm still afraid I could accidentally hurt or kill her. When the baby was only a couple weeks old, Jessie had caught her tiny thigh in the zipper of her sleeper. Oh, and there were more terrible incidents. She had dropped her twice, dear God. And knocked her tiny head on the door frame, the poor thing crying out in her baby goat voice. She was more substantial now, but Jessie still hated holding her. On Halloween night, she had left her in that ridiculous elephant outfit because the cushioning felt safer. Plus, she might have broken her arm taking the suit off.

Me as a mother is all wrong. Me as a wife too. Too bad I happened to be outside that day Doug came into our yard–and wound up with me ruining his life.

"Marry this guy, Jessie," her mother had told her a

month later. "You will never have another chance. Never."

If not for all that, I'd still be there on Brookside in my quiet house, cleaning and painting. Except the house is gone to make way for fancier buildings. And so is my mother, gone. C'mon, get a grip, she sighed, getting up to wash her plate and glass.

"How much did it cost?" Kelly asked Jessie, returning to the topic of her divorce when she stopped by Roderick McCoy's house.

"Two hundred ninety-nine dollars with forms Doug got off the computer," and she answered the rest of Kelly's questions. Ten minutes in the Cook County Courthouse on Euclid with a lady judge. Full custody of Fiona for him, unlimited visitation for her. She took her name back, Jessica George again. Afterward, Doug had taken her straight to the photo I.D. window, so she was all set with that. *I know he's a good man. Too good for me, with all his religion and doing everything the right way and wanting lots of kids.*

Kelly broke into her thoughts. "Did you cry?"

"No, but he did, and he wanted us to go out and eat."

"Did you?"

Jessie shook her head. She had just walked away from Doug. It was all she could do.

The formal portrait hanging over the mantle in the living room fascinated Jessie, helped her get to know Roderick McCoy and his wife, as far as appearance. Handsome couple, the wife seated, wearing big jewelry with a formal gown of an unusual shade of red. *That's Red Violet, I remember the paint tube.* Roderick was in uniform standing behind her gold-painted chair.

That morning, Lauren had mentioned that he was in a good mood because a buddy from Vietnam had been in touch about visiting. So Jessie decided to ask him if she could get rid of some cartons stacked in the breakfast area: a dusty and collapsing box of Campbell Soup labels, another of long-expired canned corn, and a third filled with yarn. She made her way down the stairs to his den like she was stealing through the woods, hand on her palpitating heart, and peeked around the doorway. He was in his recliner facing the TV on the back wall, his big arm in a brown plaid flannel shirt resting on the arm of the chair, his square, salt-and-pepper haircut jutting above it. She planned to say, "Mr. McCoy, is it okay to get rid of the boxes in the breakfast area?" hoping he would grunt okay. But when she began to speak, the cat jumped out of his lap with a loud meow and hiss and spooked her. She heard him snort with laughter as she vanished up the stairs. *Who cares? All I want is doing the job and getting the money. I'm just moving the boxes to the garage.*

"American Chartered on Euclid," Lauren said the next day when Jessie asked about a bank within walking distance. "Go whenever you like, Jessica, and good for you, getting your infrastructure in place. You can go right now, if you want to."

She put on her coat and set out, her money tucked in an envelope and her photo I.D. in the small, flat wallet that fit in the back pocket of her khakis. She had not been in a bank before and quivered with both anxiety and excitement, walking up the brick sidewalk past the neatly trimmed shrubs and struggling through the heavy door.

"Hello. Welcome to American Chartered," voices called from different directions, confusing her as she took in the place with its crystal chandeliers and rich furniture.

"How can we help you today?" asked one of the voices, a woman at a nearby desk.

"I want to open a bank account," Jessie said, moving toward the desk.

"I'll be glad to help you with that. Have a seat," the woman said, and Jessie sat down in the pretty chair in front of the desk. "Checking or savings?"

"I just need a place to put my money."

"Will you be writing checks?"

"Maybe. Yes."

The woman unfolded a brochure in front of her and started throwing around banking words—interest and low minimum and high yield. When she stopped talking Jessie said, "I'll take the Free Checking Account that is actually free."

The woman filled out the forms as she supplied the information, then asked, "And how much will you deposit today, Ms George?"

"A thousand," she said, handing over the envelope with fifty twenty-dollar bills. *Gosh, I hate letting go of all that.* But while the woman went to the counter to deposit her money, she reasoned with herself again. *Yes, you'd rather have it at home with you— but stop acting silly—this is a bank—most people put their money in banks—it's normal, it's safer,* and she beamed inside at the feeling of adultness that came over her. She picked out checks—pretty ones, nature scenes— happy to think she could now pay her rent by check. She wanted no part of the free credit card or the services available over the telephone and on the computer. *I don't know how to do any of that—though it would be nice doing business without people.*

After shaking hands with the woman—smoothly, this time—and them thanking each other, she exited into the crisp, sunny day and saw a whole shopping center she hadn't noticed on the way in. Exhausted from the ordeal—and hungry—she rewarded herself with a hot dog and coleslaw lunch at the grocery store restaurant, even sitting down in a booth, then bought a plastic file box at the drugstore. She also went by Zimmer's and found a small hammer and little gold nails perfect to hang her pictures, linoleum tacks they were called.

"You must be laying a whole house of linoleum," the clerk commented.

Uh oh, am I in trouble? I took every box on the shelf, a dozen of them. Maybe you're only allowed to buy them if you're using them for linoleum.

"Um, I'm using them for something else."

"Sure," he said as he scanned one twelve times, twelve beeps chirping out. "Looks like quite a project."

Relieved, she nodded.

27

And then she took a deep breath and asked if they had step stools. He showed her on a computer the different kinds they could order, and she picked one, and they ordered it and said she could get it next week. It cost over fifty dollars and wasn't the same as the one at Roderick McCoy's. She had picked a taller one.

How accomplished she felt as she walked back to Harvard Drive, making a major detour to stick a note on Doug's mailbox that she wanted to see Fiona.

4

Polishing the dining room table and glancing out the window, Jessie felt as colorful and clear as the blue November sky. When her reflection in the shiny wood twinkled at her, a lightning of memory flashed of first seeing herself in a mirror, in kindergarten. *One of the biggest shocks of my life so far. Huh.* Now, she searched for her face in the glossy grain—the close-set eyes, the small round nose, the knob of a chin. The doorbell rang, and she jumped but ignored it as usual. On the second ring, Roderick stumbled down the hall from his bedroom. He tripped over the cat and opened the door cursing.

Faintly, Jessie heard a stammered sentence. "I'm looking for a girl, a woman. She recycles." *Oh, no. It's that guy again.* "I'm eager to express my appreciation for her conservational efforts."

"The cleaning girl?"

"Oh. Perhaps. I once saw her mopping the floor."

Roderick shuffled to the dining room. "Somebody's here for you," he told her and walked back down the hall.

Jessie entered the foyer, back-lit by sunshine, and looked up at him in the wide-open doorway. He beheld her a moment, then said, "These are for you, in gratitude for your conscientious recycling," and held out a water bottle and a tote bag.

She neither moved nor spoke.

"Please accept them. They're Groot Green, which is more than a color at Groot, where earth day is every day."

"Who are you?"

"Oh, shoot, that's how I meant to begin," he said, slapping his head causing Jessie's eyes to open wide. "Oh, and also, I apologize for startling you at the window last week."

He breathed in, wrinkled his brow, and started again, looking at the floor. "Jakob Otteson is my name. Two weeks ago tomorrow, I saw you at the recycling center in Rolling Meadows. I simply want to pay homage to your efforts on behalf of the environment. I believe we share a passion for the beauty of the earth, for the glory of the skies," he said. He stopped and grimaced, face flushing, and began a gentle rock back and forth.

"Oh, gosh," he mumbled.

Silence, and then she said, "I don't get it."

"Nothing to get," he laughed with a nervous, braying laugh. "Do you drink water?"

Jessie squinted and nodded.

"Well then here—uh, what's your name?"

"Jessica."

He placed the water bottle in her hands. "Do you ever buy groceries, Jessica?"

Another nod, and she took the bag when he handed it to her. Still rocking a bit, he glanced toward his motor scooter, parked in the drive, then back at the ground at their feet.

Next, more silence, followed by both of them speaking at once.

"So you..." he started, as she said, "Okay. Um, thank you."

"So you clean this house here for Roderick McCoy?"

"How did you find that out?"

"He told me. Just now. I got this address off envelopes

you dropped in the business mail dumpster."

A car turned into the driveway. They watched as Lauren got out.

⸺

"I work at Groot Industries where 'Earth Day is Every Day," Jakob said in answer to Lauren's invitation to "tell us about yourself." They were seated at the dining room table, also at Lauren's invitation, even serving cookies and lemonade.

What's happening? I didn't want this. I've got work to do.

He continued. "I'm trying to be part of the solution, not the problem. Trying to be the change I want to see. I live in hope that the planet can still be saved, though I have my doubts, especially when you consider that in fifteen years there won't be any glaciers in Glacier National Park at the rate we're going. The signing of the treaty in Paris showed progress, but then we backed out, and will the countries even fulfill their commitments..."

And then, gesturing in his earnestness, Jakob knocked over his drink. "Oh no, not the abominable spill," he moaned. "After you were so nice to invite me in, now I dump my lemonade. Oh gosh." Jessie pitied him in his distress despite her irritation at his presence.

"Don't worry, don't worry, not a big deal," Lauren said, dabbing with napkins. "I'm concerned about global warming and all too, naturally."

He went on and on until Jessie was thumping her feet on the floor so loudly that he stopped talking and looked at her.

She stopped thumping and said, "Sorry. I need to get to work," but Lauren asked another question.

Finally Jakob said he had to get back to work too.

Thank God, and Jessie sprang from her chair like Jack bursting out of the box. Lauren pulled her along to the front door where Jakob apologized for his spill again, thanked Lauren again, and then looked down into Jessie's eyes and said, "May I come back?"

She shrugged.

"Okay then!" he laughed and made his way through the gate and back to his scooter. The women watched him start up and take off, and he and Lauren exchanged jaunty waves. When he had scooted out of sight, Jessie looked up at Lauren and shook her head like someone waking up and trying to figure out where they are. Lauren shut the door and followed Jessie into the dining room.

"Are you upset, Jessica? Have I totally overstepped my

bounds?"

"I don't know what's going on."

"C'mon, he's sweet on you, can't you see that? He's nice and seems authentic. Yeah, different, but in an okay way."

"I don't want a man."

She felt Lauren eyeing her as she wiped up more thoroughly from Jakob's spill. *I did not need another mess. I spent hours this morning clearing stuff off this table.* There had been mail, some opened, some not. Shipping boxes, some opened, some not, from L.L. Bean and Amazon and several from Vet Friends. Scattered pens, paper clips, rubber bands, clumps of cat hair. Half-eaten Cracker Jacks, the syrupy kernels and peanuts trailing across the smooth surface. *I'm amazed there aren't roaches all over the place.* She had found an open box of checkbooks under dried cat vomit and wiped them off and spread them out to dry. Lauren had pushed them aside while entertaining Jakob, and then he'd dumped his drink, and the puddle had quickly surrounded the checkbooks.

"Don't you ever get lonely, Jessica?"

"No."

"Well, huh. Sorry then. I thought maybe you liked him and would make a cute couple. Okay, I'll back off. Sorry.

"And say, I need to talk with you about something else. Uncle Roderick's surgery is coming up pretty soon, you know, and..."

"He took a gun down by the school this morning."

Lauren had been going through the door to the kitchen with plates and glasses. She looked around at Jessie and froze.

"I was crossing Illinois Avenue—it was after nine o'clock because I stopped at Zimmer's on my way—and I saw him walking toward me next to that row of big, tall pine trees and I recognized him and I saw he had a gun, a long one."

"By the elementary school?"

Jessie nodded.

"Oh, my God," Lauren said, clattering the dishes back onto the table and plunking into the chair. "Then what?"

"I asked him what he was doing out there with that gun, and he looked all confused and walked back to the house with me and went to his bedroom."

Lauren put her hand over her heart. "Did anyone see him?"

"I don't know."

"Probably not if nothing's come of it by now. Oh, my

dear God. Jessica, do you realize how serious this is?"

Jessie nodded.

"Weren't you scared?"

She thought. "Um, no. He wasn't acting scary."

"Have you talked to him since?"

"Yeah. I went in there to ask him about the checkbooks the cat earped on and asked him if we should save them or throw them out. He asked what bank they were from and I said Palatine Bank and Trust and he said they were good. I saw the gun on the floor beside the bed and carried it out of there and started cleaning the checks."

"Where's the gun now?"

"Between the refrigerator and the wall."

"Oh, my God, my God, I'm getting it out of here," Lauren said and jumped up and ran to the kitchen muttering under her breath, "This is it. I've got to go, I've got to leave." When she came back in the house, she called her office, said she wouldn't be back that day and headed for her uncle's bedroom.

"The V.A. hospital admitted him, and he went along with it, which surprised me, but thank God," Lauren told Jessie the next day. "As a matter of fact, he was the old

Uncle Roderick through intake and assessment and all that. The one who hasn't been around much lately—articulate and calm, strong enough to cry." Blinking back her own tears, she got a glass of water and sat down across from Jessie at the table, snapping the lid off her Chinese take-out and slurping noodles.

"But I'm tired of it. Hitting me the other week was the last straw, but that's not the worst part. The worst part is not his rudeness, not his dependency that's devouring me, not even his hopelessness."

Keeping her eyes on Lauren, Jessie swallowed the last bite of her sandwich and bit a chunk out of her apple.

"No, the worst part of Uncle Roderick is the slow burning rage coming from secrets I don't want to know."

I wonder what she means by that, but I don't want to know either.

"I don't know if this had anything to do with him taking the gun outside," Jessie said, "but I heard him talking on the phone the day before with somebody named Wayne. It didn't sound good."

"Right. He mentioned it to the psychiatrist yesterday; it probably was part of the trouble. Wayne's his army buddy—more of a brother to him than my dad ever

38

was—and cancelled his annual trip to come and see Uncle Roderick in January. I think he's come every year since Aunt Vevie died. But his wife broke her leg and will be having surgery and needs him to help with recovery and all."

She wiped her mouth with the paper napkin, held it there, closed her eyes. Jessie thought she might be falling asleep. But then she opened her eyes, moved her head ever so slightly back and forth, and seemed to go to the very bottom of her body to draw up breath, then took another bite, chewing and swallowing before she continued.

"I feel bad in all this. Uncle Roderick was my rock for so many years. When my parents divorced and my mother all but disappeared from my life, when my father moved to Arizona with his new wife and forgot about me and..." Tears streamed into her noodles, but she kept eating and talking. "...he was always there for me, until the last few years." She looked at Jessie. "Honestly, I wish you could have known him, the real him, the real McCoy," she smiled.

Hard to imagine him that way, but I can tell she's telling the truth.

"I think it's the war that did it, mostly," she went on, Jessie's eyes still on her. "Combined with Aunt Vevie. I liked her, she was fun and good to me—but not to him. They were a terrible mismatch. I thought he'd be better off without her, to tell you the truth, but..."

"Imagine this," she said to Jessie like she was talking to her best friend. "I almost moved in here! I thought maybe I could help him get through whatever it was that was sinking him lower and lower. I tried to police his drinking, get him in rehab or AA; that was futile. Eventually, I realized I couldn't save him. It came clear to me one day when I got caught in a thunder storm. 'Lauren, can you stop the lightning?' I asked myself. 'Can you stop this rain from falling on your head? No more can you stop Uncle Roderick from living his life the way he chooses.' Then the PTSD started up, flashbacks and all that..." She stopped talking like she was bored with her own story.

Jessie's apple was so crisp each bite cracked, and it sounded to her like she was eating into a microphone. She took smaller, more careful bites.

"Well, this is it," Lauren said, standing up and eating her way to the kitchen sink. "I've been thinking of moving back to L.A. for a while. Now's the time. I've booked a flight for Saturday to go out there and see a few friends and get my networks going. And I'm not going to put it off because of his latest crisis," she said, rinsing out the empty container. "And it's a shame Wayne had to cancel right when so much is falling apart. But I can't help that.

"I'm glad you're here, Jessica. Oh, and listen, he's having knee surgery on December eighth. Would you maybe want to earn some extra money by helping him out with..."

"No," Jessie said, louder than she meant to.

"That's what I figured," Lauren sighed.

5

———✺———

"Fiona?" Jessie called. "Fiona! Where are you?"

Doug knocked, and she ran through the utility room to let him in.

"I can't find her," she told him. "I had to use the bathroom, and she was sitting in the living room with the toy dragon and..."

"Oh geez, Jessica, you've got to be kidding." He dashed into the living room calling her name. They rushed from room to room looking behind curtains and furniture. Jessie expected to find the baby's flat body under something heavy. She could hardly breathe.

"You didn't let her go outside, did you?" Doug demanded, running to the back door again.

"No!" Jessie said. And then she heard Fiona's soft

babble, and there she sat, in the corner of the utility room on the far side of the washing machine, next to an outlet, picking at some torn linoleum.

Doug swooped her up and her baby brow wrinkled to mirror his. He held her to him, rocking back and forth, his eyes closed, then walked back into the living room and sat down. Jessie followed and sat down too. He picked Barney up off the floor and cuddled Fiona and the stuffed animal to him, and she was soon asleep.

"I'm waiting for you, Jessica. I don't know what to say anymore." He shook his head from side to side like a teetotaler looking at their beloved alcoholic.

"I don't either. I didn't mean to lose her."

"Did you hold her?"

"I tried, but I don't think she wanted me to. She twisted away and wanted to crawl."

"Did you talk to her? Did you read her books?"

Why would you talk to a baby? "I read her the one where the duck goes to the zoo, but she didn't listen, just played with the dragon."

"It's a dinosaur."

"Oh."

"I don't know what God wants me to do for you now.

I've forgiven you for the gravest sin, but I've run out of ways to help you. We got you mothering classes, and Stephanie Nordstrum tried to help, she tried hard."

Yeah. It was hard for both of us.

"I know you don't think you can be a good mother and it doesn't come naturally—boy-oh-boy do I know that," he said, pausing to stare at the floor, then shaking his head back to the moment. "But are you even trying? With Fiona? I mean, is there any point in me bringing her over?"

Jessie looked at the floor and shrugged.

"I'm seeing someone, a godly woman named Alicia. I wanted you to know. She has a two-year-old, and she's crazy about Fiona. But you'll always be her biological mother, and..." he choked up "...and Jessica," he looked at her so hard she had to look away. "...this is your chance for redemption."

They sat in silence again until Doug got to his feet, shifting the baby as he rose. "Here," he said, laying her in Jessie's arms.

She looked into the sleeping angel face while Doug stuffed the books and Barney into the diaper bag, the grinning purple head sticking out, and slung the bag over his shoulder. Leaning down to take Fiona he said, "We'll

44

talk more," then walked out the back door with her child.

Instead of the usual relief, Jessie had a different sensation. *Maybe this is lonely.*

―――

Intent on cleaning cat hair off the upholstered dining room chairs, Jessie ignored the doorbell. Soon, there was a tapping on the window. That guy again. Jakob. Not as startled this time, she stood up and motioned with her head to the front of the house, went and opened the front door, and returned to her task. She heard the door close, then there he was.

"Hello, Jessica."

"You know, you're liable to get in trouble for taking people's mail out of the recycling and knocking on their windows."

"I know. I could. I don't do this normally, but I feel safe with you. You seem like you're not going to call the police."

"I don't want to call the police. You don't seem dangerous," she said, looking at him. "I just think you should think about what you're doing."

"Oh yes. I'm thinking about it."

He stood awkwardly while she worked.

"Looks like you're sure getting Roderick McCoy's

house cleaned up."

No response.

"Who lives here anyway?"he persisted.

Without looking up, she said, "Nobody right now." *I could explain about Roderick being in the V.A., but there's no need for him to know that.*

"Oh. Well, have you always been a recycler?"

She shrugged. "I was just getting rid of stuff."

"Oh," he struggled on. "Nonetheless, your actions registered in the universe. And if more people recycled, our environment wouldn't be in dire danger. Did you know that the U.S. comprises five percent of the world's population but generates thirty percent of global garbage? Why, if we would all reduce, reuse and recycle we could save the planet, Jessica! Did you know that if everyone drove fifty-five miles per hour we would save a billion barrels of oil a year? Did you know that if just five percent of us installed solar panels it would equal taking seven million cars off the road? Listen to this—do you know how many pounds of carbon dioxide a recycling household saves every year?"

He knelt on the floor and looked up into her eyes. "Do you?"

She looked back at him and shook her head.

"Forty—eight—thousand."

She released his gaze and moved on to the next chair, scouring it with the rag and coming up with a great yellow tuft.

"In my work at Groot," Jakob continued, looking out the window, his words coming faster and faster, "I'm trying to get the recycling rate in this area up to seventy-five per cent. But, alas, I fear all efforts are too late. Maritime waste threatens to..."

"Yuck! Get away from me!" Jessie cried.

"Oh, no," Jakob moaned, heading for the door. "I've bored you, I've irritated you. Darn it all to heck..."

Jessie jumped up and followed, but the door shut in her face, and he was gone. *Oh gosh, I wasn't talking to him. I was talking to the cat, pressing its wet nose on my arm.* She wanted to open the door and yell that to him. But she couldn't. She couldn't open the door.

Annoyed with herself, she finished cleaning the last chair and ate her sandwich and fruit at the kitchen table. Then she set out for Zimmer Hardware for supplies to clean downstairs, planning in her head as she walked back and forth how she could have everything fresh and clean by the time Roderick McCoy got back. As the day's sun faded, she delighted in organizing, but thoughts of Jakob kept flying through, sparks in her consciousness.

———

"Too bad Doug came back before you found Fiona all safe and sound. Dude's uptight. Doesn't he know that's what eight-month-olds do?" Kelly was saying. She strained forward to see through the driving rain and worn out wipers. "I learned that from subbing at the day care center, which hasn't called in a while, by the way. I need work, Jessie. Anyway, once those babies can go, they go. You're gonna' lose track of 'em here and there, but they're usually fine. Except that one time I read where a mom thought her baby was in the crib, but then she found it, too late, in the..."

"Un-uh," Jessie said, and Kelly hushed briefly.

"Well, cousin girl, what would you have done if I hadn't picked you up?"

Jessie shrugged, her cloth coat and sneakers soaked.

"You would have been a drownded rat, that's what. Man, this storm dumped a load of snow out west. We're lucky it's just rain—as long as it doesn't freeze. But I figured you'd be out in it with no umbrella or raincoat. Hey, wanna come to Mom's? You haven't been there since I moved in.

We can TGIF."

I don't know what TGIF means, but I do want to see how Aunt Barb's house is doing.

"Okay," she said, surprising both of them.

6

"Oh no. The roaches are back."

"Oh. Well, the syrup spilled between the stove and the cupboard. Maybe that's why," Kelly said, pointing to the overturned bottle.

Jessie started tugging and rocking the stove forward, Kelly sputtering, "What in the world?" She fixed soapy water to clean up the syrup, then worked side by side while Kelly fixed dinner, wiping up after her and sweeping crumbs at her feet as soon as they hit the floor, eliciting, "Good grief!" and "Stay out of my way! How am I supposed to cook?"

An hour later the kitchen was as clean as she'd left it a month ago. They sat down to spaghetti, garlic bread, and red wine. *This wine doesn't taste very good, but I like the feeling it gives me. The dry socks Kelly gave me sure feel good too. Mmm. Relaxed.*

"I'm lucky getting this house, all paid for, no mortgage," Kelly said. "I'm astonished, no kidding. Knock me over with a feather." Fork mid-air, she thought for a minute. "No crap, this is the only nice thing my mom ever did for me I can think of." She took another bite and said through the food, "But it's a big one. Thanks, Ma."

They went on eating and Kelly asked, "Did she ever mention it—leaving the house to me?"

Jessie shook her head.

"I thought maybe you put in a good word for me, for old time's sake."

Jessie shook her head again.

"We got raw deals with moms, didn't we?" Kelly said, gulping wine. "How about Tommy? Do you and him have much of a relationship?"

Jessie shook her head. "Nope. My mother's funeral was the first time I met him."

"What? Are you kidding me?" Kelly shrieked, staring at Jessie, both of them shaking their heads. "Which I didn't even know that your mother died. Living right here in the same town, I didn't even know! Oh God," she groaned, "my own mother didn't even tell me my aunt was killed in a car accident blocks from my apartment. What a bitch!" she yelled, then collapsed on her arms on the table. "None of the stuff I did was bad enough to deserve that," she wept. "Not the drugs, not the stealing, not the lies I spread around about her. I'm a better person than my behavior," she said, blowing her nose. "Ma could never see that."

"That really was weird," Jessie said. "...you showing up the morning your mom died not knowing about my mom."

"Ya' think?" Kelly said, looking up at her. "After me and Ma not speaking for two years, I didn't know anything about family." She sunk back down, her head between her arms like a bird under its wing in a storm. After a minute and a big sigh, she looked up again, asking Jessie, "Did you know we have a grandmother named Raven?"

"Not until the obituary."

Kelly sat up and blew her nose and wiped her face with her napkin, then started rifling through a lopsided stack on the table and pulled out a newspaper clipping. It got away from her for an instant, floating on to her plate. She wiped off the spaghetti sauce and read out loud:

Palatine – The Mass of Christian Burial for Nancy Loretta George (nee Justine), 59, will be held at 10 a.m. Thursday, at Holy Family Catholic Community, 2515 Palatine Road, where she will lie in state from 9 a.m. until the time of Mass. Born December 16, 1958 in Santa Fe, New Mexico to Gerald and Raven (nee Hatahle) Justine, Mrs. George passed away July 18, 2013 in Palatine as a result of an auto accident. She worked as a medical records clerk at Northwestern Memorial Hospital in Chicago. Survivors include her mother, Raven Justine, in Kalamazoo, Michigan; a son, Thomas Justine of East Moline; a daughter, Jessica Marie Stewart (Douglas) of Palatine and granddaughter, Fiona; and a sister, Barbara Gleason, and niece, Kelly Gleason, also of Palatine. She was preceded in death by her husband, Bruce George; a daughter, Reneé; and infant son, Blake. In lieu of flowers, donations can be made to Little Sisters of the Poor, 80 W. Northwest Highway, Palatine, IL 60067-3580 or Masses in her memory.

"Who wrote that?"

Jessie shrugged. "Tommy, I guess."

Kelly sipped some more wine and put her head back down and snores soon followed, leaving Jessie to her thoughts. *My mother's funeral was horrible.*

"I'm not going to the visiting part. I can't do that," she'd told Doug.

"You have to, Jessica. Honor your mother and father, it's a commandment. I'll stand right by you and do most of the talking. You have to say only two words: 'thank' and 'you.'"

In the church parlor before the service, Doug had steered her next to Tommy in the line to receive guests.

"Sorry we had to meet this way," Tommy had leaned over and said. "I knew about you, but—I'd lost touch with Mom over the years, and then Dad just dying in February..." He might have said more, but people had started coming.

Someone had asked her if she felt like an orphan now. *Yeah, since the day I was born,* and she nodded her head. A woman named Lisa had told her that she and Jessie's mother had been good friends in days gone by, "...before she had you. And now you have a baby of your own, right?"

Jessie had nodded.

"I can imagine Nan took a lot of joy in being a

grandmother. What's your baby's name?"

"Fiona."

"Oh sweet. How old is she?"

Jessie wasn't sure. Doug had put in that she was five months. "My mother never saw her," Jessie had thought about saying, but hadn't.

In his talk, the priest, who didn't seem to know her mother, had stuck to God and Jesus and eternal life—"being fully in the presence of God" was how he'd put it. A thirty-something guy had paid tribute, recollecting having Mrs. George for a Sunday School teacher and how she "let the little children come unto her every week, Christ-like, with Cheetos and apple juice." Lisa had called "Nan" her guardian angel through tough times. *How can this woman they're talking about, this Nan, be the same woman as my mother?* had run through Jessie's mind.

Kelly rustled awake. Yawning, groggy, she said, "Man, it all blows my mind. You know what, Jessie? How do families get in such pitiful messes?"

Jessie's silence rendered that a rhetorical question. She changed the subject, fumbling for words. "Um, at the recycling center—um, well, something happened—and, um, ever since—well, there's this guy that's been coming around Roderick McCoy's."

Kelly looked at her.

"To see me."

"What? What happened at the recycling center?"

"He helped me put cardboard in the dumpster."

Kelly rubbed her eyes, ran her fingers through her hair, and said, "Do you mean to tell me you are fresh off a divorce and you have another guy already? I mean, let's face it, you're hardly the type."

"I know. And I don't want another one—I don't think."

"Ha. You gave yourself away with that 'I don't thi-ink,'" Kelly said in a sing-songy voice. "Let's have it, the whole and nothing but. C'mon in the living room. What's his name?" She filled her wine glass again and slopped it on the floor getting her bulky self up. Jessie got a paper towel, wiped up the wine and followed her.

"Jakob."

"Where'd he come from?"

"I told you. The recycling center. He likes me because I recycle."

"Seriously," Kelly said with a snort. "To think I was there when this love story started. Well c'mon. Dish. Is he cute?"

Jessie nodded. "But I don't think he'll ever come again because I yelled at the cat and he thought I yelled at him and he left before I could tell him."

"Oh my gosh, that's hilarious," Kelly laughed, until she saw Jessie's expression. "Aw, c'mon, Jessie. Don't you see how funny that is?"

Jessie shook her head.

"Good grief. Well, anyway, do you want to see him again?"

"Probably not. I don't know."

"Then you do. Do you have any idea where he works?"

"At the recycling center."

"Oh yeah, okay. If you want, I'll drive you over there so you can set the record straight."

"I could never do that."

"That's true. You want me to?"

"No!"

"Well, if he really likes you, he might come back."

"Maybe."

"By the way, how'd you meet Doug? I've always wondered."

"He was reading our meter—he's a meter reader—and I went out to get the mail and he started talking to me."

Kelly waited, then said, "Oh, I see. He started talking to you and then you got married."

"After three months," Jessie said.

"Where'd you go on dates?"

"We only went to his church."

"For what?"

"For church. You know—services. And then there were suppers, game nights, music shows."

"Was it fun?"

"Not really."

"Who came to your wedding?"

"My mom and his parents."

"What'd you wear?"

"A white dress my mother got me."

"And then nine months and five minutes later, Fiona was born?"

She shrugged.

"How was your sex life, if I may ask?"

She shrugged again.

"Uh-huh. Oh well. Maybe Jakob will be better."

"I need to go home," Jessie said.

"Oops," Kelly said, rolling straight through the parking

space into the cyclone fence. She backed up a bit and turned off the ignition. Mellowed by wine and weather, they sat in her cab behind Jessie's building talking more about their mothers and fathers.

"Once, I saw her wedding dress," Jessie said, her reverent tone drawing Kelly's gaze. "Her bedroom door was unlocked when I got home from school. I went in. It was getting dark outside, but I was afraid to turn on the light. I walked around looking at her pretty things and then opened the closet door and something fell on top of me. I thought someone was in the closet and was attacking me and I ran out screaming..."

"Oh man, that would stop my heart."

"...but when everything was quiet again, I peeked in and saw it was a plastic clothes cover that had fallen down off a hook. I pulled a bench over and hung it back up and unzipped it. There was her wedding dress," Jessie said, and saw it again in her mind. *It was so beautiful. I wanted to tell her it was beautiful, but...*

"Wow. That would make a great scene in a haunted house movie," Kelly said. "A bride ghost that got jilted at the altar. Your character would wind up headless."

They sat staring at the rain glinting in the streetlight.

59

Kelly lit a cigarette.

"You may not know this, Jessie, or don't remember," she said, rolling the window down a crack and sitting up straighter, "but at one time, our mothers were tight. Nan and Barb, Barb and Nan. When I was a kid, they hardly went a day without seeing each other and talked on the phone constantly. I'd be at your house or Renee would be over at our house. All that changed when Renee got killed in that motorcycle crash. And now, Nan and Barb, Barb and Nan—gone." She looked at Jessie. "You knew about Renee before the obituary, right?"

Jessie nodded. "I didn't know about a baby named Blake dying, but I knew about her. But I didn't know how she died until your mother told me."

"That's the first you heard of the motorcycle accident with her boyfriend?"

Jessie nodded.

Kelly let out a low whistle. "That's what I'm talkin' about—craziness, that they didn't talk about stuff." She took a drag on her cigarette, blew smoke out the window, and turned sideways in the seat to look at Jessie. "Your mom and Renee had this terrible fight and Renee took off on the bike with Richie and—it was awful. She totally lost it—Aunt Nan. I was ten. Then, when I was thirteen, Daddy shot himself and Ma lost it. God, that's a lot, Jessie."

The cousins sat in chilly silence except for the drumbeat of the rain. *Yeah, that's a lot, and what to do about any of it now?*

"He did it because she was such a witch," Kelly went on. "Plus, he was a drunk and a drug addict. But at least I had fun with Daddy. With your dad too. He used to do tricks with his hands for Tommy and Renee and me, with coins and cards. Did he for you?"

"I didn't know him."

"What do you mean?"

"I only saw my father once. He didn't live at our house."

"I'm not believing this," Kelly said, flicking a long ash out the window. "Then where did he live?"

"In Moline, I think, where Tommy lives."

"You mean you and me have always lived within a couple miles of each other, and I didn't know he was gone from Palatine all those years?"

"I guess so," Jessie said, then added, "It's weird, all that people don't know about us."

"Like what else?" Kelly asked, stubbing her cigarette out.

61

Jessie took a breath, then said, "I'm too tired," and slipped out into the rain and past the picnic table to her apartment. Doug had stuck a note on the back door: "Where in the world are you?"

"I don't know," she whispered, exhausted by too many people and too much life. She went straight to bed.

7

Thanksgiving morning Jessie walked to work on hushed streets, the only one out. She stopped across from the reservoir, chewing her gum, to watch a shadowy figure wander about. A coyote. *Wild,* she thought, moving on, breathing in the still, chilly air. No rush hour traffic, no school buses or delivery trucks. People were at home sleeping in or tending to turkeys. Light after light glinted on through house windows, warming her along with the slow dawn. By the time she reached South Harvard Drive, the world was awash in pale pink. *I feel pink, just like the world, happy and kind and beautiful—and thankful. Pretty good for Thanksgiving Day, I guess.*

Unlocking the front door like she owned it, she began her morning ritual, walking through the rooms she'd straightened, admiring her work and cleaning up after the cat. The furry mess had stopped using the litter box altogether this week, perhaps because her beloved master was gone. Despite that disgusting development, Jessie floated down the staircase to Roderick's den like a blossom off a tree because, after three back-breaking days, the time had come for final touches.

Books and artifacts she had cleaned and set on the floor could be put back on the polished shelves. She would wipe out the small refrigerator and arrange the piles of snacks in a basket she'd found in the basement. Pictures she'd removed from the walls so she could treat the wood paneling had been wiped down and could now be re-hung. She placed a wastebasket she'd gotten at Zimmer's next to the recliner and also a floor mat to protect the freshly shampooed carpet around his chair. She'd been so pleased with the transformation of the bathroom, former cesspool, she'd eaten her lunch in there one day.

This reminds me of putting the last dot of paint on a picture and laying my brush down, she thought, placing extra rolls of paper on the back of the toilet, and then looking around the big room. *I can think of absolutely nothing else to do. It is finished.*

65

When Kelly honked her horn around four o'clock, she ran upstairs and waved her in like she was in a contest and Kelly was the judge, sure to award her first place.

"Whew, sure smells clean," Kelly said, starting down the steps.

Jessie watched her face as she entered.

"Looks good, cousin."

You have no idea.

"This him?" Kelly asked, picking up an eight by ten framed photo of a well-built young man in a track uniform.

"I don't know. He sure doesn't look like that now. Maybe it's his son."

"Look closer; this is from 1964. Hey, you didn't tell me he was black," and she handed the picture to Jessie. "Nice home theater system. Man, that screen must be fifty inches."

She moved to the bookshelves. "Wow, he's a pretty big war hero," she said, fingering first the Silver Star Medal and then the Purple Heart. Jessie trailed her, polishing the fingerprints off the awards while Kelly examined the photos, flags, commemorative coins. "Cool compass, in Army green, no less." She checked out the saber in its case on its display rack and studied the photographs. "Look at those sweet young hunks, shoulder to shoulder, all of 'em squinting into the hot Vietnamese sun. Hmm," she sighed as she put it back in place.

"Pretty impressive, but, yikes, there are ghosts here, dontcha' feel 'em? Let's go."

Jessie turned off the light and followed her up to go to Thanksgiving dinner.

"Oh, and Kourtney's trying to get Khloe to move in right next door," Kelly told Jessie over their holiday meal. She'd been talking about this family for a while. "Khloe says Kourtney's talking about digging a tunnel between the houses if she moves in. And Kris is wanting to be on Broadway, been taking song and dance lessons behind their backs. Caitlyn's the big news, of course."

"Where do they live?"

"The Khardashians? Search me. Probably Hollywood."

"Oh. Well, how do you know them? Did you graduate with one of them?"

Kelly narrowed her eyes at Jessie. "You take the cake for not knowing things, girl," she said, with a shake of her head. "Hey, whatsamatter; you don't like turkey?"

"Not too much. Sorry. I'm not used to it."

"Didn't you have it every Thanksgiving growing up?"

Jessie shook her head. "The only time I ever had turkey was at Doug's parents' house for Thanksgiving dinner last year, when we were married."

"So wha'd your mom fix?"

Jessie shrugged.

Filling their wine glasses, Kelly said, "Before Renee died, we'd go back and forth every year. Whoever's house it was at would do the turkey and stuffing and pies. The other one would make the green bean casserole and mashed potatoes and rolls."

They chewed for a while.

"Didn't you and her go to somebody else's sometimes?"

Jessie shook her head.

"Tommy and your dad never came?"

"I told you, I didn't know them," she said, serving herself more green beans.

"Yeah. I was just checking cuz it's so hard to believe."

They ate on.

Kelly shook her head again and took another serving of mashed potatoes and gravy.

"What about your boyfriend from the recycling center?"

Jessie shrugged.

"Well, has he come back?"

"No," she said. *But I saw him in the hardware store yesterday.* She had turned down an aisle in the quiet old store with its polished wooden floors and smells of oil and screws, and there he was, walking toward her. He was focused on products to his right, and she approached on his left. She had to turn sideways so they didn't touch, but she felt his electricity. *What if I had spoken to him, explained the mistake with the cat instead of hiding until he left?*

"I saw him yester..." she started, Kelly interrupting, "Want more wine?"

Her speech was slurry, and Jessie didn't like how things were going, and then, sure enough, before too long, Kelly started weeping and laughing crazy, and then she flung her second piece of pie with extra whipped cream across the room, yelling, "Oh, Jesus and Mary, I'm going to eat myself to death like Ma and die right here in this house, just like her.

"Yes! That's what I'll do. I'll go sit in mommie dearest's recliner and wait to drop dead of obesity," she gasped, clutching her massive bosom as though she were having a heart attack. She filled her glass and staggered into the living room.

I should do something, but what?

She finished her dessert, then peeked at Kelly: reclined, eyes closed, puffing on a cigarette.

Jessie cleaned up, starting with the pie mess, and gave the kitchen a thorough, anti-roach treatment, figuring she would walk home when she got done. It wasn't yet seven o'clock. She took the garbage out and when she came back in, saw smoke snaking into the kitchen through the living room door.

"Kelly!" she screamed, running to her, rousing her from a dead sleep. The upholstery smoldered, the fumes noxious, and both women were coughing as Jessie got them to the kitchen and dumped Kelly on a chair. She grabbed the scrub bucket from under the sink, filled it with water and dashed the fire out.

Back at home, putting her pajamas on, she began to tremble.

Kelly had cried and coughed and kept hugging her, a totally new sensation, prickly and pleasant at the same time. Jessie had aired out the house and cleaned up the mess, then made coffee and listened to Kelly for hours until she'd sobered up and calmed down. It was going on midnight when Kelly drove her home.

Jessie felt an urge to cry and an urge to laugh but did neither, and then—something broke loose inside her, like a stubborn cap on a paint tube, twisted and twisted, and finally giving way. *I feel special and normal at the same time. Not that putting out a fire is normal, but that—I did it. I did something that mattered, something important. Kelly kept saying, "You saved my life," and maybe I did.*

As she lay down, Jakob popped into her thoughts. A sensuous tremor took her over, and then she was asleep.

8

Squeak! Beep! Rattle! went Fiona's colorful ball rolling across the floor, her scrambling after it to roll it again. Doug had brought her over to spend the whole day on this holiday weekend. Jessie sat on her couch watching. *Having her around for so long makes me think of when she was first born.*

During the week, alone with the baby, she wished it would sleep all day long. But when it did sleep Jessie would go into a panic if she couldn't hear it breathing, and every few minutes, she'd poke it until it moved.

She hated breastfeeding. Her nipples cracked and bled and she didn't use the salve because she wanted an excuse to stop. At her three-week check-up, Fiona still hadn't gained any weight, so the pediatrician switched her to full formula. Doug enrolled Jessie in a mothering class, which was like trying to give swimming lessons to a person while they were drowning.

She would see looks pass between the two instructors, saying, "Wow, this girl just ain't got it." One of them said to her once in an exasperated tone, "Has there never been a baby in your life, a niece or nephew or a friend's child?" as though Jessie were at fault for never having had a baby in her life. And it didn't help when they said things like, "Interaction is crucial because the brain grows as much in the first year as it will grow during the rest of her life."

Doug had also arranged for Stephanie Nordstrum from church to hang out with Jessie and Fiona. "You can pick up lots from her," he'd said, "so you'll be more at ease with mothering." *He probably also didn't think it was safe for Fiona to be alone with me. For good reason, I guess.*

The Nordstrums were the type family Doug hoped for: four kids, so far, homeschooled by the mother, church-centered, always happy, it seemed. Jessie's mouth fell open in awe watching Stephanie swing her baby and her toddler around like beanbags. She swung Fiona around too, and held her up in the air and talked silly to her and got her cooing. *I always wished Doug would take Fiona to Stephanie's house on his way to work and pick her up on his way home.*

Fiona tired of the ball and started fussing, so Jessie put the pacifier in her mouth. She sucked until her eyes glazed, and she fell over asleep. Jessie covered her with her blankie and started getting nervous over how she might choke at feeding time.

Then, she went into a daze herself and stretched out on the couch in the winter sun. Next, Fiona was pulling on her, one baby foot on its tiptoe and the opposite knee raised as she tried to climb. Drowsy, Jessie pulled her by the arm, and the child plopped up and snuggled into her. Afraid to move, Jessie stared at the ceiling. And then she felt Fiona's heartbeat. And then she felt her own.

This is it. He's coming home today. I hope Jakob comes—but I also hope he doesn't. I'm nervous around him. I hope Roderick McCoy will like his den, but he might not. Worse, he might decide he doesn't need me anymore. I can hear him telling Lauren, "Since the roaches are mostly gone and the downstairs is pretty well in order, I don't think I'll need her anymore,"

At a quarter past noon, the doorbell rang. She felt herself flush as she opened the door, but it wasn't Jakob, only the exterminator.

"Wow, you're getting this place shaped up," he said as

he stepped into the front hall where mail lay neatly sorted on the side table. Rugs vacuumed, furniture dusted, light bulbs replaced. Glistening.

Jessie nodded. The guy went about his work, and she returned to the den for the final vacuuming after the last treatment of stubborn stains in the carpet. Thinking she'd heard the bell again, she shut the vacuum cleaner off and listened, heard nothing, started it up again. And then, positive she'd heard it, switched off again and let the vacuum bounce on the floor with a dull thud as she ran up the stairs.

She jerked the door open and yelled, "Hey! I'm here," to Jakob's back.

He turned around and did a funny jig step. "Oh wow. I thought you probably didn't want to see me after all my gloom and verbosity the other day."

"Huh? No, no. I was talking to the cat when I said get away from me."

"Aha. For real?"

Jessie nodded. "Her snotty nose on my arm and everything. She's gross."

"I am relieved beyond words."

Her heart fluttered.

He apologized for being a pessimistic bore and talking too much and not listening.

"It's the darnedest thing. I can tell you the causes of climate change for the past sixty-three million years but saying hello and starting a conversation is highly challenging," he lamented, looking down the sidewalk behind him, half turned away from her.

"That's okay. I'm not that good at talking either."

His head turned quickly to look into her eyes. Her gaze dropped.

"Um, may I tell you about that day when I knocked on the kitchen window?"

"I guess so."

"Well," he breathed in, "You had the same expression on your face as Hannah Smithson had outside the Jewel one time when I tried to talk to her." He turned away, then back. "She called the police."

Jessie studied his face, red and distressed. "What for?"

"I was too happy to see her, I guess, and scared her. I don't talk to girls very well." He turned away again, then back, and said, "So thanks for being nice."

"It's okay."

"Nonetheless, I do worry on a daily basis where we are

headed as a planet, and people's irresponsibility and indifference shock me. Jessica, we could reverse the situation if we had the will. Do you know what is found in sea gulls' stomachs these days? Oh, you name it: cigarette lighters, foil, plastic..."

Jessie shifted from one foot to the other.

"Oh no, there I go again." He pulled out a pack of gum. "I noticed you chew this all the time," he said, and gave it to her.

Spearmint. Oh, gosh, that burns my mouth. I should say thank you but it prickles my mouth so bad. Should I tell him and give it back? That seems rude. They stood in silence with the door still open and cold air rushing into the house.

"Perhaps not the right flavor?"

"It hurts my mouth."

"Oh, no, never. What kind do you like?"

"Only Doublemint."

"Noted," Jakob said, holding out his hand, and she handed back the gum.

After more silence, he said, "Well, I should move on," and he took a step down the sidewalk, "and get on with my duties, such as they are in the fight against..."

He was unlatching the gate when Jessie stammered out,

"Thank you."

He raced back.

"Did you have a nice Thanksgiving?"

Jessie nodded.

Jakob laughed. "Okay. Details, please."

"I worked here and then ate supper at my Aunt Barb's house."

"Aha. Did Aunt Barb cook a delicious dinner?"

"No, she's dead. My cousin Kelly cooked. Aunt Barb's daughter."

"Aha."

They turned silent again. *I want to tell him about putting out the fire and Saturday with Fiona but—I hardly know him—I don't know how to get into it. I think he wants to tell me things too—I can see it in his eyes and his mouth is half-open—oboy, we're just no good at talking.* He said another goodbye and turned to leave again.

"Um, did you?" Jessie said, half yelling.

"Did I what?"

"Have a nice Thanksgiving?"

"Oh. Yes, indeed. My father's clan gathered at the Leif Ericson monument in Humboldt Park, as is our tradition, and then we went to Farmor's—that's my grandma,

Norwegian for grandmother—assisted living facility. Nice dinner, I only wish they'd had tofurkey. That would have been perfect. You know, eating animals as our main source of protein is unsustainable. My heart aches at the rain forests that have been... uh-oh..."

He squeezed his eyes shut in concentration. "Did you go to Fremd or Palatine?" flew out of his mouth.

"Fremd."

"Oh, no," he laughed, reminding Jessie of a horse neigh. "Forest green and gold vs. scarlet and gray. We shall have fun with that silly rivalry."

"Were you in special ed?"

"Oh yes, big time."

"What was wrong with you?"

He laughed again. "There is nothing wrong with me, dear girl. I am, however, neuro-atypical."

"Oh."

"Yes. I'm on the autism spectrum. Part of it is I'm a word thinker. I often see words as I say them, sometimes in color. When under stress, I talk excessively and use big words."

Jessie gazed at him.

"Were you in special ed?" he asked.

She shook her head.

"I thought not."

"But I have problems."

He nodded.

They stood looking at each other, exhausted.

"May I come back?" Jakob asked.

Jessie nodded.

His horsey laugh burst forth again, and he yelled over his shoulder as he ran to his scooter, "Soon! I'll be back soon. With the right gum."

She smiled, inside.

<hr />

"Jessica, yoo-hoo," she heard Lauren call.

"Oh, no," she said out loud in the master bedroom. They were a couple hours earlier than expected. She'd been playing her and Jakob's conversation over in her head while pulling the sheets off Roderick's bed, making a face at the odors. Peeking down the hall, she saw him heading her way. She panicked at being in his private quarters and ducked into his bathroom, but that was exactly where he was going. In a second, he loomed over her, unzipping his pants as he entered. "What the..." he said. She twisted past him and hurried to the kitchen.

Lauren was looking at her time sheet on the counter.

"I didn't know you were coming so soon," Jessie accused.

"If you had a cell phone you would have," Lauren said, her irritation matching Jessie's. "Anyway, how's it going around here?"

"Only two medium and seven tiny roaches under the fridge last Friday. And, I've cleaned the den downstairs."

"Wow. That was a job. Well, it remains to be seen if ten days at the V.A. did him any good. He grouched and complained all the way home. Man, I hate it that Wayne's not coming. That would have done so much to lift his spirits," she said, opening a checkbook. "But none of that's my problem. You have a bank account now, right?"

Jessie nodded.

Lauren began to write. "Jessica Stewart, right?"

"No. It's George now. Jessica George."

"You changed your name?"

"Yeah. I got divorced a couple weeks ago."

Lauren stared at her, shook her head, finished writing the check and handed it to her.

Roderick stood in the doorway, his eyes riveted on his niece.

"Are you going back to L.A.?"

She looked him in the eye for a long moment. "How did you know?"

"I've been able to add two and two for a long time, Lauren."

"I was waiting for the right..."

"When are you going?"

"Next week."

Boy, he's mad. He looks like a furious bull with that hard look in his eyes and his wide-open nostrils.

"I'm sorry..." Lauren started.

"No. No sorry. Just go. "

"I will not just go," she said, her voice rising, arms flying. "I will tell you how hard it is for me to leave you," she choked up. "And why I have to."

She breathed slowly in and out, Jessie taking it all in from the other side of the counter. "Uncle Roderick, you've taught me to be a straight shooter, so here goes. My move is happening fast because the company has been in search mode for a long time. I got in right at the end. They want me in place for tax season, ready to go, no negotiation as far as timing.

"And I'm moving because..." She sounded like she'd forgotten lines in a play. "...because you're sinking. I don't know why, but I can't help you, and I don't want to sink with you. It's not all because of you. I've needed this change for a while. And I hope and pray you're going to be okay. I think you have what it takes to straighten yourself out, to get to the bottom of what you're drowning in. You have financial resources and a support system of professionals and... oh, I don't know... I love you, Uncle Roderick, and I will still be in your life, but not as close. That's it."

"Okay, baby," came his words through tight lips.

"I'll help you get lined up for your surgery and..."

"Enough. Go." He hobbled past her to sit down at the table.

Lauren stared at his back for an instant, then pulled on her gloves, grabbed her purse and left.

"Home is where when you have to go there, they have to take you in," Roderick quoted. "Except there's nobody here to take me in."

Jessie edged quietly out of the room to finish his bed. Floating a sheet in the air, she heard him making his way down the stairs, and wondered what he would think of the cleaned-up changes.

After a minute he hollered, "Where the hell are the remotes?"

She froze, but then thought of Kelly and the fire: *I saved someone's life. I put out a fire. I can talk to him.* She raced down the steps.

"They're in the side pocket of the recliner. If you put them back there each time you won't lose track of them." She pulled them out and handed them to him.

"You're Jennifer, right?" he asked, looking up at her.

"Jessica."

"Oh. Jessica," he said, struggling to his feet. "Well, Jessica, you have done a beautiful job cleaning up my pig sty," and he swept his arm across the room.

She nodded.

He laughed, then sobered. "It's sad, the state I'm in. I keep trying to get back on track, but... Now, my niece is moving to California. Can't take her old uncle any longer. Truth is, I'm not sure how much longer I can take him."

"Um, who's going to pay me when she leaves?"

"I'll pay you."

"Okay. If you can't find anything else, let me know," and she turned to leave, then said, "I'm making your bed up fresh, and starting tomorrow, I can work on your bedroom, if you want."

"Fine. That's good." He fell back into his chair with a

grunt and a groan.

"Oh, and I noticed boxes of Christmas decorations in the basement. Shall I..."

"I don't care. You can if you want."

"Okay."

Tasks of the day completed, she went out into the weather, dark moving in fast. She could feel the temperature dropping but didn't care, glowing from the inside with the satisfaction of talking to him and knowing her job would continue.

The next morning, however, her head ached so bad she had to stop chewing gum. Too many thoughts. *Jakob said he would come back soon. Lauren's moving. Fiona's coming Friday night. Roderick will have that surgery pretty soon, and I'll have the house to myself again.*

He had asked her if she knew anyone who could drive for him, take him to the hospital and run errands while he was in rehab and so forth. Twenty-five dollars an hour. *Wait, who is it that needs work? Oh, yeah. Kelly.*

9

"You got picked on in school, right? Tell me some stories," Jakob said in another midday get acquainted session. They were getting more at ease with each other, but Jessie shook her head no.

"They probably ignored you most of the time," he went on. "You little quiet ones stay out of the spotlight most of the time, not like my type. Although you do have that scared rabbit look that whets their appetites. C'mon, tell me; it'll be good for your pretty soul." He was leaning over the kitchen counter, his eyes bright and eager, as she washed dishes from the china cabinet in hot, sudsy water.

She stayed intent on her work until he said, "Okay, I'm not going to force you even though I wish I could squeeze it out of you." He turned to leave.

"No, wait," she said, rinsing the last fancy candy dish and placing it in the drainer. She dried her hands and turned around and leaned against the counter next to him, hugging herself and taking a deep breath.

"This one time was in Chemistry when we were in small groups to tell each other about experiments we had to do—individual experiments we made up ourselves. I said I was going to mix vinegar and baking soda and explain the energy or something. I remembered that from fifth grade and thought it might be okay for a C, at least. But then someone said..."

"'... that's not an experiment, that's a demonstration,'" Jakob completed for her.

"Yeah," she said, looking at him. "And I wasn't sure what that meant. I'd been absent some and didn't much get chemistry. And then this guy named Josh said real quiet to the girl next to him how I could do an experiment about how many ugly midgets it takes to change a light bulb."

"Yeah, scoff-scoff-snicker-snicker," Jakob said, and she nodded.

"And then the teacher came from the front of the room and stood over us..."

"Yeah, Josh was watching; they sit so they can see the

teacher."

"Yeah," she said, looking at him again.

"So what'd you do for your experiment?"

"What I said, the vinegar and baking soda. I went to the library that afternoon to look on the computer so I could make it better, but I'm not very good at the computer, and I was all..." she stopped.

"I know: sick and disgusted and nervous and overwhelmed."

"Yeah. And then I wanted to print something, but I didn't have any change..."

"Oh, geez."

"So I stayed home the next day. Well, for a few days."

"Did you look online at home?"

"We didn't have a computer."

"What? An American household without a computer in the twenty-first century? Poor Jessica."

She shrugged. "So I did the project and wrote it up, and the day I came back the teacher called on me to make my oral presentation—I thought maybe they would be all done with that, but they weren't—and..." She couldn't go on.

"Pretty bad, huh?"

She nodded. "He stopped me and told me to come back

at lunch time and talk to him. And then after class, Josh got right next to me when we went into the hallway and patted me on the head and said, 'Good job, Jessie,' and everybody laughed.

"But you're right. Mostly, they ignored me."

In the stillness, Jakob started to put his arm around her, but she moved to the utility room and got the broom.

"So do some people call you Jessie?" he asked as she swept.

She nodded.

"Which do you prefer? Jessica or Jessie?"

"I don't care."

"Aw, c'mon. Care."

She stopped sweeping long enough to look right at him and say, "Don't judge me," then focused on the floor again, relieved when the doorbell rang into the awkward moment.

"That's my cousin. She's coming to talk to Roderick McCoy about driving him to the hospital."

Kelly entered the kitchen in bumbling grandness, her hair fluorescent blue now. Her colorful outfit, including tights the same shade as her hair, revealed every crack and roll. The three of them stood silently until Kelly said,

"Okay, I get it. Everybody's too shy to introduce, so I'll do it. You must be Jakob. Yeah, Jessie's right, you are cute. Well, I'm her long-lost cousin Kelly, reunited after..."

"You're the one who might drive me?" Roderick's voice broke in from the doorway.

They turned toward him, Kelly saying, "Yessir, at your service."

"Can you drive me to Lovell V.A. Hospital in North Chicago next Monday morning? Have to leave at 5 a.m. You'll drive my vehicle, then bring it back and park it back in the garage."

"Yessir. Wow, that's early, but sure I will. I heard you'll pay twenty-five dollars an hour."

Roderick nodded, and Kelly whipped out her phone. "We should have each other's numbers."

"Good idea," he said, "but there's a bit of a problem. My niece talked me into letting my landline go, which seemed a good idea at the time, since telemarketers were the only ones who ever called. I don't even know my number on this blankety-blank thing," he said, taking his cell phone out of his pocket.

"Let's see," Kelly said, taking it from him and punching buttons. "Here it is. I'll call you now and put myself in your directory."

"Good enough," Roderick said and turned to Jakob. "Who are you?"

"Jakob Otteson, sir. I stop by on my lunch break sometimes to see Jessica—or Jessie. We're becoming friends—I think."

"Yeah, he's my friend," Jessie put in.

"Okay." Roderick turned to Jessie. "How much am I paying you?"

"Fifteen dollars an hour."

"Okay. Could you start doing my laundry too?"

She nodded. *Oh, this is great. More to do.*

"Good. I'll be in my den if you need anything."

When he was out of hearing range, Kelly said, "So that's Roderick McCoy. Man, he looks depressed, he smells depressed, he walks depressed. Like Dad. That guy's not okay. You be careful, Jessie. He could do anything, to himself, to you. Are there any guns in the house?"

A sound came from the dining room.

"Oh yuk. The cat's earping," and Jessie went to the sink and reached underneath for cleaning supplies.

"The cat's what?" Jakob asked.

"Earping."

"What's that?"

"Do you mean puking?" Kelly asked.

Jessie nodded.

"I never heard that word before—earping," Jakob said.

"Earping's not a word, Jessie. Where'd you ever hear that?"

"My mother said it once, when I got sick. She was talking on the phone the next morning and said, 'Jessie earped last night.' Are you sure it's not a word? I think it is."

"Maybe she said vurp, like when you think you're going to burp and then there's stuff."

"No. She said earp, and that's what I did."

"My mom says vomit and my dad says regurgitate," Jakob said.

Kelly hooted. "Well, I say puke. Tell it like it is."

"My grandma says retch. I say hurl," Jakob said.

"Oh, this is fun," Kelly giggled. "Heave, spew..."

"How about disgorge?" Jakob said.

Kelly said, "Listen to this one I heard once: pray to the porcelain god."

Jakob guffawed. Jessie said she didn't get it.

"Porcelain god's the toilet," Kelly explained.

"Oh. Well then, there's upchuck," Jessie said.

"Oh yeah, upchuck," Kelly giggled. "Upchuck! Oh cripes, that's hilarious. Whaddya do, up your chuck? Toss your cookies sounds much more lady-like," and they all laughed.

Gagging noises came from the dining room again and silenced them for a split second until they exploded, Jakob braying, Kelly whooping, and Jessie emitting a heh-heh-heh sound like a vibrating phone.

"OMG," Kelly laughed, wiping tears away. "What's the cat's name?"

"Precious," Jessie said, going to clean up. "Precious the Fourth. Lauren said the wife named every cat Precious."

A couple minutes later Roderick surprised them by coming into the kitchen again. "Sounds like you're having a good time up here. I thought I'd show you this," he said, and handed the picture of him in his track uniform to the closest person, Kelly.

"Wow, sir. Looking good. High school?"

"Right, a hundred years ago. They pressured me pretty hard to play football, but I didn't care a bit for the tackling part, hitting or being hit. So I went for track and field. Broke the shot-put records, conference and state."

Passing it to Jessie, Jakob said, "It's hard to believe that's you."

"You're right about that, young man," Roderick said, taking it from Jessie. "Just thought I'd show it to you," and he hobbled away.

After a minute, Jakob said, "I don't think I spoke very well."

"You got that right," Kelly said, "but at least he wasn't p'd off. I wouldn't want to make that dude mad."

10

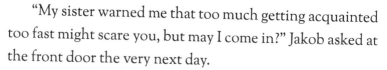

"My sister warned me that too much getting acquainted too fast might scare you, but may I come in?" Jakob asked at the front door the very next day.

Even after all they'd been through yesterday—the painful confiding all the way to the fun with Kelly—Jessie hesitated. But the eager hope she saw in the way he cast his eyes down and then looked back up at her won her over.

"Is this your lunch hour?" she asked.

He nodded.

"Do you have your lunch with you?"

When he said he did, she invited him to bring it in, and they sat down across from each other at the kitchen table. They emptied their lunch bags, arranging their sandwiches and fruit and carrot sticks, blushing at the intimacy of this simple act.

Jakob paused, focusing on his food, then picked up his sandwich and took a bite.

"Um, did you just pray?" Jessie asked, picking up her sandwich.

"Oh. Yeah. I did. I prayed. After all, there are many without food. The least I can do is thank God that I have some."

"Okay, well don't talk with your mouth full," she said. "What kind of sandwich is that?"

"Sorry," he said, swallowing. "Peanut butter and mayonnaise."

"You must like it."

"I'm crazy about it—and about you too."

Gosh, I can tell by the look on his face he didn't mean to say that. She smiled so he wouldn't feel bad. That made him laugh too hard and long, and the smile left her face, and then the smile left his face, but he seemed used to this and went on.

"Speaking of prayer, may I ask—do you believe in God?"

"I guess so."

"I think if you're guessing, maybe you don't."

"Stop judging me." *I didn't mean to say that, but it's how I feel.* "Please."

A low growl came from Jakob. "I meant no offense. I don't even agree with what I said. I probably said it because I'm having disturbing doubts regarding my faith, and—would you talk with me of God, however briefly? Because you see, I am questioning God's existence for the first time in my life." His voice caught. "And I am deeply distressed."

Yeah, I can see it in your eyes, like your mother's about to catch you doing something wrong. She could see it in the rounding of his shoulders as he drew into himself even as he leaned toward her, and in the way he abandoned his sandwich.

"I guess it's okay—for you to talk," she said.

"Before," he started out, his voice tight, "I never felt alone. Never. I always felt loved. Always." He closed his eyes and held his head and began to weave back and forth.

"And now?" Jessie asked urgently, wanting to break the spell he was going into.

He sat still and looked at her. "Now I don't always feel that way."

Their eyes locked. And then, he crumpled, and he cried.

98

Roderick appeared in the doorway, looked and listened, quickly retreated.

Jessie watched Jakob until he had spent himself. He stood up and started stuffing his lunch back in the bag, his face red and wet.

"No. It's okay. Sit down," Jessie said.

He did, and they were silent together until Jessie said, "I don't know much about love. Doug is the only one who's ever said they loved me."

"Ah, but it's not about the love of mere mortals, Jessica. As much as my people love me, it's not enough. I'm referring to a love way beyond that."

Jessie shrugged. "I don't know about it." She started eating her sandwich again.

Jakob took a huge breath and said, "Oh."

They heard the cat gagging and smiled.

"Well, who's Doug that loves you?"

"My husband, but..."

"What? You're married?"

"No, no. I mean my ex-husband."

"What? You're divorced?"

She nodded.

He stared.

"Pardon my astonishment, Jessica."

She hesitated, then went on. "I did something really bad that he couldn't handle."

"I can't imagine you doing anything so terribly bad."

"Well, I did," she said. She took off her glasses and rubbed her eyes. *Do I tell him or not? I think I will.*

She put her glasses back on and took a couple more bites and chewed them well and then wiped her mouth with her napkin. "I took a Plan B pill so I wouldn't have any more kids after the first one."

"You have a kid?" Jakob squawked.

She nodded. "And then I might have had another one, but I stopped it. He said I killed his second child."

"Good God."

"But I couldn't do it, I couldn't have another baby," she went on, looking at her lap, talking in a voice that seemed to be shriveling up inside her.

Stretched over the table hungry for every word, Jakob hunched like a vulture, his head sunk between his shoulders.

"This one time in the locker room after gym I heard girls talking about somebody going to Osco and getting a Plan B pill so she wouldn't get pregnant after she went all the way with her boyfriend." She felt her face heating up, knew it must be red. *I should just stop. I can't believe I'm telling him this. I hardly know him. This is hard and embarrassing, but he's the first person I've told, and... I want to tell him.*

"Okay." She rolled her eyes up to focus her thoughts and took in air. "So—the baby was still new and Doug—well, I was afraid I might get pregnant again—and that's when I remembered Plan B. Somebody got it for me—I can never say who—and I took it but had a terrible reaction. I could hardly breathe and my mouth and tongue puffed up and red bumps broke out on my skin. Doug took me to the emergency room, and they asked me what I'd eaten and if I had taken any medicines. I didn't want to die—I felt like I might—so I told them."

She peeked up at him, shifted in her chair.

"He held everything in until we got home and the neighbor who was there with the baby left. Then he cried and cried and shook me shouting that I had killed his second child and maybe I wanted to kill the baby too."

In her head, she heard Doug's anguished cries. "You've broken God's commandment to be fruitful and multiply, you've wasted my seed, you've broken trust between a man and his wife! I thought I could save you, I thought I could bring you into the fold, but you have done evil. You have to go, Jessica. You just have to go." *That was the awfullest and best minute of my life.*

Jakob's mouth hung open, his eyes riveted on the top of her head. She heaved a tired sigh and looked up.

"Fiona is our baby's name and I..." she groped for words. "...I'm getting to like her and getting better at taking care of her, but—I just don't know how–to take care of a baby. I think Doug is starting to figure that out, because he told me that he forgives me for taking that pill." She turned her head slowly side to side and said to Jakob, "That's probably love, him forgiving me."

Jakob thought and nodded. "In a scenario such as yours and Doug's, that may well be love." He put his uneaten apple and his sandwich box back in his bag. "I have to get back to work," he said, "but, if I may ask, do you think perhaps you might reconcile?"

"Get together again? No. Our divorce was final a couple weeks ago. He has a girlfriend he might marry. He wants me to be Fiona's mother, but no, we're done."

"My good luck, then, because I am growing quite fond of you, Jessica. Even as I sit here in shock at your past, I am hoping we may have a future."

"Maybe," she said. "But I don't know. You're pretty weird. I don't mean that in a mean way, only that I might not be smart enough to, um..."

"I know exactly what you mean. But you're the first one I've ever gotten this far with, all the way to maybe."

<hr />

Carrying cleaning supplies, Jessie tried to step silently into Roderick's den and sneak over to clean the bathroom without him noticing. But then she froze at the sound of his voice on the phone.

"Lauren, precious girl, this is your uncle. Please listen to this message, baby girl. I couldn't stand you leaving with ugly words from this old fool ringing in your ears, and I called to say I'm sorry. I'm sick and sorry, and I took it out on you. Follow your dream. Go get 'em, Lauren McCoy."

Jessie took a step but jerked like she'd been shot when his cell phone crashed into the TV. The cat leapt out of his lap with a shrill meow.

Roderick lurched from his chair, yelping in pain, and went to the small fridge next to the shelves of war relics, got a beer and pulled the tab. At the hiss, his huge shoulders rose and fell. Taking a gulp and turning around, he saw her.

"What?"

"I'm going to clean the bathroom."

"Why are you looking at me that way? I owe that ungrateful woman nothing; that's why I erased the message. Listen," he snarled, "I picked up her college tab when my brother had his heart attack. For thirty-five years, I've made sure her birthday was special, and on and on, and this is the thanks I get? Her running off right when I need her most?"

Jessie moved toward the bathroom, but he kept talking.

"She's never deserted me before. Everybody else has but not her. She came the day Vevie died. She made coffee after they took the body away, and that's when we saw Chico, a black speck in the corner of the backyard. We dug his grave, and I cried on her shoulder," he went on, and while she knew he wasn't talking to her, exactly, Jessie stood there. "Easiest dog to talk to, understood every word I said, I swear it.

"I'm a decent man—at least I used to be," he said, with another swig of beer. "But, 'I have sinned most grievously,' like we used to say in church." He picked up the phone parts and sank back down in his chair. "Most grievously," he repeated and turned the TV volume up.

Jessie hurried to the bathroom. That she could handle.

Snow sifted down as she pulled Roderick's door tight and locked it. *I should go back in to wish him the best with his surgery to get in good with him so I can keep this job. But that feels phony. Plus I'm too tired.*

Rounding the corner at the end of the block, she heard music, voices lilting into the frigid, dark air through an open door at the high school. HOLIDAY CONCERT TONIGHT was posted on the billboard sign on Illinois Avenue. *That place seems friendly and nice right now, but I know better.*

Traffic was backed up on Quentin. Marching on, she saw flashing lights ahead at Illinois and Plum Grove. Sirens wailed as emergency vehicles wove their way through Friday night commuters inching this way and that to make a path. At Cedar Street she walked left into the neighborhood, and many drivers turned there too, bumper to bumper. Still, these side streets were darker and quieter.

Her mother's fatal crash nearly six months ago haunted her now, the image of her battered, dead body vivid. She shivered from the cold. *I have no sadness over her death. It's all so strange. It feels bad not to feel.*

Despite her fatigue, she passed her building and moved carefully between blocked traffic on Plum Grove to cross over to Jewel-Osco. She put her coleslaw in the small cart, then cheese, hot dogs and buns. *I think I'll get an onion,* and she headed to produce, swerving to miss a kid darting in front of her, yelling, "Bananas, Mommy!" A taffy apple glistened deliciously, and she put that in the cart. *Look at you, Jessie, buying all these extras, right here in this busy store!*

Standing in line gave her time to think. *Fond, he said. I'm growing quite fond of you. That's a special word he saved for that exact moment, for me,* and a glow went through her. *But then, all that trouble he poured out. Yikes. Oh, well, then I poured out my troubles too.*

Into this kaleidoscope of feelings, the checkout person asked, "Isn't your name Jessica?"

She looked sharply up to see a thin-faced, fair young woman with honey blonde hair who looked vaguely familiar. She nodded.

"George?" the girl asked. Jessie nodded again. "We graduated together. I'm Tonya Henderson. We were next to each other in some classes," she said.

"Oh, yeah," Jessie said.

"Five thirteen," Tonya said, bagging the items. "Well, how've you been? What have you been up to?"

Digging in her wallet for exact change, Jessie said, "I'm

divorced now, and I have a little girl."

"Seriously? That's a lot in a year and a half. Who'd you marry?"

"Doug Stewart."

"Did he go to Fremd?"

"No, he's from McHenry."

"Oh. Do you have a picture of your little girl?"

Jessie shook her head, stuck her wallet in her pocket and picked up her groceries. "I'll get one and show it to you next time."

"Cool. Take care, Jessica."

"You can call me Jessie," and Tonya said okay as she turned to greet the next customer.

Jessie crossed back between the jammed cars. *That was nice, talking to Tonya. It was—what?—ordinary—like I'm joining the world of humans. And Doug's dropping Fiona off soon—and I'm happy about that. And Jakob. It's all as weird as can be.* She let out a half laugh.

11

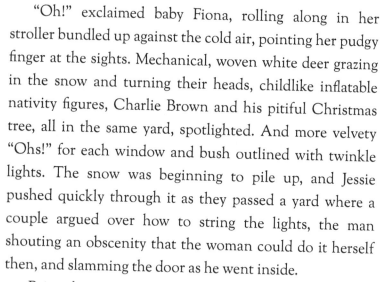

"Oh!" exclaimed baby Fiona, rolling along in her stroller bundled up against the cold air, pointing her pudgy finger at the sights. Mechanical, woven white deer grazing in the snow and turning their heads, childlike inflatable nativity figures, Charlie Brown and his pitiful Christmas tree, all in the same yard, spotlighted. And more velvety "Ohs!" for each window and bush outlined with twinkle lights. The snow was beginning to pile up, and Jessie pushed quickly through it as they passed a yard where a couple argued over how to string the lights, the man shouting an obscenity that the woman could do it herself then, and slamming the door as he went inside.

Being alone is easier. And that baby Jesus back there—full of hot air, and Mary and Joseph are like cartoon children. What's the point? Ridiculous.

That conversation Jakob and I had about God is the longest one I've ever had with anyone about that. Doug had asked her on their first date if she believed in God and if Jesus was her personal savior. She had said yes, knowing that was the answer he wanted, and the topic hadn't come up again. Thinking back to lunchtime with Jakob, she felt she could reverse his statements: "I've always felt alone. Always. I've never felt loved. Never." She acknowledged this unemotionally. But Jakob being so upset over losing his beliefs made her wonder if maybe she was missing something. What had he said? "...a love way beyond human love...." *I'm seeing a big question mark, like Jakob sees the words he thinks. It's black.*

"Hey! Let's go see Tonya," she said to Fiona. They were turning back on to Plum Grove now, the streets back to normal after the accident that had surely messed up somebody's life.

Tonya was wiping up her conveyor belt and squealed when she saw the baby. "Ooh, can I pick her up?" and she had Fiona unbuckled and cuddled in an instant. Fiona looked up at her and then looked at Jessie and smiled. "Oh, Jessie, she looks just like you!"

"Oh gosh, let's hope not," and they all laughed, including Fiona.

———

Around nine, Doug came, and Jessie asked to keep Fiona overnight. "Could have saved me a trip, if you had a phone," he chided, "but I'm happy you want to have more time with your daughter. That's righteous."

He'd packed extra clothes as well as a baby toothbrush and baby toothpaste for her four teeth, two white squares on top, two smaller ones on the bottom. Jessie felt clumsy putting pajamas on her, but they managed, and she'd cuddled right into Jessie's chest, and they'd both fallen straight asleep.

Saturday morning hadn't gone as well. Fiona kept crying and crying. *This is my fault, but I don't know what to do.*

"Did you use the Numzit? Did you try the teething rings I put in your freezer?" Doug asked when he came to get her.

"Oh no. I forgot all about them. Sorry," she said, and again, "Sorry," as she told Fiona goodbye. Her stupidity stalked her the rest of the day, which she puttered away musing again on how being alone is easier—*but being with people, especially Fiona, is more—what? Fun. Interesting.*

Doug had gotten her out with people some, mostly

through church. He'd said to her once after a cookout at Stephanie Nordstrum's, "Jessica, you've got to talk to people. Can't you speak once in a while or at least smile and nod your head? And you can't stay in the bathroom so much. People thought you were sick."

"I was."

He'd hugged her to him and said, "It's okay, don't worry. God will get us through."

But God hadn't, as far as Jessie could tell.

Restless on Sunday, she walked for miles through streams of melting snow in the fifty-degree sun. She trotted along Brockway Street, intent on a run-down yard, imagining how it would look if she could have fifteen minutes to pick up trash and trim bushes and sweep the porch and straighten the decrepit rocking chairs. Organ music blasted forth from across the street, turning her around to see the red doors of a church swing open. The minister walked out in white garb to greet worshipers, the first one of whom was Jakob.

Joy rushed through her in an irritating way, and she lined up behind a tree to peek at him. A gray-haired couple came behind him followed by a young boy and his parents.

111

They gathered around Jakob. *His family!*

Clusters of people soon filled the sidewalk, and rings of laughter lilted and chirped above the murmur. An elderly couple approached Jakob, who looked like a bumble bee in a swarm of butterflies, and began talking. Jessie could hear him: "...global injustice of climate change..." Heads turned his way and as quickly turned back to their circles; it was only Jakob. He was focused not on the people but the distance, unwittingly looking her direction. Intent on his face, wondering how she could endure his obsessions, it took Jessie a second to realize he'd seen her.

"Jessica!" he yelled. Horrified, stomach lurching, she watched him gallop across the street. No place to hide.

Jubilant, radiant, he tried to drag her back over to the crowd. She pushed him away, and said, "Stop! Leave me alone!" as though he were a stranger. He came at her again, and she swatted him in the face. His hurt look hurt her as well, but anger and humiliation propelled her down the block and around the corner.

"No! I'm not going to," she said out loud when tempted to scurry back to her apartment and lock herself in for the rest of the day. *No! I'm going to go through with my plan.*

112

Roderick was unloading groceries from the back of his SUV when Jessie walked up.

"Hello," she said, her voice so quiet he didn't hear her and almost ran over her when he turned to walk into the house, his arms full.

"What in the world are you doing here?" he demanded, and her idea suddenly seemed like a bright and beautiful balloon deflating.

She had to say something, though. "I wanted to tell you good luck for tomorrow. I hope your operation goes well, and your therapy goes well, and healing up and all that goes well too."

He looked at her like she was speaking a foreign language.

Oh gosh, I feel so dumb and phony. "Here, I'll get these," she said, and grabbed a couple bags.

"Thank you," he said, staring at her, and she followed him through the garage, glancing with satisfaction at the order she had given it, and into the kitchen she'd saved from ruin, though it was a day and a half messier since she'd left, including a couple cat accidents. They set their loads on the counter and stood there, looking straight ahead out the window into the backyard.

"Do you like lasagna?" Roderick asked, still staring out into the backyard.

"What's that?"

He looked down at her. "What's lasagna?"

She nodded, looking up at him.

"What's lasagna? Really? It's an Italian dish with pasta and tomatoes and cheese. I put sausage in mine."

"Something like spaghetti?"

"Yeah, sure."

"I'd probably like it."

Is he inviting me to eat with him? Not knowing, she said she'd better be going, and he said that she could stay and try some lasagna, if she wanted, and she said okay, and a little oxygen seemed to spurt into the room. *Man, this house seems so different than normal, and it's so quiet, I guess because it's Sunday afternoon. But it feels okay.*

Roderick sorted the groceries, putting lasagna ingredients on the counter next to the stove and salad items next to the sink, then started pulling out pans and dishes. Feeling in the way and not enjoying the odors from the cat turds and puddles, Jessie asked if he wanted her to clean up after the cat "since I'm so used to it." He said that would be fine, and one task led to another until she was chewing her gum, cleaning out the litter box and wiping up the cat's bathroom, right off the kitchen. She checked his den, too. Beer cans and other trash overflowed the wastebasket. *He still needs me,* and she put them in the trash bag and carried it up. Wonderful aromas from the cooking took over the house as she happily straightened up, scrubbed up, and then returned to the kitchen, standing on the far side of the counter out of his way, intrigued by his layering of the lasagna ingredients.

"The sage in the pork sausage flavors it just right," he commented, then went on after a brief hesitation. "I had planned this as an appreciation dinner for Lauren. Now she's gone, everything between us blown up. But this morning I took a notion to eat healthy before surgery tomorrow, a 'last supper,' I guess." He put the lasagna in the oven. "There."

Looking at the stovetop, slopped with tomato sauce, and the dirty pans and empty cans, Jessie offered to clean up.

"That would be great," he said, "while I fix the salad and garlic bread." And so, they worked in silence beside each other, the bulky Roderick and the tiny Jessie.

"I can't remember the last time I sat down to a meal

with someone else," he said as they sat down.

"Me, either," Jessie said, "except Jakob at lunchtime. Oh, and with my cousin Kelly."

"Lauren's birthday in June was my last time, I guess. Cheers," and Roderick held his glass up, then put it back down when Jessie didn't respond.

After some quiet eating, she said, "I like lasagna."

"What's not to like, right?" he said, wiping his mouth with his napkin. "Your friend—his name is Jakob? And you're—hmm—Jennifer?"

"Jessica—or Jessie."

"Jessica. Why can't I get that through my head? Jessie. Okay. Anyway, I heard some sounds from the kitchen the other day. He sounded pretty upset."

"He's upset over God."

"Who isn't?" Roderick snorted.

"I mean over his beliefs. He's always believed in God and now he's not so sure."

Long silence.

"What's it matter, really? It's mostly a philosophical issue to me and, in truth, I think I'm pulling for nonexistence because if there is a God, I am in a heap of trouble."

116

What's he mean by that? I don't want to be nosy, but he brought it up. "What kind of trouble?"

Unable to speak at first, he wound up sighing, "War can ruin a man.

"What's odd," he went on, as though talking to someone else again, "is that all those years passed relatively okay. Successful career supervising huge construction projects from here to Timbuktu. Literally, Timbuktu. Plenty of friends. Family good, outside of the marriage. No kids of our own, but we had Lauren.

"So was all that a lie?" he asked, gazing out in the backyard with the look of a worried child. Jessie put a chunk of lasagna in her mouth—*Man, this is so good! I wonder if I could learn to cook it*—and peered up at him, her head still oriented toward her plate, intrigued because of the faraway sound of his voice. She watched him shake his head, as though to clear it.

"Retirement came, too much time on my hands, and dreams started up. Nightmares again, after forty years, for God's sake." He speared a cherry tomato with his fork and shook it at the window. "Your letters..." he said

My letters? What, that one note I left on the microwave?

"Why in God's name did you not mail them?" he asked,

his face twisting hard.

Jessie glanced over her shoulder to see if someone was standing out there. *Maybe he's seeing things. That wouldn't be too surprising with all the pills he took.*

"Mailing those letters instead of the ones that glossed over everything could have made all the difference." *Uh-oh, he's going to cry.*

"Genevieve," he went on, and she knew that was his wife, "I'm sorry. But Vevie, it wasn't our fault, it wasn't. We were pawns in a horrendous drama..."

Jessie was trying to think what she could say to bring him back when she heard Jakob's motor scooter outside.

She jumped up from the table and said, "Oh, no. That's Jakob. Send him away."

Roderick looked puzzled, but in a few seconds the doorbell rang.

"It's that boyfriend of yours?"

She nodded.

"You don't want to talk to him?"

"No!" she said. "We had sort of a fight. Get rid of him."

"Might be better if you talk," he said starting down the hall.

Oh gosh, I've got to hide. She ran into the cat's bathroom, then dashed back out and grabbed her plate from the table and rushed to the counter to pile on another piece of lasagna and hide again. Then she darted in and out one more time to get her drink, closing the door quietly as Roderick and Jakob entered the kitchen.

"Sir, my devastation has no bounds," she heard Jakob say and rolled her eyes at his stilted language and whiny tone. "I have erred most drastically with Jessica and she has rejected me publicly. I apologize for disturbing you, but I knew not where to go except here, where I have known her."

"Slow down, son, stop beating your head and stand still. That's not going to help. Calm down here and let's try and sort this out."

In a higher more agitated pitch, Jakob said, "I fear there's nothing to sort out. I am doomed to a lonely existence because I can't..."

"Stop! Stop rocking," Roderick commanded. "Do you need food? Have you eaten lately?"

Apparently, Jakob had to think about that. "Not since breakfast."

"Well, it's two o'clock in the afternoon. Alright. Go over there and sit down at the table. I'll bring you some nourishment."

Jessie heard him set the meal before Jakob, who said, "I'm vegetarian."

"Eat."

Jessie ate too, and the atmosphere calmed, back to more of that mellow Sunday afternoon feeling.

"Okay," Roderick said quietly. "What's happened?"

"I saw her across the street from my church this morning. I thought she had come on purpose because she wanted to see me. Naturally, I was ecstatic. But I misjudged, and when I ran over to her..." Pause. "...she rejected me—and—she struck me."

Jessie, perched on the toilet seat hearing every word, lost hold of her fork. It clanged against the sink before she could grab it.

"The cat. It's just the cat," Roderick said.

"Well, you can tell there's no hope," Jakob continued. "Girls reject me. Let me count the ways," and he gave a half-hearted laugh. "But none of them ever struck me before."

Did I strike him?

"Women are never easy, that's well-established. Being on your own has its advantages."

Right.

120

"But right when it seems God is exiting, she has entered."

"Wait now. Have her take the place of God? I don't think that's a very good start for a..."

"No, no, no, that's not what I mean. I wouldn't think that way. A companion on the journey, that's all my heart desires."

I feel bad. And that idea, a companion on the journey—that does sound nice, the way he says it. Kind of nice.

Roderick whispered something.

"What did you say?" Jakob asked.

"I had a companion on my journey once. Her name was My Phuong." He pronounced the name reverently. "I hear you, man."

Then, he spoke up so Jessie would hear, it seemed. "You're good kids who could use somebody else." He picked up some dishes and headed for the sink. "Believe me, I'm no one to give advice, but I will say this: don't give up the battle if you're sure of your objective. Change your strategy maybe, but don't give up. And honesty's the best policy. I've learned that by not doing it. Now, how about some spumoni?"

Jessie wanted some, whatever it was.

121

12

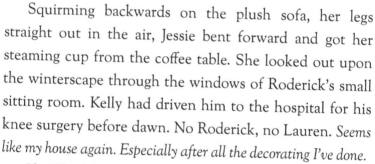

Squirming backwards on the plush sofa, her legs straight out in the air, Jessie bent forward and got her steaming cup from the coffee table. She looked out upon the winterscape through the windows of Roderick's small sitting room. Kelly had driven him to the hospital for his knee surgery before dawn. No Roderick, no Lauren. *Seems like my house again. Especially after all the decorating I've done.*

She'd had fun tacking up twinkle lights at the windows and setting around singing angels and funny snowman candles, even in the bathrooms. A tall, skinny, artificial Christmas tree graced the landing halfway up the staircase, the first sight to see coming in the front door. It looked perfect with the newly-shampooed carpet on the steps, clean and fresh as new fallen snow.

Sipping cocoa, she recalled all the strangeness of yesterday. The incident at Jakob's church. The lasagna dinner with Roderick. *Oh my gosh, so weird.*

She had decided to leave the house for a while, in case Jakob came. *I think I do want to keep trying with him, but I'm not ready yet. I'll walk to the bank and get money, buy new sneakers, find a Christmas present for Fiona, maybe try to buy a sandwich somewhere.* In the afternoon, she would start arranging the living room for Roderick's return, since he wouldn't be able to climb steps for a while. They'd discussed it over the spumoni ice cream yesterday, after Jakob had gone.

The musical ceramic Christmas tree on the table turned, its teensy lights twinkling and its tinny arrangement of O Tannenbaum offering cheer. The cat wandered in and jumped up on the couch with a pained grunt, settling in beside her, and she allowed it, stroking the poor animal's fur.

She set her cup down and stretched her limbs to the limit, like the cat often did. *I hate to leave, but Jakob will probably come pretty soon and I don't want to be caught within blocks of this house or he'll scoot around and find me.* Five minutes later, the tree unplugged, the rinsed cup in the drainer, she ventured out into the cold, gray day.

Wow. I got my money, bought my new sneakers and Fiona's present, and ate lunch out, all with no problems. And no Jakob, thank heaven. I need this time. His tire tracks snaked up the driveway in the newly fallen snow. Footprints, too, that went to the back of the house. A little scary, his persistence, but feelings of deep satisfaction prevailed as she unlocked Roderick's door and went into the relatively clean-smelling, orderly house, at ease and alone.

And she loved what she'd gotten for Fiona, a baby pantsuit in maroon velvet with a white collar decorated with flowers and lace. She'd seen it right away on a faceless dummy Fiona's size. A salesperson had walked by, and Jessie had actually tapped her on the shoulder. "I want that outfit for my daughter, the shoes and socks, too." She thought the lady would take the outfit off the dummy and hand it to her, so she had a shopping lesson when the clerk found a nine months size on the rack and then took her to the shoe section and handed her the plastic box with the tiny patent leather shoes shining inside and pulled fancy white socks off a hook. "Would you like it gift-wrapped? That's an extra five dollars." She said yes and was glad. It was so beautiful! Even so, when she got back to Harvard

Drive, she couldn't resist carefully unwrapping the box, standing the socks up in the shoes and working the tiny buttons down the back of the top. She smelled the clothes, held them to her cheek and up to a mirror, imagining Fiona wearing them, then re-wrapped.

Okay. I'm ready for Jakob, came to her while cleaning the living room. *He can come whenever he wants. Tomorrow would be okay.* Enjoying her gum, sugarfree raspberry from Jakob, she bit her tongue, hard. She hardly noticed the pain, though, and revved up the vacuum. *Raspberry is just right for how I'm feeling inside. Man, it's yummy!*

"I know what a dog is," Jessie snapped.

She had seen Jakob coming up the walk and had grabbed her coat and stepped out and said, "Hi. Want to go for a walk?" because she wanted to have the house to herself, at least for another day or two.

Jakob had looked down at her. *I see suspicion in his eyes. I need to be nice.*

"Sure. Walk. Okay," he'd said.

In short order, they'd disposed of Sunday's incident.

"I'm sorry about what happened Sunday."

"Me too."

125

"That's okay."

"Yeah."

They had startled when a dog, barking furiously, raced along the other side of a fence.

"A dog came in our yard once, my first time to see one. It didn't bite me, I don't think, more licking, but it scared me," Jessie said.

"Was your mom or dad there?"

"No."

"How old were you?"

"I guess four or maybe three. It was before I started school."

"Wait a minute, how could you be that old and not have seen a dog? You mean nobody ever taught you woof-woof? Nobody ever taught you what a dog is?"

"I know what a dog is!"

"Now you do. Were you out in the yard alone? You shouldn't have been, at that age. Unless it was fenced in. Was it fenced in?"

When Jessie didn't answer, Jakob said, "Uh-oh. You want me to stop judging your life, right?"

She nodded. They walked on in silence for a block.

"I don't want to judge your life, Jessica, and when you

say that, it makes me nervous. I'm trying to get acquainted. Is it judgmental for me to ask you questions about your childhood?"

After thinking it over, she said, "I'll just tell you. I was on my own. My mother went to work and came home every night. She was there, but I was on my own as far back as I can remember."

"Didn't you have a father?

"No."

They walked on, occasionally jostling against each other. *Doug felt rough and bony when we bumped into each other. Jakob's soft.* She took a piece of gum from her pocket, unwrapped it, and put it in her mouth.

"You chew an awful lot of gum," he said.

She shrugged. "I got in the habit at Aunt Barb's, she offered me a piece. Chewing helps me think and keep myself organized."

Jakob started up with statistics he'd seen in a dentist's office related to gum and decay, gum and TMJ (whatever that was), gum and gums. *Does he ever stop? I don't know what TMJ is, and I don't care. He's ruining everything.* She was about to blast him when wild honking overhead drew their eyes to a graceful V of geese in the winter sky.

"They're late. Eons of evolution have established instinctive patterns, now violently disturbed by the rapid onset of climate change."

"That's too bad," Jessie said, meaning it. *I do care about nature and the environment, but it's too bad he sounds like a science textbook so much.* They watched until the birds were specks.

More silence until Jakob said, "I saw pretty-looking lights through Roderick McCoy's windows. They're pretty."

"Yeah, I found some decorations and put them up."

"They're pretty."

"Yeah. Thanks. I saw your family, I guess," Jessie said. "On Sunday."

"Oh, at the church. Yeah. That's my family—my mom and dad and my sister Martha and her husband Nathan and their son Simon Peter Joel."

"Yeah, I thought it was your family." And then Jessie decided to say, "Your mom's pretty."

"Lydia. Yeah, she's pretty. She drives us a little crazy, but she's a fine person, and she sure does love us. And she runs a very energy-efficient household."

"Why does she drive you crazy?"

"Oh, she doesn't have much of a light side. She's always trying to be righteous and expects everybody else to, too."

"So she's a lot like you."

Jakob stopped and looked down at her. His eyes were serious and his mouth opened, but then a smile took over his face. "Okay, you got me a little bit. By the way, what's your mother's name?"

"Nancy. Some people called her Nan. She was killed in a car accident in July."

"Oh, I'm sorry, Jessica," and he patted her cheek, and they looked into each other's eyes. Jessie got flustered and looked away. They were at the end of South Three Willow Court. They headed back, resuming the rhythm of their walking and talking.

"I'm very happy right now," Jakob said.

"Does that mean you're not so worried today?"

Jakob wrinkled his brow. "Yes, I think it does. Having pleasant company helps," and they bumped against each other again as they stepped off the curb.

"How about God today?"

Wrinkled brow again. "Yes," he said. "God is great and God is good today."

"That's good," Jessie said.

"Yes," Jakob said again. "But don't get me wrong. I'm still..."

"I didn't get you wrong."

Jakob frowned. "Did Roderick McCoy get to the hospital okay this morning?"

"Kelly said yes."

Kelly had said a lot more, too, and as she and Jakob walked, Jessie lapsed into a mental review of it all. Roderick's mood was swinging around "like a trapeze at a circus,'" Kelly had said. "First off, when I'm barely awake, he's all gung-ho about 'life after new knees,' how he's going to get his act together and big plans to go to California to see Lauren and track down 'that rascal Wayne,' whoever that is."

"That's his army friend," Jessie told her.

"Okay, and then he expected Lauren to call last night, but she didn't, and he started to cry, Jessie, actually cry, and then snapped out of it and said—as though he'd discovered gold—he was better off alone because he wouldn't have to worry about any more 'desertion in the ranks,' those were his exact words. And when he got out of the car, he acted like he was telling a hilarious joke and said, 'If I get lucky and don't wake up from this, you won't have to come back and get me.'"

"Wow," Jessie had said.

"Yeah, wow. He talked about you guys, too," Kelly had said. "He called you—sorry, Jessie—'my strange little cleaning girl and her strange boyfriend,'" Kelly had said, stifling a laugh.

"What'd he say about us?"

"Other than that? He said you would be strictly an employee. Me too, he said. 'I'm alone in this broken-down world, and I might as well start acting like it.'"

Jakob's voice snapped Jessie back to the present.

"I hope everything goes okay for Roderick McCoy."

"Me too."

Maybe I should tell him I was in the bathroom Sunday and heard everything he and Roderick said. No, no need for that. But I will tell him how I'm feeling about Roderick and my job and everything. "I hope everything goes okay too, but I just work for him, that's all. And, um, I've been feeling a little bit bad because I want this job to keep going so I've tried to be nicer."

"Aha. Brown-nosing you mean?"

She nodded. He shrugged and she felt better.

"If I may ask," Jakob said when they crossed the street

on to Harvard Drive, "what did you do as a child, when you were on your own, as you say? TV? Did you have friends to play with? Toys?"

"I painted."

"What did you paint?"

"By number."

"All the time?"

"Pretty much."

"Jessica, you are most intriguing."

"Call me Jessie."

"Okay," and they blushed a little.

"Your mother got you the paint-by-number kits?"

She shook her head.

"Oh. Then who got them for you? Did you go to a store or order them off Amazon or what?"

She shook her head again. "I don't know who gave them to me. It's a mystery."

They were back at Roderick's front door, and Jessie dismissed him with, "You can come for lunch tomorrow if you want."

"Ooh, the keys to the kingdom!" he said, which raised her eyebrows. "Oh, don't worry," he said. "It's only an expression to say I'm happy you're letting me into your life a little more."

Hmm. I'm not sure I want him to think he can unlock me. Hmm...

Near the end of their walk Jakob had commented that something stank. Jessie had smelled it too, and the smell had persisted in the house. Finally, she thought to check her shoes. Her brand-new shoes. Dog poop. *Oops. I should have checked them outside.* The soles were intricate with squiggly treads and dots and deep grooves. She soaked them in soapy water and spent a good while using a brush and a nail to work it out. She cleaned and sanitized floors and carpets all through the house where she had tracked it, humming O Tannenbaum and smiling once in a while as she worked. *Oh well, that's life,* and she sprayed pine scent air freshener through the house and as she backed out the door.

13

Jakob came on his lunch hour for the next three days, and Jessie was always ready for him now. Mornings were a luxury of cleaning in splendid isolation and looking forward to his ring of the doorbell. Afternoons, she went over their conversations as she worked. Walking home in her new shoes, she joyed in the holiday streetlights—colorful snowmen, decorated trees, and choo choo trains glistening into gently falling snow. She greeted people on the street sometimes, and then enjoyed her cozy apartment. Friday nights with Fiona were getting better.

"Sounds very beautiful," Jakob said when she described Fiona's outfit on Wednesday.

"And this guy wrapped it up in blue and silver paper with angels and a shiny blue bow on top with silvery lines shooting out all around like a star."

"Fiona's pretty little, huh?"

Jessie nodded.

"I can't get over you being a mother."

She nodded again.

"I'm not being critical," he quickly added.

"I know."

Their lunches tasted ever more delicious, and they covered a wide range of topics, often family, mostly his. In one conversation, he said that he had wounds from childhood like anybody else.

"But you talk to each other and go places together all the time. Your family sounds perfect," Jessie said.

"Me? My family is nutsy nutso. I think what you mean is that I have a family."

"Oh. Yeah. I guess that's it. And Jakob," she said, "thank you for not asking me about mine all the time."

"You're welcome. I can tell it's hard for you. I don't want to put you on the spot."

"I can tell you can tell. Thank you," she said, and the look that came across his face filled her throat with longing and a velvety fluttering within. Her passions startled her so much—her mouth watering and heat working up her face—that she got up and started for the cat's bathroom to regain her composure. Jakob jumped up too, but she passed by, saying, "I have to go to the bathroom. Be right back," and sat in there for a few minutes. Cooled down and breathing normally again, she went back to the table.

Jakob confided to her that he'd been thrown off the Environmental Concerns Task Force at church for being overly fervent.

"Not to be mean," she said, "but that makes sense because you get so carried away." *Oh gosh, it's sad when he hangs his head like that. Maybe I shouldn't have said that.*

"True. It's all tied up with my doubts about God. Well, and my condition."

Neither of them knew what to say after that. Jakob brought up the weather and having to decide each morning if he'd wear coveralls or his coat. Jessie nodded in sympathy, but good conversation was over, the depth of their time together this day spent.

On Thursday she opened the door, and he said, "I'm having it bad today."

She nodded and opened the door wider.

"But I am happy in this moment, Jessie," he said as he entered, "because you have opened your door to me."

136

He helped her carry Roderick's TV up to the living room, holding the front corner and backing up the steps while she steadied the bottom corner. They rested it on each step. *He's strong, and I love how he asks me if I'm ready before moving to the next step.* But it was heavy, and when they got to the top, they hurried down the hall. Her arms were aching, but she and Jakob were still in perfect step. They set it in place, and looked at each other, moved to each other. Jacob leaned down, and she stretched to him, and they kissed.

"That was nice," Jakob said as they released.

Jessie nodded.

"I can taste your gum," he said.

"Is that okay?"

He nodded.

She smiled and looked at the floor. "Do you want to have lunch now?"

They gobbled their sandwiches and went walking, chomping on their apples in sunshine as bright as the air was cold.

"Maybe we should go out somewhere. On a date, I mean," Jakob said.

Jessie shook her head. *I don't want to go out. Eating and*

talking and walking—and gosh! now kissing... that's enough.

They walked on in silence until Jakob asked, "By the way, are you a church-goer?"

"I only went with Doug."

"Didn't like it?"

"Too many people."

"Aha. That would be hard for you."

"Not for you?"

"Sure, sometimes, but starting as a baby helped, I suppose. It's like a second home, like my extended family."

She nodded. "You went to college, right? What was that like?"

Jakob's expression clouded over. "Socially, challenging. Some really bad scenes. Not as bad as high school, though. In fact," he said, "I made a couple friends. But—it was intense. I'm still recovering, really, which is frustrating. I was too emotionally exhausted to go straight on to my Master's in Earth and Environmental Sciences; I will someday soon, though."

Jessie looked up at him and nodded.

"Academically, I was in my element," he continued. "Interestingly, I enjoyed my English classes more than the environmental classes. Less stressful. My electives were mostly literature and linguistics. Hey, listen to this: many languages give lots of information in one word—for example, in some languages the word aunt can tell you whether she's the mother's sister or father's sister or married into the family."

"You know so much," Jessie said. Admiration tinged her words.

Jakob ducked his head and gave it a funny little twist and smiled. Jessie sensed his heat. She had a vision of the two of them stretched out on Roderick's bed, embracing. She almost made a sound at the excitement tickling her.

Oh gosh, I'm thinking about sex with Doug—the burning when he came into me—holding my breath at the pain—he felt too big—and then it would be over, thank heaven. "Intercourse is for procreation, Jessica," he had advised, so they had only had sex enough to get pregnant with Fiona and then once more—and then Plan B—and then the end of the marriage.

I think sex with Jakob would be different, she imagined. *But that's way too much to think about, like a mountain I could never climb, at least not right now.*

They were about finished eating on Friday when the doorbell rang.

"You come too, okay?" Jessie requested as she got up.

She opened the door to Kelly. "Hi, kids. Gotta get some things for Rod. A deck of cards, his cell phone charger, and a heavier coat."

Jessie knew where to find the cards and had seen his charger when she'd pulled the nightstand out to vacuum. They went to the entryway closet to find a coat. She'd been delighted recently to find the closet stuffed to overflowing, knowing it was probably good for several hours of cleaning.

"How is Roderick McCoy?" Jakob asked Kelly.

"Okay, I think. Surgery went well. He'll move to rehab over the weekend. Any messages?"

"Um, yeah. Tell him I, uh, I've been thinking of him and, you know, hoping everything went well," Jessie said. "And tell him Precious is okay," she said as the cat padded through the foyer.

"So how you guys doing? Haven't seen you for a while. I guess you're doing good, I mean, at least you're doing, I mean, here you both are."

"We're doing good," Jessie said.

Jakob smiled and patted her head.

"Don't pat my head, Jakob."

He stopped patting but kept smiling.

"I'm going now and leaving you lovebirds to yourself," she said, laughing herself out the door.

Fiona woke Jessie up with her babbling. She was sitting up in the bed and looking around. When Jessie opened her eyes and said, "Hi, Fiona," the baby squealed and fell over on her. They rolled around laughing and cuddling. *Is this really my life? I feel like I'm in somebody else's body, some very lucky person.* She curled around her baby, wishing she herself were a baby again. But when memories and questions about her young years started swirling in her head, she scooped Fiona up and headed for the kitchen.

"Here's your new chair," Jessie said, fitting Fiona into the little plastic seat Doug had buckled and strapped to a kitchen chair.

She alternated between feeding her bites of baby cereal and strained fruit and feeding herself Cheerios and bananas, and they conversed a bit, such as it was. Whenever Jessie laughed at Fiona's utterings and expressions, Fiona would laugh back. After breakfast there was a loaded diaper to change and Fiona's twisting around didn't help, but Jessie managed, thinking the same as with the dog poop—no big deal. They were having fun reading a book—*What? She knows how to turn pages?*—when a rap came at the back door.

"Who could that be?" she said out loud, and Fiona answered her with baby talk. "Seriously, your daddy's not coming until two o'clock, and the only other person who knows where I live is Kelly."

"Give me that baby!" Kelly said as she entered, grabbing her out of Jessie's arms. "You must be Fiona. What a cutie pie squeezembeezem little dollie girl you are," she cooed, in a squealy baby voice. Fiona reared back and looked at Kelly in alarm, got intrigued briefly when Kelly stuck her tongue out and wiggled it, but then turned and reached for her mother.

"Already a mommy's girl, huh? Oh, come on, little dollie, you can get used to cousin Kelly," and she started jiggling the baby and walking into the kitchen, but at Fiona's first fuss Jessie took her. "Okay, raise yourself a spoiled brat," Kelly said, and started looking all around the kitchen and wandering through the other rooms.

"Pretty nice, cuz. Needs pictures on the walls though. Make it your own."

Jessie and Fiona were following her.

"Hey, I came over with an idea," Kelly said, plopping

down on the couch. "You know how you're trying to get in good with Rod so you can keep your job? Why don't we bake him some cookies, and tomorrow I can take you to the hospital to deliver them?"

"Um—okay."

Jessie talked Kelly into walking the half-block to the Jewel, Fiona leading the way in her stroller.

"Wait a minute," Jessie said as they neared the store. "Look at all those people, all those cars! Let's come back later, when it's not so busy."

"It'll probably just get busier all afternoon, c'mon," Kelly answered her, pushing the stroller steadily ahead. And they had a good time, Kelly making all kinds of eyes at Fiona and getting her to laugh in her grocery cart perch while they moved through the crowded aisles to find the ingredients for chocolate chip cookies.

And then, disaster.

Jessie had gone off for eggs and paused behind a heavy woman with several children who was checking her eggs for cracks and dropped a couple coupons. Jessie knelt to pick them up and give them to her at the exact moment the woman began to move on and tumbled backward over the stooping Jessie. A nanosecond of shock, and then

143

pandemonium, a perfect mess of flying eggs cracking onto jars of peanut butter across the aisle and screaming children and the groaning woman trying to get up, Jessie at the bottom of it all. The woman cussed Jessie out and the kids slid around on egg yolks. Mumbling "Sorry," Jessie hurried away. Soon a code fifteen in aisle twenty-two came over the loudspeaker.

"What's that on your cheek?" Kelly said when she rejoined her and Fiona.

"Egg. There was an accident," she said, wiping it away.

"Oh. In aisle twenty-two?"

Jessie nodded.

"Oops. Well, did you get the eggs?"

"Oh. No. Would you go get them? I'll stay here with Fiona. I can't go back there right now."

"Good grief. What'd you do? Were you the accident?"

Jessie had wrapped her arms around Fiona and laid her head on the tiny shoulder, and Fiona was messing up her hair with both hands. She nodded.

"You alright, Jessie?"

Jessie nodded, even though she felt like her knees were going to buckle.

"Okay, okay, kooky cousin. I'll go get the eggs. Then

we'll have everything. And you know, accidents happen."

While they waited for Kelly, she huddled with Fiona, on the lookout for the family. They rumbled by but didn't turn down her aisle.

"Fiona," she said, fighting tears, "I'm an idiot." The baby turned her head slightly and squinted at her as if weighing up her words.

When they went to check out, Jessie saw Tonya but wasn't up to conversation and guided their cart into another line. Shaken and shaking, she paid and Tonya saw her as they rolled by her counter and called out, but Jessie kept her eyes down. Outside, transferring Fiona back into her stroller, she saw the family from aisle twenty-two and heard one of the kids say, "There's that girl that made you fall. Oh my God, she's got a baby?"

They started walking, Kelly chattering and Jessie repeating to herself, *if I can just make it home...* That was a left-over line from one time when her mother had had a flat tire on their way back from the doctor and kept driving, saying, if I can just make it home. She'd made it, driving on the rim, the tire shredded. Jessie now felt like that tire, but they made it, finally. She was behind her building again, safe from the world.

14

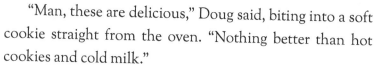

"Man, these are delicious," Doug said, biting into a soft cookie straight from the oven. "Nothing better than hot cookies and cold milk."

"Absolutely. Got any cold milk, Jessie?" Kelly asked, opening the refrigerator, finding some, and serving Doug a nice big glass.

"It's very nice meeting you," she purred to Doug, "even if you are my cousin's ex now. Jessie amazed us, getting married and all. And now, this precious little princess on her little throne." Fiona sat in her plastic chair and Kelly rubbed her fuzzy head. She spluttered a raspberry at Kelly, eyes dancing. Kelly and Doug laughed at the baby. Jessie washed dishes at the sink, her back to them.

"Yeah, she's a keeper," Doug said.

What a stupid thing to say, like maybe he's been thinking of giving her away. But I shouldn't talk bad about him when he's been saying how well I'm doing with Fiona.

In a leading-the-witness manner, Kelly said, "And she thinks you're a good guy, so we were surprised when you split." Sitting down next to him and looking him directly in the eyes, the two of them talking as though Jessie wasn't there, Kelly passed him another cookie.

He munched for a minute and then said, "Yeah, it was tough. I thought I could—I hate to say fix her—how to say it?—help her live a more normal life, after all she'd been through."

"You mean with her mother?" Kelly prompted.

"The mother who wasn't a mother," Doug said. "The way that woman neglected her and kept her isolated, it's a wonder she's doing as well as she is. And Jessie," he called to her, "you are doing great."

That may be true, what he said, but still, she was my mother. She bought my clothes and food and took me to the eye doctor for glasses. Nobody has the right to talk about her that way.

"Jessie has the makings of a fine woman," Doug concluded. "And by God's grace, I've forgiven her for..." His eyes closed briefly. "...for everything."

147

Right. Thanks. Now please go away.

"But now Fiona, little one, it's just about nap time, isn't it? We'd better head home," he said, unbuckling her and dressing her for the cold until she looked like a baby Sasquatch, and, in a flurry of farewells, they were gone.

"I still can't get over him marrying you, Jessie."

"Shut up, Kelly."

"Oo-oo, testy. Okay, I'm outta here," she said putting the last cookie in the shoebox from Jessie's new sneakers, the only container they could find. "I'll pick you up around noon tomorrow," she called as she went out the back door.

Jessie didn't answer and couldn't imagine going. She scoured the greasy cookie sheets in the lukewarm, gray water with no suds. *I should get fresh dish water. Too tired. Feel awful. Shredded, I feel shredded.* A bright winter sun streamed into the kitchen and in its rays she saw every dust mote in the air and crumb on the table she'd just wiped. *Those particles look so heavy. Like my life. Full of mess and problems nobody can see most of the time, but they're there,* she sighed, a sour fatigue on her face, in her bones.

She went to bed, making a cocoon of her sheets and blankets and trying not to think of the accident at the grocery store, but all she could see were flying eggs, and she heard again the soft smash and crack they made and picked dried egg white off her cheek and refused the tears forming behind her eyes.

⁓

Turning her truck on to Plum Grove in sparse Sunday traffic, Kelly said, "Hey, Jessie, wanna' see if Jakob wants to go?"

"No." After they'd kissed on Thursday and not on Friday, Jessie was confused. She still wanted weekends off from Jakob.

"Aw, c'mon, the more the merrier. You two are doing good, right?"

"I don't know where he lives."

"You got a phone number for him?"

She shook her head, wincing at a sensation of sharp little blades cutting through fuzziness in her throat.

Kelly turned into a parking lot and pulled out her phone. "What's Jakob Otteson's address?" she said to it. "Unknown. Do you know his parents' address? Do you know their names?"

Jessie had done a lot of thinking after the grocery store incident about how bad she was at being out in the world, how hard it was. *Even dangerous. I feel like a zoo animal who got out by accident. What street do I run down? Will I get hit by a car or what other terrible thing might happen? I just want to be safe in my cage.* But after sleeping soundly through the night she decided, again, that venturing out was worth it. In that spirit, half-hearted as it was, she said, "His mother's name is Lydia." And they were soon parked in Otteson's driveway.

Jessie was considering going to the door, but Kelly jumped out saying, "I'll go since you're so shy." The dad answered and Jessie watched Kelly start jabbering, not hearing Jakob's scooter until he was squinting through the window at her. They beheld each other carefully for an instant, and then she rolled the window down as Kelly scurried up.

"Jakob! Perfect timing. Wanna' go see Rod with us? We baked him some cookies, and we're headed over to the V.A."

"Hi, son," the father said, trailing behind. "Nice to meet Kelly, but I haven't met your other friend here."

"This is Jessie," Jakob said with a big smile. "Jessie, this is Leif Otteson, my dad."

Lydia came out, pulling her coat on. "Hi, everybody. Jakob, let me meet your friends," and he introduced again and said, "We're going to see Roderick McCoy at Lovell

V.A. hospital for knee surgery. He's in rehab now. I'm going to put my scooter in the garage."

Lydia held her hand out to Jessie. "How nice to meet you, Jessie. Jakob says you're a special friend."

Jessie blushed and nodded and said thank you. *Does that make sense, to say thank you? I don't know what else to say.*

"You're welcome here anytime. We hope Jakob will bring you by for a visit soon."

She nodded and Kelly and Jakob climbed in, sandwiching her, and everyone waved. Kelly talked through most of the drive with only an occasional question to Jakob and Jessie, but they didn't care. They weren't listening, just sitting quietly against each other. Jessie smelled him, a not unpleasant smell of—of what? Of Jakob and his scooter.

She watched stores and restaurants fly by, and Christmas decorations, and water towers painted with flowers and designs and the names of towns. *This is the farthest I've ever been from home, but I'm not saying anything because they'd make a big deal out of it.*

The day had grown increasingly gray and windy. She saw a man struggling to control his large dog. The animal lurched around, garbage gusting by it. As they passed the scene, she craned her neck looking through the back window and saw the man trip over the leash and hit the ground, causing her to relive the brutality of that first bam when you don't know what's happening. If Kelly hadn't been rattling on, she might have told them, "This woman in the grocery store yesterday fell down on top of me with open eggs that smashed everywhere. It was awful." She might have.

"There will be signs in the sun, the moon, and the stars…" Jakob mumbled.

"Huh?" Kelly said. "What'd you say, Jakob?"

"Trying to remember what was preached this morning."

"Preached? Spare us," and she got back to her gossipy account of something or other.

Jakob leaned his head back, closed his eyes, a faint groan escaping his mouth.

"What about the sun, moon, and stars?" Jessie asked.

Jakob looked out the window, concentrating. "Oh, man. What did Jesus say? People would be fainting from 'fear and foreboding' because of what's coming upon the world. The 'powers of heaven' would be shaken over it. Naturally, it's throwing me back into grappling with the dying of the planet and…" He hung his head, shook it. "And though Jesus' point was redemption and the preacher tried to spin a message of hope out of all the weirdness, my soul isn't buying it," and he slunk down in the seat and went into himself, even with Jessie right there.

They filed into Roderick's room, Jessie feeling like they were three clowns, rotund Kelly at the head of the parade in a multicolored tunic top with her fluorescent hair and red-as-red-can-be lipstick, handing her silver helium "Get Well Soon" balloon to Roderick.

"Hey, Rod!" she said. "We came to cheer you up."

Then came her, "the strange little cleaning girl," as Roderick had called her. She felt tinier and weirder than ever, carrying the shoe box of cookies. "Hi," she said, with a self-conscious wave.

Jakob came last, flashing a nervous smile at Roderick, who was sitting up in sweats, legs stretched out on the bed.

"Well, for crying out loud, who would have thought," he said, reaching his hand out to Jakob to shake. "Sit down, sit down, people. What a surprise. Take a seat now, and tell me what's up."

The TV showing a football game provided the only light in the dark room. Jessie handed him the shoe box and perched in a chair under the TV.

"For me? Well, what a nice surprise. Thank you, thank you." He sniffed, wrinkling his nose, and Jessie knew it smelled rubbery from the sneakers. But he held the box out anyway, and they all took one.

"Mm-m-m, good as Mama's," Roderick pronounced.

Putting the box aside, he said, "Watch this," and slowly, grimacing, lifted his leg and bent his knee. "That's seventy-eight degrees or close to it. When I get to ninety I go home, probably Thursday. That is, if I don't eat all these cookies. I've got to lose weight."

They laughed and Roderick was about to say something else when Kelly pulled her phone out of her pocket and exited, saying she had to take this one.

"Jessie, Lauren said to tell you hi."

"Oh. You talked to Lauren?"

He nodded. "She called Monday night to see how surgery went but my phone was dead—I'd left the charger behind—so I didn't get the message until it got charged up on Friday. She had left another message, which I accidentally deleted along with one from somebody else—I'm no good at this—but I finally got her Friday night."

"Oh. Is she okay?" Jessie asked.

Roderick considered. "I don't know really. 'I am fine. How are you?' That was about it. Perfectly perfunctory." He looked toward the door where a cart rattled by, then looked out the window. "I can't find my loving uncle self anymore. I'm alone, that's what I need to get used to."

A deadly tickle in her throat sent Jessie rushing into his bathroom, the heavy door thunk-slamming behind her. Heating up, she tried to slurp from the sink spigot and hold back her cough long enough to blow her nose, but finally had to throw up in the toilet. The siege over, she drank more water and washed and dried her face with paper towels and blew her nose one more time. *Oh, I don't even want to go back out there I'm so embarrassed. I wish I was home in bed.* She re-entered the room to hear Jakob say, "If I were going to take my own life, I'd take pills."

"A pistol for me. Done correctly, no pain, no complications," Roderick stated.

"Oh, Jessica, Jessie, we're talking hypothetically," Jakob quickly said, then asked if she was okay.

"I think so," she nodded, clearing her throat. "Sorry for all the noise and everything."

"Just so you're okay," Jakob said.

155

"Right," Roderick said.

"Your house is decorated for Christmas," she told him.

"Great."

"And the living room is ready for you once we move your recliner up. Jakob and Kelly are going to help. Maybe we'll do it today."

"Sounds good." He reached for the water pitcher. "I'm thirsty from those cookies." Jessie quickly grabbed the pitcher and poured him a cup of ice water, then went into action discarding used tissue and cups and arranging puzzle books, pens, nail clippers, while the men watched football. She threw the newspaper in the wastebasket and folded a blanket.

"Appreciate you cleaning up, Miss Cleaning Lady. And hey, how nice of you kids to come, no joke. But I feel a nap coming on, post-surgical fatigue, I think."

Jakob shook hands again, Jessie said she'd see him soon, and they walked down the hall, surprising Kelly sitting in a lounge, chips in one hand, candy bar in the other.

"We going already?"

15

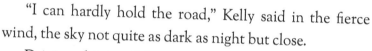

"I can hardly hold the road," Kelly said in the fierce wind, the sky not quite as dark as night but close.

Driving, driving. Silence, silence.

"Hey, Jessie, will you remember me tomorrow?"

Hesitation. "Yeah."

And then Kelly kept asking and back and forth they went.

"Will you remember me next week?"

"Yes."

"Next month?"

"Yes!"

"Next year?"

"What's wrong with you? Of course I will."

"Knock-knock"

No response.

"Knock-knock."

"What? Oh—who's there?"

"See, you forgot me already."

Jakob laughed.

And then knock-knock fest, one after the other.

"Knock-knock."

"Who's there?" Jessie and Jakob giggled.

"Amazing."

"Amazing who?" they sang together.

"Ah may zing off key, but at least I know the words," Kelly quipped.

Their laughter way too much for the jokes, they laughed at the darkness, at the wind, as though they could obliterate all problems with their joy.

"Knock-knock," said Jakob.

"Who's there?"

"Abraham Lincoln."

"Abraham Lincoln who?"

"Aw, c'mon. Everybody knows who Abraham Lincoln is."

Guffaws and groans and then Kelly said, "Your turn, Jessie."

"I don't know any."

"Oh, sure you do. You must. Think."

She concentrated, then started. "Knock-knock."

"Who's there?"

"Merry."

"Mary who?"

"Merry Christmas."

"Hmm," Kelly said. "I guess you don't know any."

"I told you."

"Nobody ever taught her any," Jakob put in.

"Don't start talking that way, Jakob," Jessie ordered, and silence set in again.

"So Rod's doing good with his therapy?" Kelly asked.

"Yeah. Might be home Wednesday," Jessie said.

"You don't sound happy."

"I like when he's not there. But it's his house, so..."

"Are you going to run out of work anytime soon?"

"There's the upstairs, but it's not so bad. No roaches up there, I don't think. Might take a couple weeks to do it. But at some point he's not going to need me that much."

"Maybe the cookies helped butter him up."

"Still, the work's not going to last forever."

"You'll find other jobs. You're a good cleaner," Jakob

put in.

"I sure am glad I got this driving gig for Roderick. Aluminum cans only pay so much and still no calls to sub at the day care center."

Jessie asked Kelly, "Have you ever thought of having one good job instead of different little ones? Maybe in a bank or store or..."

"Oh, since you've got your life all figured out, teenage divorcee who's afraid to talk to people, you can be my advisor, huh?"

"I didn't mean..."

"Not nice, Kelly. Jessie's doing great at coming out of her shell."

"Be quiet, Jakob," Jessie said, and he growled.

"I didn't mean to criticize you, Kelly," Jessie said.

"Well then, what did you mean?"

"I don't know. Maybe—I don't know—maybe I just want to know what your life's been like for all these years we haven't known each other."

"Huh," Kelly said, straightening up in the seat and putting her other hand on the steering wheel. "Well —hmm—actually, there's not a lot to say, I guess. I graduated from Fremd like you. Laid around the house for a couple years like a lot of kids do. Ma made me get jobs at fast food, but that was like an alcoholic being a bartender. She paid for a semester of cosmetology, and I think I would have been good at it, but they said I spent too much time coming up with new ideas instead of studying the stupid muscles of the face. I learned enough to do hair and facials and manicures for my friends, though, so that was a little money coming...

"Red light!" Jakob yelled.

"Whew, that was close. Sorry," Kelly said, as they all lurched backward after lurching forward. "I got a day care job, but the place got closed down over some silly rules after just a couple months. By this time, Ma and me were fighting constantly. Nothing new. One morning..."

"Green light," Jessie said, and they pressed back against the seat as Kelly took off.

"One morning she greeted me with, 'You threw the last straw on the haystack last night, Kelly. Your ass is out of here. Today. And don't come back. I no longer call you daughter.' Something like that."

The three of them stared through the windshield like it was a movie screen. *What did you do? What happened next?* Jessie wanted to ask, but waited.

"I don't even remember what I'd done to deserve that." She gave a sad clown chuckle. "There was quite a shit list to draw from. I was a mess. You guys might not believe it, but I was homeless in Palatine for a while. Stayed with friends—well, with one friend, slept in the park, hit all the shelters. One place got me the day care job I have now—except for being laid off—and paid a month's rent on the apartment I had until I moved back into the so-called home place. After she died.

"So, yeah, I'm piecing it together—and proud of it. I'm a survivor, that's me."

No more talking, only thinking, until they were back in Palatine.

"Could you guys help me move his recliner up into the living room?" Jessie asked. No response. "I don't feel like it either, but I need you."

Jakob said okay, and Kelly drove to Roderick's. They squabbled over how to move the chair, combining methods to carry the heavy thing up the stairs and into the living room, grumbling and accusing each other of pushing or pulling the whole way.

Kelly reclined in it. The cat sprang clumsily into her lap.

"Egad, this feline looks like death warmed over. I don't think it weighs a pound. Hey, where's the remote? Does Rod have any popcorn? Let's watch a movie."

Jessie nixed that, and they trooped back to the truck. At his house, Jakob said goodbye and thank you, he had had a good time, mostly. Jessie tried to say she'd see him tomorrow but could only cough. Home at last, she drank orange juice and went to bed. The aluminum fold-in windows above her head rattled from the mounting storm. Calm crept over her. *Maybe this is how my mother felt that one night when the wind was blowing so hard, and she called to me to come and get in bed with her, but I was too scared.* And then she pretended her pillow was Jakob and hugged, and fell asleep hoping he would come the next day.

He did, and after lunch Jessie asked, "Why were you and Roderick talking about killing yourselves yesterday?"

"He started it. I think he's pretty depressed. But let me just say, suicide is a toy in my mind when I'm having it rough. And it's been rough lately. A few years ago, I had hope for ecological sustainability, but now multinational corporations seem more intent than ever on... oh never mind," he said, putting his trash in his lunch bag and zipping it up.

"But AI—artificial intelligence bothers me too, how computers will be smarter than humans soon." He got up and started walking around the kitchen, his arms waving. "Computers will be to us what we are to mosquitoes. They'll exterminate us."

"You know too much stuff."

"Maybe so," Jakob said, leaning on the counter next to her. "By the way, since you're interested, could we go back to suicide?"

She handed him napkins and a plate of cookies and picked up the steaming mugs. "Let's go to the front sitting room." *I love saying "the front sitting room." It's so cozy with the warm sun shining in after last night's storm. I love the sparkles in the snow through the big window.* She turned on the Christmas lights, they arranged themselves on the love seat, and each took a bite and a sip.

"Okay, back to suicide," she said.

"Would you rather not?"

"Go ahead."

"I do think it's important for us to express our deepest..."

"Go ahead."

He hung his head. She waited.

165

"If I still believed in God the way I used to, I could tough out whatever comes."

"Why don't you believe in God the same?"

His brow furrowed deeply, and Jessie saw other signs of stress: clenched fists, a little rocking motion. *Uh oh. Maybe I shouldn't have gotten him going.*

"Reason being the mighty force of our culture, everything having to make sense, and—so many finding it ludicrous to believe in anything transcendent—and living in the post-Christian era—and what else? Mystery. I used to be better with mystery—I could pray and trust—but lately my words mock me, as though I might only be praying to myself. And, well, more than anything, I—I—I felt safe before.

"Jessie, do you feel safe?" he asked, and turned his eyes from the window to her.

"I'm trying to. When I was a kid at home I did, but never at school. With Doug, sometimes I did and sometimes I didn't. Fiona was dangerous at first, but she's getting safer. I usually feel safe when I'm locked in my apartment. I feel pretty safe here, at least when I'm alone. Sometimes being with you feels safe."

In quietness they drank their cocoa until Jessie said,

"I guess I'll tell you what happened at the Jewel the other day," and recounted the accident with the lady and the eggs. "That's why I say I'm trying to feel safe, because I'd rather stay in my apartment most of the time, all alone, but..."

"But you'd miss so much."

Jessie put her cup and napkin on the table and did something she'd never done before. She stretched her arms and hugged another person. The person hugged her back.

"I don't want to kiss because of my cold," she said, her head resting on his chest.

"Me too," he said, his chin resting on her head.

"What does transcendent mean?"

"Beyond ourselves."

"Oh."

Jessie's cold got worse, Roderick came home, and her and Jakob's friendship lurched ahead through the holiday season.

"Have you finished your Christmas shopping?" he asked.

"I only have Fiona." She glanced at him. *Oh. Is he giving me a present? Whatever. I'm not giving him one.*

One time, Jakob was going on and on criticizing people

167

who don't recycle and Jessie told him to stop whining. *Darn, I wish I hadn't said that. I will never say it to him again,* she resolved, because it triggered a memory of her mother saying it to her. She was maybe five, tears and snot coated her face, warm and salty. *What started me crying? Something about—about—that doll with one arm? Was that it? Or was it that time I pinched my finger in the drawer? Or...* She couldn't capture precisely what had happened, only her mother's sharp "Stop whining!" She had stopped whining and stopped crying too, from that day to this.

The next day they kissed again, thanks to Precious escaping out the back door. "Oh, no, Roderick will kill me if it gets away," she cried, and they tromped through the snow and cornered the cat and Jakob picked it up. She looked up at him with such gratitude that desire overcame fear of germs. They leaned into each other with passion over the nice surprise of who they each were and who they were together.

On Wednesday afternoon, Kelly brought Roderick home. *House-wise, I'm ready for him with his bed freshly made up and the furniture rearranged. But in other ways, I'm not ready at all. I feel invaded.*

"Welcome home," she greeted him at the front door,

nevertheless.

"Well, ho-ho-ho," he replied, entering on his walker. "Looks very festive with all these lights and decorations."

She and Kelly helped him out of his coat and he moved along, sinking into his recliner with a big sigh. "No place like home," he said, and then, "Thanks for the transport. Can you come back tomorrow? I'll have a grocery list ready."

Kelly saluted.

"You can go now. You can have the rest of the day off too," he said, looking at Jessie.

"Kicking us out, huh? Sure you don't need anything before we go?" Kelly said.

"I'm good, ready to be on my own," he said, his voice definite.

Jessie got her coat, and she and Kelly went out the door together.

"Want a ride, cuz?" Kelly invited.

Jessie climbed in saying, "Just what I was afraid of. He doesn't need me anymore." She coughed, her throat on fire.

"Oh, he's going to need you for awhile yet. But hey, what are you taking for that cold? You better get some of that buzzy cough syrup that paralyzes the tickle in your throat."

Jessie nodded and gasped between coughs, "Let me out at the Jewel-Osco."

"Get better," Kelly called as Jessie slipped out of the truck and walked toward the store past high mounds of snow in the parking lot.

And then she stopped, her head and heart pounding. *I can't do it. I just can't do it. Something could happen again.* She did an about-face and crossed the street and headed down the sidewalk toward her apartment, her shoulders drooping.

16

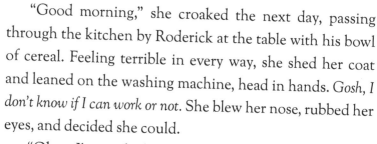

"Good morning," she croaked the next day, passing through the kitchen by Roderick at the table with his bowl of cereal. Feeling terrible in every way, she shed her coat and leaned on the washing machine, head in hands. *Gosh, I don't know if I can work or not.* She blew her nose, rubbed her eyes, and decided she could.

"Okay, I'm ready for you this time," he said when she asked what she should do. "The funk had me bad last night when I let you walk out without getting me so much as a drink of water. There I sat, thirsty, hungry, couldn't find my damn cell phone, in serious pain, but determined to be Captain Self Sufficiency."

I don't especially want to hear all this, but I'd better just listen.

"I'm my own worst enemy." A bitter smile crossed his

face. "In Nam there was a sign on the claymores, these landmines that sprayed steel balls far and wide. Know what it said?"

She shook her head.

"Front Toward Enemy." He laughed. "God almighty, I've got it turned on myself," he uttered, and then cried out in pain getting up on his walker and heading for the living room to recline.

Jessie filled a glass with water and followed him, setting it on the table at his side.

"So what do you want me to do?" *I see his stuff from the hospital still by the front door. Should I unpack his bag? Seems too personal.* "How about your suitcase? Do you want me to do anything with it?"

"Yeah, go ahead and unload my duffel bag. You know, there was a time when I would have put all that away myself if I'd had to drag it down the hall with my teeth. Where'd that guy go?" They looked at each other until she turned and left.

She found some laundry in the bag and got it going, then carried it to his bedroom and put the other items back in place and stowed the bag on a shelf in his closet. His bed hadn't been slept in, but his bathroom needed attention, and she made it glisten.

Grouchy all week because of her cold, she kept biting a cold sore by accident, pain shooting through every part of her body from that one little point. Jakob came for lunch, greeting Roderick as he passed by. After she and Jakob had eaten, she started fresh gum, intending to suck mostly and chew gently, but nicked the sore and shrieked.

"Another reason not to chew gum," Jakob said.

She got his coat and pushed him down the hallway and out the door. She rubbed her hurting face and spit out the gum. *Okay, I'm ready for the afternoon,* she sighed to herself. *What to do? No cup of tea and staring out the window for a spell now that he's back.* She got his dirty dishes from the living room and cleaned up the kitchen, then decided to attack the quagmire in the entryway closet and started pulling stuff out: a busted umbrella, a large lightweight box still sealed, boots...

"What are you doing?" boomed down the hallway.

Her breath caught, which made her cough. "Cleaning out the closet," she choked out.

"I need you in the kitchen."

He was standing at the open door of the refrigerator on his walker. "I tried to pour myself a glass of milk and knocked it over. What a mess."

That's for sure. Milk splattered all over everything. Thanks, Captain Self Sufficiency. And I honestly don't know if I have the strength to clean it up. But she did, working out of a bowl of soapy water, wiping and rinsing, wiping and rinsing, the bottles and jars as well as the shelves and the floor. With a final burst of energy, she stretched to push the box of deodorizing baking soda to the back of the top shelf, and then backed out and straightened up fast, not quite clear, and hit her head on the bottom of the freezer door so hard she thought there must be blood.

"Ow!"

"You alright?" Roderick yelled.

"Yes," she yelled back, rushing to the laundry room. She closed the door and buried her face in her coat to muffle her sobs.

"Lovely home," she heard the home health care nurse say. Then the chirp of the thermometer. Putting the contents of the closet back in, Jessie listened to their conversation.

"Lived here long?"

"Thirty-some years," Roderick answered.

"Someone's a gifted decorator."

"My wife. She died some time ago."

"Oh, I'm sorry. That's her in the portrait with you? Handsome couple. Your blood pressure's high. And I'm concerned about that bruise on your leg. Is it tender?"

"Not too."

"Are you wearing compression hose? They gave you some, right?"

"Yeah, but they're the dickens to get into."

"I know, but you're still at risk for clotting. I'll help you with them, if you like."

"Hey," Roderick called to her. "What'd you do with those heavy stockings that were in my bag?"

"I'll get them," she called back, and retrieved them from a dresser drawer and handed them off to the nurse, an attractive grandmotherly type.

After a minute, she heard Roderick murmur with pleasure, "You've done this before."

"A few times. Anyone here in the mornings to help you with these?"

"No. The cleaning girl's here, but I don't think she could."

That's right. She could not.

"Okay, there you are. Try to wear them for at least a couple hours a day. And is Monday afternoon okay, Mr. McCoy? Three o'clock?"

"Oh. You're coming back?"

"One more visit, assuming all goes well."

"Yeah, fine. Makes no difference to me." He echoed her "Merry Christmas" as she left, saying the same to Jessie who also echoed. Merry Christmas all over the place.

On Friday over lunch, Jessie asked Jakob if he was mad at her for shoving him out of the house.

"No, because it taught me some lessons. For example, don't criticize your gum chewing and don't ask too many questions. Also, no suicide talk."

She thought for a minute. "Okay."

"You throw me off a lot, though, with your fickleness. No, not fickleness—you're not fickle—with your pre-dictable unpredictability. But I'm intrigued that a person of your age, a high school graduate living in metro Chicago, who's been married, had a baby, and divorced, is so unexposed. I would love a lifetime of getting to know you, Jessie. And you're not dumb, you're unexposed."

Hmm. I don't know what to say to that.

"Uh-oh. Are you going to kick me out again?"

"I'm trying to decide," she said. *Oh dear, he looks so serious.* "That was supposed to be a joke."

"Oh good. Whew," he said. "I have to say, I'm feeling more secure since we've started kissing."

"Kissing doesn't always fix things, Jakob."

"It does for me," he kidded.

Jessie smiled. "I like it, too, but it doesn't always fix things."

He went around and sat in the chair next to her, trying for some kissing, but her coughing and nose-blowing put a stop to that. Instead, he put his arm around her and said, "I got you a paint-by-number for your Christmas present. It's about us."

And she couldn't resist kissing him on the cheek, and he couldn't resist laughing in his joyful, crazy way.

Bundling to start her walk home, she heard Roderick talking in the living room and went to check. He was staring at the painting of him and his wife and didn't notice her in the doorway.

"What a farce," she heard him say, an ugly look on his face. "Who were we, Vevie? Who in God's name were we?" His face twisted and tears trickled. "And who am I now?

Who am I?" he shouted, rising from his chair with a terrible sound escaping his throat and hobbled over to the mantle. With a mighty effort, he lifted the portrait off the wall, then fell backward with the weight of it, shouting out with pain as it crashed down on him.

"Oh, my gosh," she gasped and ran over, grasping the painting and tipping it away. She leaned it against the wall and asked him if he was okay.

"No!" he cried, holding his knee and rocking back and forth in pain. "Anybody can see I'm not okay. I'm pathetic. Crippled in every way. Help me get to my chair, and you can go."

With fumbling efforts, they managed to get him back in his chair. Huffing and puffing, he ordered her to leave again.

After a long moment, she said, "I want to fix your dinner before I go."

"Suit yourself," he finally said, turning the TV on.

An hour later, calm prevailed and Jessie said, "I'll go now, if you're sure you're okay,"

"Young lady, I think it's well-established that I am not okay. I'm well enough for you to go, though. Call a cab since it's getting late. I'll pay."

She stood next to his chair thinking of all they'd been

through together. Seeing the picture knock him down told her what she already knew: *Look out for relationships. They can do a lot of damage.*

"Go on now."

"Alright. See you Monday," and she stepped out into the dark, cold night in a state of confusion.

17

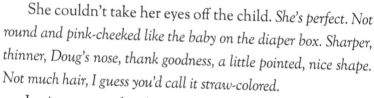

She couldn't take her eyes off the child. *She's perfect. Not round and pink-cheeked like the baby on the diaper box. Sharper, thinner, Doug's nose, thank goodness, a little pointed, nice shape. Not much hair, I guess you'd call it straw-colored.*

Jessie was on the floor on her stomach, watching her daughter concentrate and fumble, figuring out that pushing a button made a little toy radio play, and she saw something of herself in Fiona's eyes and shivered. She snuck away to get the present and laid it in front of the baby. Fiona looked at it, then looked at Jessie.

"Go ahead. Open it."

She shrieked a happy shriek and pulled the fancy bow off, and it went straight to her mouth.

"Oh no, oh gosh!" Jessie snatched it away, and Fiona

shrieked an angry shriek. "It's what's inside," Jessie told her, tearing the paper. "See? Grab it, pull it off." She opened up the box and held up the clothes. "This is for you. Let's put it on and see how beautiful you are." But Fiona wanted only the bow, and after a little struggle Jessie gave up trying to put her in the new outfit and picked her up and took her to the kitchen for supper, where the chubby fingers squeezed a pouch of asparagus into her mouth.

I want tonight to be like that night a couple weeks ago when we walked around, and she acted like the Christmas lights were magic. So, despite her fatigue and sickness, out they went into the even, still cold. The sidewalks were mostly clear and the lights bright, especially the full and brilliant moon which Fiona would point to and utter a syllable filled with both wonder and everydayness. This time, they wandered through the neighborhood that lay on the other side of Plum Grove, and Fiona oohed and aahed and clapped her hands, a new trick Jessie hadn't seen, and she clapped hers too. An older couple stopped to admire Fiona's cuteness. Jessie had seen them approaching, hand in hand, silhouetted by the street lights, happy and gentle with each other. *I wonder if Jakob and I could ever be like that.*

On their way home, raucous Christmas music blasted

out and frightened Fiona. Jessie pulled her out of her stroller and pressed her to her until she stopped crying. *I feel like Mary with Jesus.*

"Don't cry, little baby," she said. "When we get home we can try on your beautiful clothes."

Fiona protested being buckled back in and Jessie loved holding her, so she gathered her to her chest again with one arm and pushed the empty stroller with the other. Soon her back began to ache, though, and the wind was kicking up, and she had to force Fiona back in—not easy— and the child screamed all the way back to the apartment.

She had thought of wheeling into the Jewel to see if Tonya was there and show her how Fiona could clap, but not tonight. Now, Fiona's cries were stressing Jessie into a cough spasm that made her head feel like a melon just split with a cleaver.

Oh gosh, I'm afraid I'm going to earp, and she tripped down the three steps and unlocked her door, and when she opened the storm door the wind whipped it out of her hand with a crash. She had trouble with the buckle on the stroller, Fiona twisting and squalling, but she got it and jerked her out and set her on the other side of the door, then turned back and grabbed the stroller, flinging it inside.

She gave the door an extra push against the wind.

Fiona stopped crying abruptly, and then came the scream. Her fingers were shut in the door.

Jessie yelped and opened the door, scooping Fiona up and running back into the night.

"Help! I've hurt my baby," she screamed in the parking lot. "Somebody help me! Please, help me!"

What do I need to do? Where do I need to take her? To the grocery store to see if Tonya could help? To Kelly's? To Doug's, so far away?

A beam of light shone from above and then a voice. "Hey, what's wrong? Whatsamatter?" A back door on the second floor had opened and a guy ran down the steps. She ran toward him.

"Dude, what's wrong?"

"I shut her hand in the door," she wailed. "I'm afraid she's going to die."

"Dude, she's not going to die," he said with a lazy laugh. "Calm down here, let's have a look," and he took the little hand in his, Fiona screaming louder at his touch. "Woo, that's a mess. You gotta' get her somewhere. You got wheels?"

"No. Please help me!"

"Hey, listen here, calm down, dude," he said, resting a hand on her shoulder. "Your bellerin' ain't gonna' help her none, is it? Now, I just smoked a couple joints, but I think I'm good. I'll get my stuff and be right back and we'll get little baby to a doc-in-a-box, okay? Is that cool? You get what you need, maybe a diaper."

She ran and grabbed Fiona's bag, and they were soon in the guy's little truck, Fiona mere inches from the windshield in her mother's arms.

"Hey, maybe we should know each other's names. I'm Barrett, I'm in Two North."

She was trembling violently and she couldn't stop the tears seeping out of her eyes. Fiona's cries had turned to whimpers.

"So you got a name?"

"Jessica George."

"Okay, Jessica, neighbor. Good to meet you, except for the circumstances," and he extended his hand, but she didn't see it.

Urgent care was less than a ten-minute drive. Dropping them at the door, he said, "Look, baby's going to be okay. I seen this before. Them tiny bones is soft, dude. You'll be amazed how she bounces back. I'll be waiting for you right here."

That's what the doctor said too, and the insurance card Doug always had in the zipper pocket worked like magic. They were back in the truck in half an hour, the staff turning off the lights as they made their exit.

"Was I right? Everything okay?" he asked as she got back in the truck.

"I don't know." Her voice quivered. "I guess so."

"So you okay now? Feeling better?"

She nodded. "But now I have to tell Doug. We have to go to Doug's now."

"Who's that? The dad?"

She nodded and started trembling again. Following her directions, he drove to Doug's apartment complex and parked. "You staying or what? You want me to wait?"

"I don't know. I might be here for a while. You go ahead."

"Okay, well I'm Barrett, and you know where I live, so if I can..."

Jessie nodded and headed up the shoveled sidewalk, coughing the whole way into the vestibule, Fiona asleep. She pushed the button under the card saying Douglas Stewart.

187

"Who is it?" came Doug's voice.

"It's me, with Fiona. She..."

Doug was down the six steps leading up to his apartment before she finished the sentence.

"What's wrong?"

"It's her hand."

"Oh, God, Jessica. What happened? Oh, no!" he cried, picking up the purple fingers. The child woke up and started screaming again. He took her.

"I accidentally shut them in the door," Jessie said quietly. Doug rushed up the steps to his open apartment door where a plump woman with short brown hair was holding a child and watching.

"How could you have been so careless? She's a baby! You should be watching constantly, you should always know where her fingers are, always. I can't believe..."

"What happened?" the woman asked.

"She shut Fiona's fingers in the door."

Jessie looked at Doug and the woman with the other child, all of them hovering over Fiona, soothing her. She smelled baking in the air. Moving up the steps, she saw a Christmas tree sparkling behind them. A nativity scene on the coffee table with a sleeping baby in the manger made her

188

think of Mary again. *She probably never shut baby Jesus' fingers in a door.*

"I took her to a doctor," she said, clearing her throat between coughs.

Doug looked at her. "Where?"

"It was on Dundee Road."

"What did they say?"

"She said there appeared to be no fractures, but even if there were they would heal okay because the bones are so soft. And she said two fingernails might fall off but they would grow back. She said to give her the baby drops for pain. They already gave her some—they're in the bag—and she said to apply ice if pain persists." She set the bag down on the floor. "The papers from the place are in there."

Doug nodded and looked at her intently. "Who took you? How'd you get there?"

"A guy that lives on the second floor." She couldn't remember his name and didn't mention that he'd been smoking marijuana.

"Without a car seat?"

Jessie shrugged. *How could we have the car seat when it was in your car?*

Doug shook his head again.

189

"Why don't you guys come on in," the woman said, and they moved into the apartment. The woman sat down on the couch with her little boy, Doug sitting down next to them with Fiona.

"Introduce us, Doug," the woman said.

"Oh, this is Alicia and her son Lucas."

"Hi, Jessica. Sorry to meet at a not happy time." A timer dinged. "Oh, the cookies," and she went to the kitchen.

Jessie stood in the doorway, not knowing what to do. She watched Doug looking at Fiona like a father hawk, Lucas snuggling into them. A coughing spasm hit, and she choked out that she guessed she would go, and started down the stairs, hacking and gulping for air.

"Jessica, is your neighbor driving you back to Plum Grove?" Doug asked over the banister.

Coughing too hard to talk, she shook her head. Her eyes were watering and her nose running, but she had nothing to wipe it.

"Well, come back up here and get a drink of water, and I'll drive you home."

Oh God, I just want to get out of here, but I don't think I can make it that long way. She went back up, accepted a drink of water and a tissue, and finally stopped coughing.

190

"Ready?" Doug asked.

She nodded, and Alicia handed her warm cookies wrapped in foil. "Merry Christmas."

"I'll be back shortly," Doug said, depositing Fiona in Alicia's arms. That was the last sight in Jessie's mind, Fiona in another mother's arms, as Doug drove in silence across the freezing streets.

He parked at her place, cleared his throat, and said, "I want you to know something, Jessica. Alicia and I are not sleeping together. She has her own place. We wouldn't do that. Not until we're married. I wanted you to know."

I don't care. "Okay," she said.

She left the cookies on the seat and slid out. Doug went with her to get the stroller, flung on its side next to the washing machine. He folded it up and turned to leave, then said, "Um, maybe it would be better if you didn't have Fiona for a while, since you're not that crazy to have her anyway and... you know..."

Jessie nodded.

"I'll be back in touch after the holidays, okay?"

She nodded, looking at the floor.

"Merry Christmas, Jessica."

She locked the door and made her way into the dark

191

apartment. In the living room, the ray of light from the streetlamp shone through the curtains on to Fiona's velvet pant suit and the torn angel gift wrap. She put it back in the box and slid it back under her bed.

This shouldn't have happened. None of it should have happened. I shouldn't have let Fiona come tonight. I should have canceled because of my cold. I shouldn't have taken her on the walk. I shouldn't have done any of it—gotten married, had a baby, gotten involved with Jakob. She lay face down on the bed, regretting every relationship and every step out into the world she'd ever taken.

18

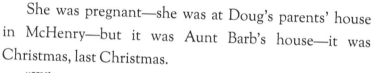

She was pregnant—she was at Doug's parents' house in McHenry—but it was Aunt Barb's house—it was Christmas, last Christmas.

"What are you going to do with the baby?" her in-laws asked her at the same time.

Doug laughed behind her. "What do you think? She's going to love it."

"Well then, if she's not going to kill it, let's eat," his father said.

They sat down at the table and now it was their house in McHenry, their table decorated as it actually had been, a dark green tablecloth and centerpiece of three large pine cones sprayed with fake snow arranged on a circle of mirror. Tiny glass balls—aqua, shiny pink, off-gold—hung from these miniature trees.

Doug held her chair for her and as she sat down, she bumped her belly on the edge of the table. All three of them yelled, "Be careful!"

She saw her face in the mirror and panicked. Something else had happened in the dream, something important, and Jessie lay there trying to replay the ending, but couldn't get back.

Burning up, she threw the covers off, but by the time she came back from the bathroom she was chilling and pulled them up again.

Next, she dreamt that the full-length dress bag that held her mother's wedding dress was hanging on the wall behind her, on her right and above as she lay on her back in bed. She knew her mother was inside, her mother's corpse. The bag was unzipped, and she reached up and opened it so she could look in. The corpse was hanging there, decayed into a substance like popcorn in light shades of blue and gray. She touched her mother's foot, and it crumbled like a popcorn ball but wasn't sticky or messy or smelly. "Hi," she said, looking up at the corpse. That was the end of that one.

Towards daybreak, Mary, the mother of Jesus, was in the room with her. She didn't have baby Jesus, but she was laughing. Jessie sat up in bed scanning the room for her, trying to remember what she had looked like. The image was gone, but she still felt her presence and could hear Mary's laughter in her memory. *Why the laughing? What, Mary? What were you trying to tell me?* She lay back down to ponder the visions, re-playing them in her mind until they faded completely away, like rainbows do while you watch.

She forced herself out of bed and worked around the house in her pajamas, cleaning this and that. Frequent resting, staring into space, dozing, coughing until she threw up, twice. The afternoon passed as miserably, then a fitful night.

By Sunday morning, she was a hot and cold, sputtering, hacking mess of mucous, and ached from coughing, from breathing, from swallowing. Her khakis and T shirt lay on the floor and she pulled them on, then socks and sneakers, and struggled into her coat to go to Jewel for orange juice and medicine, then took it all off and went back to bed because she could not go back to that place, not yet, not now. *I should go to urgent care probably. Maybe that guy in two north who took Fiona to urgent care would take me,* but she knew she wouldn't, couldn't ask him.

When she spread grape jelly on her toast—the knife so

heavy— she saw Fiona's crushed, purple fingers. Amethyst really. The horror at the door Friday night took over her senses and she couldn't eat for hearing Fiona's scream and imagining her pain. *How is she doing? Will I ever see her again? Should I?*

Roderick snored in his recliner as she passed the living room Monday morning, but he soon came into the kitchen, wincing and panting.

"Well, I accidentally flushed that stupid cell phone down the toilet last night. What a mess. So it's official: I am an island unto myself. Just as well. Nobody calls me and I have no one to call."

Jessie tried to say she was sorry but could only cough.

"Even after the portrait fiasco the other night—and before the phone fell in the can—I fought off the blues enough to call my buddy Wayne, but no answer and his mailbox was full. So, yeah; who needs a phone?"

She nodded, and he leaned on his walker and started leaving, then said over his shoulder, "My bathroom needs a thorough disinfecting. The toilet overflowed. I also need to borrow your phone if I could, to call the plumber, and then call your cousin to see if she can take the cat to the vet."

"I don't have a phone."

"You don't have a phone?" He stared at her, but took no notice of her flushed face or wheezing.

She shook her head.

He let out an expletive.

"Well anyway, get the bathroom. The kitchen needs attention too."

Dirty dishes, spills, trash all over the place. *The roaches will be back in no time. He does need me whether he thinks so or not.* She cleaned up cat messes and tended to the litter box, always disgusting after the weekend. She started on his bathroom next, resting for a spell on the closed toilet seat. Not much sleep last night and she certainly felt no better, but had chosen working over being cooped up another day. Now, she realized she'd chosen wrong. *I'll clean the kitchen and tell him I have to go.* She had done everything but the floor when the doorbell rang. Roderick called a loud "come in," and she soon heard the nurse talking with him in the living room.

You're not going to be able to finish this until you take a break, Jessie. Stop. Go and sit down, she ordered herself, and walked slowly down the hall to the front sitting room, collapsed on the couch, and closed her eyes.

"So, how have you been doing, Mr. McCoy?" she heard.

"Pretty well for a geezer, I guess."

"How are the exercises going?"

"Still hurts. I thought I'd be through the pain by now."

"Exercising regularly?" she asked.

"Er, uh," he fudged. "The physical therapist has been here twice, so—but, no, not quite regularly, I guess. I had a fall a few days ago and twisted the other knee," he said.

Yeah, you had a fall, you and Vevie, Jessie thought, recalling that catastrophe.

"Okay, I'll check that knee before I leave."

"The cat's pretty sick," Roderick said. "Doubt she'll last much longer."

We can only hope. Shame on me. I take it back.

"Oh, dear. This can be tough around the holidays. I'm a cat lover too, I understand. How's your appetite?"

"Off and on. Not much fun eating alone."

"Do you have anyone to talk to, Mr. McCoy?"

"Besides you and the P. T.? No, not really."

I guess I'm nobody. Jakob's nobody to him. Kelly's nobody. But he talks to us all the time, tells us every weird thing that comes into his brain. Whatever.

"You're medicated for hypertension, right?"

"Right."

"Your reading today is higher than last week. Depression often correlates with that. Do you think you might be struggling with depression?"

"Oh, yeah. I'm medicated for that too. In fact, I checked into the psych unit at the V.A. last month. Yeah, I'm struggling. Not unusual after what I've seen."

"Vietnam?" she guessed, and Jessie heard him grunt.

"Let me take a look at that leg."After a minute, "Way better. The hematoma is fading and the joint you fell on doesn't look too swollen or inflamed so exercising is okay.

"You know, Mr. McCoy, I've had bouts with depression, and I believe in action plans and to do lists. Usually, if I can force the first item on the list to happen, the others happen too, and I can rise up. Not telling you what to do, but the holiday season can make matters worse if you don't fight hard. You could also call the V.A., couldn't you?"

"Oh, I hardly think that will be necessary. Maybe an action plan."

The nurse left, and Jessie forced herself back to the kitchen and fixed sudsy water. *I should just mop, but those moldings haven't been cleaned since the first time I did the floor in*

October. I'll just give them a quick swipe so this room will be really clean for the holidays. She shed her sweater and gathered her last ounce of strength to get down on all fours. The cat sidled up behind her, brushing her with its mangy hair, and nuzzled her arm with its wet, cold nose. She whacked it, hard, and it thumped against the wall and landed on the floor, a motionless heap of yellow fur.

What? Jessie crawled over to it. No movement, no sound. She touched it, nudged it. No reaction. *It's dead. Okay, that's it.* She stood up, dried her hands on her pants, put her coat and hat and gloves on, picked up her lunch, and left.

All the way home, she fingered the key in her pocket. Lights flashed and sirens sounded with deafening blasts as an ambulance and then a fire truck flew past. They did not register in her consciousness. She chewed her gum harder with every step, pulled off her hat and gloves, and opened her coat wide to feel some coolness on her overheated body. A redbird perched on a post right in front of her. The brilliant sun cracked the ice and melted it into streams of water softly and steadily trickling into the drains. She neither saw nor heard. She labored at breathing and shivered as she sweated but did not break the rhythm of her stride until she stepped down those three steps and entered her apartment.

Locking the door, she breathed in as delicately as painting with one hair, trying to avoid coughing, capturing a fragile peace, a tiny victory over despair, and breathed out a raggedy sigh of gratitude for refuge. She changed into her pajamas and crawled under the covers, which felt as sweet and wonderful as she'd imagined. For a moment. But then the thoughts came. *I hurt my child. My work at Roderick McCoy's is over. What about Jakob? I'm a weird little freak and have been an orphan all my life. I never want to go outside again.* After those ten seconds, she was sound asleep.

19

At midnight, Jessie began hanging her paintings. Twelve hours she'd slept, waking up hot and sick. She'd felt lifeless but couldn't stay in bed any longer. She'd drunk a large glass of water and thought maybe she should eat something, a bowl of cereal maybe, but had no appetite. *What to do? In the middle of the night? When I'm sick?* And it had come to her: *Hang my pictures.*

She'd been planning this for the whole seven months since Doug had moved her into this place: Start in the entry/utility room with painting number one and cover the walls, then to the kitchen, the bathroom, the living room, and end up in her bedroom with her most recent ones. She got her half-size hammer and golden nails and slit the tape on the first box of paintings. The brown flaps opened to Balloon Bear, a fuzzy brown Teddy bear holding three balloons. *What a mess.* She lifted it out of the box, a weak smile on her chapped lips. The bold primary colors splotched outside the balloon lines, but she loved this one the best because it was the first.

Putting a stack of the pictures on the washing machine, she climbed up and positioned the bear as high as she could reach above the corner of the machine and tacked it in place, her mind drifting back to that day she came home from school and saw the first kit lying on the kitchen table.

I was afraid to touch it, and then the phone rang, and I jumped a mile. My mother told me the kit was for me, and I could paint the picture. I remember sliding it out of the box and reaching back in for the paintbrush and the plastic wells of paint, six of them held together by a plastic strip. I figured out that I needed to rinse the brush and filled my plastic orange juice cup with water.

"You shouldn't have used that one, but now that's the painting cup," her mother had said when she got home.

"I love painting," Jessie had said, but her mother didn't seem to hear her as she went up to her bedroom.

Every week a new kit had arrived, giving little Jessie's life form and purpose. She had saved the boxes until her mother told her to throw them out, and then she had started writing the titles on the backs of the picture boards and numbering them.

She soon filled the space over the washer and dryer to the ceiling, four rows of bright colored eight by tens, simple shapes, obviously painted by a child. In Sea Animals, a purple and pink dolphin leapt out of the water against a cloudy blue sky with yellow sun while a gold-with-black-striped fish, a two-toned green turtle, and a pink and red crab swam happily in the sea underneath. In the same style came Farm Animals, Zoo Animals, Dinosaurs and Birds. And then the puppy series featuring a light brown, floppy-eared cocker spaniel. Puppy with Soccer Ball, Puppy with Kitty, and Puppy Gardener, its paws resting on redwood boards, a butterfly on its nose. The black lines of the butterfly's wings smudged into the yellow, and these thirteen years later she was still disappointed that it wasn't perfect. Zebra, number twenty-seven, was a favorite because it had been a breakthrough. Only the cartoonish head of the animal was pictured, a tuft of black hair between its ears and a small green heart hanging over the hair. *I can still hear my mother's voice.* "You did great on that heart," *she said as she walked by. I remember that.*

On into the wee hours she worked, row after row,

stopping only for the bathroom or to blow her nose or drink water. She loved her step stool and its handy shelf and the small hammer. The entry room now looked like a circus had been whirled around and let go.

She moved steadily through the kitchen with its limited wall space. The Flower Vase Art, its five paintings now going up over the seats in the kitchen booth, had come with six tubes of acrylic paint and three natural bristle brushes. These works had moved her to a new level of artistry. The set had come on her eighth birthday, and she had been at the kitchen table painting the first one, Van Gogh's Sunflowers, when her mother came in the back door.

"Thank you, Mommy," she said, looking up with eager eyes.

"Not from me," her mother said as she passed through.

"Then who are they from?" Jessie had asked, not for the first time.

"A friend."

"What friend?"

"A friend."

"Aunt Barb?"

"Stop." Her mother's warning was harsh. "I said a friend." Questions were not welcomed in that household.

She lifted out Petal Girl, an odd figure of a young girl with long blond hair and bangs and black ovals for eyes. Her dress formed her body, a pale aqua triangle with pale legs and bare feet emerging at the hemline. Bright pink flowers, heart-shaped, on long slender green stems, some of them taller than the girl herself, surrounded her. *Oh Petal Girl, you are Renee to me. Why did you have to die in that motorcycle crash before I was ever born?* She hugged Petal Girl to her bosom and held back tears as she tacked her up.

Angel in the Forest came next. *This one was really hard. Took a lot longer than one week.* An adolescent fairy with shaggy red hair and translucent wings sat cross-legged surrounded by verdant ferns and forest. She smiled down, petting a bunny with one hand and a squirrel with the other. Now, the tears trickled out of Jessie's eyes—at the beauty of the scene and the joy on that little angel girl's face. And then she hit her thumb with the hammer and the tears were from the pain.

Her coughing woke her. She picked her head up off the kitchen table and looked wildly around the room having no idea of the time or the day or what she'd been doing. In an instant, she remembered: *Fiona's fingers. No job. Sick. Is this a life or death deal? I feel like my body is getting less and less, wasting away, as though it might not be able to keep going much longer. Like the cat, at the end.*

Hanging these pictures was her life now. What she had left.

She lugged a box into the bathroom and set it on the toilet seat, but mucous started gagging her, and she thrust the box into the bathtub and flipped up the toilet ring barely in time to heave into the bowl. Gasping, she felt like a rag doll that's lost half its stuffing. But she washed her face, brushed her teeth, and got busy again with fevered determination.

She pulled out Nativity. *Appropriate to hang in the bathroom? Why not?* A storybook starting with Christmas and ending with Easter had come with this kit, and it was the first time she'd heard the story of Jesus. In the painting, the baby, looking bigger and older than Fiona, was asleep on the hay, wearing a T-shirt-looking garment. This was the first metallic paint, she remembered, looking at the gold circle above his head. A curious lamb stood by the manger. Mary, dressed in bright red and blue with a white shawl over her head and shoulders, gazed down on the babe, arms crossed on her breast, and Joseph, wearing green and tan, looked on from behind. A cow with horns and a mouthful of hay observed from the left and a gray donkey from the right. *I saved the best part for last, that window opening to the ink blue night and rays from the bright star shimmering into the stable.* She tacked it up now, next to Flamingo Large.

The first light of dawn shown delicately across the living room as she carried the step stool in there and dragged boxes in because she was too weak to pick them up. She fit two rows between the bottom of the window looking out on Plum Grove Road and the top of the couch. The paintings were larger now and more intricate. There were two round ones—one of ocean-going sailboats, the other of a deer's head with great antlers.

Up went her favorite one of Jesus, his head and shoulders mostly in reds and browns and yellow on much of his face and on part of his robe where light shone. *He looks serious and sad and wise and kind. Wow, I remember painting this so many years ago and wishing he would come in the back door and sit down at the table with me.*

The Persistence of Memory was her least favorite, with its melting clocks out in the desert draped over dead wood and maybe part of a dead animal. *I could never figure this one out. Maybe I won't put it up—but no, I have to. My friend gave it to me, and I painted it. It's part of my life.*

"Who was it?" she demanded out loud. "Who gave these to me, especially this weird one?" She hit her thumb again and cried out and grew more furious at her dead mother for not telling her who the friend was. *For not telling me anything!* She sank down on the couch.

She had considered many times that her father had given them to her, and yet doubted so. From the only time she'd ever seen him, she had built him up in her mind. *He brought me a green and silver pinwheel and took me out in the yard to play with it. It was breezy. The pinwheel whirred and flashed. He picked me up and I smelled cigarettes on his breath, and he held me close and warm and safe.* Jessie hugged herself and rocked and wept, and then howled.

Purged, she tried to eat a bowl of cereal but the milk had soured. She put it in the sink with three days of dirty dishes and went back to bed, curling in a ball under the covers. Not asleep but not fully awake, she flopped around trying to hit a comfortable spot for her sore limbs and the way they fit with her body and her sore neck. She got caught up in a dream-like process involving other people, giving them instructions to complete some job. The work had seemed real and of crucial importance, yet when she bolted up in despair of resting and tried to recall what had been going on, all of it vanished.

I have to get all the pictures up. Now. That's all.

The hammer seemed lighter, and she was soon finishing the living room with Regal Tiger, prominent by the light switch, as she'd planned. Aunt Barb had wanted to enter this tiger in a contest.

"You are amazing, Jessie, for a nine-year-old. It looks so darn real. Look at those whiskers, Nan, little wisps, and those teeny tiny black dots that make the stripe by the mouth. Look how she's blended the different oranges."

Her mother had said no about the contest, Aunt Barb had pushed it, and they'd had a big fight. "Go to your room," her mother had ordered, but Jessie could still hear them yelling at each other.

"Nancy, how can you ignore this girl the way you do? She's your own flesh and blood, for God's sake, and you hardly..."

"Don't start with me, I mean it. I've got enough on me."

"Enough on you? Don't make me laugh. There's no excuse for the way you do her. It's abuse by neglect, as far as I'm concerned."

"Oh, really? So report me, role model momma, and I'll

report Kelly's whippings. And you know what, Barb? Get out and don't come back. And you know what else? At least my daughter hasn't ever run away. And my husband didn't kill himself, just left me, and thank God for that!"

The door slam had shaken the house, and she could hear her mother sobbing. *I wanted to go to her, to help her. But I didn't. I didn't know how.*

Sweat dripped from Jessie's face, mingled with tears. She shoved the last two boxes of paintings into her bedroom. These paintings were her friends, the bear and the deer, Jesus and the dolphins, dragonflies and leprechauns and ballerinas. Without them, she would have had no one in her growing up years. She had to get them out of the boxes and up on the wall or something in her would die for good.

Let the Children Come unto Me, another favorite. In the picture on the box, the figures were paint-by-number flat, but Jessie had brought them to life by defining their features and bleeding colors subtly into each other. By this time, the mystery friend was supplying sable brushes and high-quality paints. A little girl sat happily on Jesus' lap, her hand resting on his knee—*imagine!*—and Jessie had painted over the lines to turn the child's head so she looked up at

213

him as he spoke.

"What are you saying, Jesus?" she asked now as she tacked it up. "Please talk to me," she whispered, staring at his mouth, his dark brown beard and mustache barely separate, and thin pink lines for his lips. "Please!" Then, she began to speak for him.

"You're a good little girl, Jessie. You're beautiful and I love you. I wish you could sit on my lap. I would hold you and hug you and you would be my own little girl. We would..." and then her sadness overtook her, and then rage, and she drove a nail into Jesus' silent mouth.

"Oh!" she cried, prying the tack out, and threw herself on her bed, hot tears pouring out again. She could barely breathe for hurting.

But there was no choice at this point, no sanity to it, and she jumped up gasping and worked fiercely on, banging too hard, too fast, wounding her thumb over and over. Her arm felt it would drop off, but she grabbed picture after picture, climbing up and down, moving the ladder, opening another box of tacks and dropping it and maniacally scraping them up to put back in the box, wiping the sweat running down her face with her shoulder, her forearm, so she could see.

Laboring for breath, her T-shirt soaked, she pulled the

last picture out, number seven hundred twenty-eight, Beyond the Gate. She sat down on the bed to look at it. Hues of blue and yellow flowers lined a path leading through the gate of a white picket fence with the gate—the focal point— slightly open. In the background were trees and a couple cottages and a bit of blue sky with a cloud. *Oh my gosh, that cloud had at least ten colors in it!* She admired the careful feathering and places she'd extended beyond the lines. *This was my best*, she thought, as her breathing evened out.

In wonder, she gazed on it remembering that last week of high school, rushing home each afternoon to finish it before Saturday, her wedding day.

"Wow. That's good, Jessica," Doug had said, "but you'll have to leave your pictures at your mother's house until we get a bigger place."

And now, for the first time, Jessie caught the irony of Beyond the Gate. Fresh tears flowed, but this sadness was not so bad because she understood her tears. *I don't want to go back to my tiny life, but I don't know how to live out in the world. I don't think I can. It's too hard.*

And then Jessie laughed, recalling a story the teacher had told in Business Practices. Mailroom staff had left a

215

large stack of bulk mail for a temp worker to process overnight. When they returned the next morning, the pile hadn't been touched, and there was a note on top of it: Too hard. Went home.

20

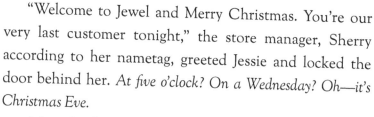

"Welcome to Jewel and Merry Christmas. You're our very last customer tonight," the store manager, Sherry according to her nametag, greeted Jessie and locked the door behind her. *At five o'clock? On a Wednesday? Oh—it's Christmas Eve.*

After she'd tacked up Beyond the Gate, she'd had a burst of energy and put the tools and the ladder away, then flattened the seven boxes that had held her paintings and leaned them against the wall next to the back door. She liked the new spaciousness of the room. It would take some time to get used to the intensity of the walls, but she loved what she had done. Her fever had broken, and she had taken a hot bath, falling asleep in the tub, soaking out some of the soreness. She'd shampooed her hair and brushed her teeth and put on her black slacks and the pretty purple sweater Doug had given her last Christmas. Ravenous, she'd felt a tiny, deep spark of confidence to re-enter the Jewel.

Oh, good, Tonya's not on duty. I still don't want to talk to anybody. She hustled through the aisles in a private holiday spirit grabbing whatever looked good. A cake with pink frosting decorated with cherries. Eight dollars! *Okay, it can be my Christmas present to myself. Oh, that spinach dip looks so good, and so do those chips right next to it.* Fruits and veggies looked beautiful. She stocked up and threw in a large coleslaw. She grabbed a couple frozen pizzas, a new item for her. Milk, bread, oh, and why not, ice cream, Candy Cane Delight. Cough syrup, cough drops, and gum.

"That will be fifty-two thirty-eight," the young cashier said.

"How much?" she said softly, knowing she didn't have that much, not quite. Her neck got hot and the heat rose up her face as she fiddled in her wallet. He repeated the amount. "I only have fifty dollars and..." She started coughing and dropped her coins on the floor, picked them up, placed all of them, every penny she had, on the little shelf, too addled to count.

"Um, do you want to put something back?"

Jessie stared up at him.

The manager, Sherry, came and started bagging. "How we doing here?" she asked. "About got it, so we can all go home and enjoy turkey dinner?"

"Um, she's a little over," the clerk said.

"Uh-oh. How much?"

"A dollar forty-nine," the kid said.

"I'll put the ice cream back," Jessie said.

"No way, girlfriend," Sherry said. "We gotcha covered. No way you're going home without that candy cane ice cream. Not on my watch. Merry Christmas, honey," and she put money on the counter and rushed off to the next task.

Jessie carried her groceries home under a gently falling snow, smiling at the kindness. And another surprise greeted her at the bottom of her steps, a Christmas bag of goodies. She put the groceries away and then took some cough syrup and ate a sandwich and some slaw and drank three glasses of milk. And then, all at once, she became fully aware of the punishment her body had taken in the picture-hanging marathon and fell on the couch.

Around ten, she woke up needing the bathroom and thinking of that fancy cake and Mary the Mother and Jesus the baby and what a magical night the first Christmas must have been. The cold medicine was doing its work, and she unpacked the mysterious gift bag. A bottle of Merlot. *Yup, from Kelly. That's what I figured.* A tin of Danish cookies, two boxes of soup, gourmet crackers, peppermint coffee, hot cider spices and cider, a box of chocolates, and a small evergreen-scented candle in a glass Christmas tree. She set the candle on the table and lit it, poured some Merlot into a juice glass, and sipped slowly, feeling the tingle, looking around at her pictures. *Too bad I don't have a musical Christmas tree like the one at Roderick's. That would be perfect.*

I don't have my own baby, but I have the baby Jesus because he's everybody's baby. What that means, I don't quite know except maybe that love is real, even if I don't know much about it. Gazing into the flickering flame, she knew, again, that she couldn't go back. *I have to have more. More what? More life.*

She started tearing the cellophane off the box of chocolates from the gift bag and heard Jakob's scooter. Standing stock still, she waited for the knock and still didn't move when it came. At the second knock, she put the chocolates on the table, walked through the utility room, and opened the door. His expression through the glass of the storm door scared her: *Too much feeling, too thrilled to see me, like he wants to grab me.* He grabbed the handle and tried to open the door, but she had locked it. She stood blinking at him in the pale light. *It's been four days since I've seen him. Actually, I've hardly thought of him, with so much happening. I feel a world apart. I don't know if I want to let him in or not.*

Jakob's smile drooped away. She opened the door.

"Jessica. Jessie. Are you okay?"

She nodded.

"I've been looking everywhere for you. Where have you been?"

"Right here. How did you find out where I lived?"

"From Kelly. Why did you leave the scrub bucket with water in it at Roderick McCoy's on Monday morning?"

"Because I killed the cat."

"You killed the cat?"

She nodded. "By accident, and I just wanted to get out of there."

He looked at her and took her hand.

Oh, no! Is he going to propose?

"Jessica, will you come with me to the Christmas Eve service at my church?"

"No," she said, pulling her hand away. "I'm not going anywhere. And you're reminding me of Doug." *Oh, gosh, he looks so hurt. I wish I hadn't said that.* "After a while I'm going to have a Christmas dinner. Pizza. I'll wait for you if you want to come back after your service."

"Yes. I will. Thank you, Jessica. I will!" The smile was back.

"Okay. I'll see you later." She shut the door and went back to the kitchen. His engine started, turned off, another knock on the door, another opening.

"Please?" he said, and started rocking a bit. "If you don't go with me, I might not go either, because of the doubts that are caving in on me, but you're more solid."

He stood still and looked down into her eyes and said, "I think you and I fit oddly and wonderfully together, and I want more love and joy in my life, and Christmas Eve is full of love and joy, and if you'd sit next to me, simple and solid like you are—oh, wow."

At her silence, he turned to leave again, but then Jessie said okay.

He swooped around and repeated, "Okay?"

She nodded, and he picked her up and started dancing around.

"Put me down or I won't go!"

She put on her coat, hat, mittens and his too big

helmet—he insisted—and climbed on the scooter. Suddenly, Renee and the motorcycle crash came into her head. But then, she leaned against Jakob's back for this amazing night ride, arms full of him, hands clasped at his navel, Christmas lights turning into bright blurs streaking along with them.

Simple and solid, she smiled to herself. *Can that be me?*

They heard bells chiming as they parked and squeezed into a bustling crowd jamming the entryway, poised to walk down the middle aisle. The minister turned and greeted them when they slipped in, "Merry Christmas, Jakob," with a nod to Jessie, and then the line of many people moved forward singing O come, all ye faithful, joyful and triumphant with trumpets blasting. Jakob joined in. Jessie wanted to put her hands over her ears.

She followed him to his family's row, and they edged in next to his dad. *Oboy, all these new people, all this noise and movement and not knowing what's going to happen next.* Playing with a hangnail on her middle finger, left hand helped relieve the tension. Yelling above the music, Jakob leaned forward and pointed to each one. "There's my dad, Leif; you met him. Next is Martha, my sister, her husband, Nathan, their son, Simon Peter Joel." Jessie peered around

Jakob to see who was who. "And then my mother, Lydia. Look, Mom! Here's Jessie." The family smiled, stared, waved, nodded. After song and prayer, they sat down, tight up against each other.

Giant nativity figures sat up front, the characters similar to the ones in her paint-by-number picture. In the message, the minister focused on Mary, saying maybe people would want to come up afterwards and take selfies of themselves with her because she is the best example of having faith. Jessie had no idea what take selfies meant, but she looked at Jakob to see if he'd caught the idea of Mary helping people have faith. He looked back at her, but she couldn't tell from his look.

Simon worked his way down the pew, squeezing in between Jakob and Jessie. He sneaked several glances at her, and after a bit whispered, "How old are you?"

"Nineteen," Jessie whispered back.

"I'm six."

"Oh."

"Do you like my Uncle Jakob?"

"Yes."

"Do you love him?"

Jessie shrugged.

"Do you want to be my friend?"

Jessie nodded, even smiled a little.

He drew pictures on the bulletin, showing each one to her, reminding her of Fiona, how one day she would do that. *But I might not see her doing it, growing up.* She focused on the Mary upfront to keep from crying. Near the end, all the lights were turned off and fire passed from one candle to the next. Light filled the place again, dim and gentle, as they sang Silent Night. When people started extinguishing their candles, Simon said to Jessie, "Let's never blow ours out, never," so the two of them stood there with lit candles while everyone else belted out Joy to the World, until Jakob bent over and blew them out. Jessie had to laugh at the exasperated look the nephew gave the uncle.

After the service, the friendliness of Jakob's family made Jessie nervous. She kept flipping that hangnail. His mother invited her to their midnight Beef Burgundy dinner.

"Please, Jessie, pleasepleaseplease," Simon said, jumping up and down.

Jessie smiled weakly, thinking, *I can't possibly. Exhausted. Afraid I'll have a coughing spell. New people asking questions. I can't possibly. All I want is to get home and lock myself away. Me and Jakob.*

"We're going to eat at her place. Pizza, right?" Jakob said, looking down at her.

She nodded. *Rescued! My hero.*

21

※

"Holy cow, you sure did paint a lot as a kid," Jakob said. They were in the living room, on the paint-by-number gallery tour.

"Yeah," Jessie said, standing behind him. *Oh man, I want to press against his back and put my arms around his middle like on the scooter. But I feel shy again. I need to think about something else.* "So how'd it go with you and God tonight at the service?"

"Better with you there. You know what they say: God's omnipresent, but sometimes you need somebody with skin."

"Jesus?"

Jakob looked at her. "Yeah, sure. But he's not exactly here, is he? I mean, we can't see him, talk to him, touch him."

Well, you can sure touch me, Jessie thought, blushing hard.

"By the way, your pictures of Jesus are very nice."

"Probably the best one is in the bedroom," she said, hot and embarrassed saying the word bedroom. "It's of the last supper. I think it was the hardest of all. And by the way," she asked Jakob, "do you think Mary could help your faith, like the preacher said?"

"What? I think I missed that."

"She said Mary is a model of being faithful for us because she kept trusting God and trying to do what God said even when she was worried and didn't know how things were going to turn out."

"She said all that? Okay, yeah that's helpful—but they weren't faced with the imminent end of the earth."

"She said it goes for today too, and any trouble that comes our way."

Jakob grunted. "Can we sit down now? I want to give you your present."

"I didn't get you anything," she said, sitting down on the couch next to him.

"That's okay. Open it," Jakob said, handing over the colorful gift he'd been carrying around, excited like a dog being leashed for a walk.

Jessie tore the paper off the flat package. "Oh! It's beautiful," she said, looking at the picture on the box. "Let me see." She opened the flap and pulled it out. Her trained eye could tell more by looking at the white board with its faint outlines and tiny numbers. She could envision The Glowing Night, a dark scene with lots of yellow, appearing as though it had rained right before sunset. A sidewalk lined on both sides by tall fir trees broadened out of the background. She could already see the glowing lampposts and knew which yellows she would use. The best part was crystal clear to her, a tiny black splotch on the sidewalk toward the back, a silhouette of a couple walking as one, no light, no space between them.

"That's supposed to be you and me," Jakob said, pointing to the splotch.

"I thought so," Jessie said, flushing and tingling, her eyes still looking down. "Jakob, that makes me happy," and he ducked under her and their lips touched—their third kiss—the best one yet.

"I've never tasted better pizza," Jakob said, his mouth full, shoulder to shoulder with Jessie in her kitchen booth.

"And listen, Jessie, Roderick McCoy wants you to come back. He doesn't care about that cat; it was his wife's, not his. He didn't even want to give it a proper pet burial. He told me to put it in the garbage can."

"You really think he wants me back?"

"Yes. He needs you. His house is back to pigsty conditions."

"That's good, then," she said. "Well, there's another reason I shut myself away these last few days, besides the cat and being sick—though I have been very sick, Jakob."

"Me too, and it's your fault. I got your cold from kissing you," and he whinnied a little laugh.

"No, I mean seriously ill, with fever and coughing, maybe pneumonia." Her voice softened. "I thought I might die," she whispered.

"Oh no, not that!"

She nodded. "But I'm getting better."

"I thank God for that, Jessie, because I don't want to go back to life without you."

Her feelings flopped this way and that at his earnestness.

"But what was the other reason you disappeared?" he asked, leaning forward to take a bite, looking sideways into her face.

"I've lost Fiona," she said in a voice so tiny she wasn't sure she'd said it out loud. "I've lost Fiona," she repeated louder.

"What? Why?"

She couldn't speak. Jakob encircled her with his arms, and she leaned on him and wept. The pain returned inch by inch, like a band aid slowly torn from tender flesh. He stroked her hair until she could tell him of that terrible night.

"She was screaming and the wind was howling and I was coughing and so sick and I thought the rug was in the door so I pushed it..." She dissolved into tears again.

"Oh God, so sorry, Jessie. That's awful," and he kissed the top of her head and squeezed so hard she had to say, "Not so tight, just hold me," and, embarrassed and comforted, she let him into her world of hurt. He waited until she was calm again and had wiped her tears and snot into a used tissue before he spoke.

"Is she okay now? Fiona?"

Jessie shrugged and nodded. "I guess so. I think so."

"Okay then, let's try to be like Mary. I'm going to say what I used to believe, before my doubts. God always makes things turn out okay, eventually. I mean, not exactly, maybe, but in a way beyond our knowledge or imagination—so that even if the earth passes away, even if our evil, stupid pollution kills it, God will still go on, and the love Jesus taught us and showed us will still be true."

"Okay, Jakob," she said, sighing. "I'll try to believe that because it sounds good—or at least the best we can do."

"A few weeks ago," Jakob said as they resumed eating, "we read that passage in my Sunday School class, Luke chapter twenty-one, verses twenty-five through thirty-three, earth passing away and the fig tree parable and so forth. What I'm saying, Jessie," and they looked into each other's eyes, "is that even if you don't get Fiona back, it's going to be okay, somehow. And hey, don't forget, Mary lost Jesus. She thought he was gone for good, but then, no, he wasn't."

Jessie sighed big again and got up and pulled the pizza back out of the oven and served them each another piece.

"Your family's nice. Simon's cute."

"He likes you. That's not usual. He's pretty choosy with people."

Bangbangbang on the door at one a.m. made them jump, but their startled looks quickly turned puzzled, and then, quickly again, comprehending, they said at the same time,

233

"Kelly."

"Cousin, this is the art institute from hell on steroids, except it's beautiful," Kelly said, in her green Santa hat, her jingle bell jewelry jingling. She made a small circle around the utility room and then the kitchen, gaping at the covered walls, fingering some of the paintings. "What in the world are all these?"

"My paintings. I've been doing them since I was six."

Kelly stared at Jessie, her head turning side to side in wonder.

"Impressive, huh? I'm flabbergasted. She's an artist," Jakob said.

"And look at her, all dressed up," Kelly said.

"She's beautiful," Jakob said.

"O brother, he's got it bad, look at him looking at her, all googly-eyed. Hey, any of that pizza left? It smells scrumpdillyicious. I'm starving here in the middle of the night worrying my head off over you, Jessica George. I've been by here four times since you vanished from Rod's on Monday. Where were you when I stopped?"

Jessie shrugged. "Sleeping maybe. At the store once, when you left the bag."

"Well, dear God in heaven, I thought you might be eaten by a coyote," she said, biting into the pizza set before her. "Hmm, I see you've opened the Merlot."

"Oh, yeah. And thanks for the nice presents," Jessie said, pouring her some wine.

"Where were you at eleven o'clock tonight?"

"At church."

Kelly's eyebrows raised as she chewed.

"With me. My church," Jakob said.

She nodded. "Oh, man, this pizza is good, even if it is veggie."

"I have a meat lovers. Should I put it in the oven?"

Kelly nodded vigorously.

"So how was church?" she asked, guzzling her wine and topping it off.

"I think you should stop drinking wine, Kelly. You're starting to act like you did on Thanksgiving."

"I am not. That was entirely different. I was depressed. Tonight, I'm totally enjoying you kids," and she raised her glass to them and giggled. "Did she ever tell you what happened on Thanksgiving night, Jakob? Me almost burning the house down?"

Jakob shook his head and looked at Jessie.

"I'd have been asphyxiated and burnt to a crisp if it weren't for her," Kelly went on. "If she hadn't been there and taken quick action, there'd a-been a four alarm at my place. Who knows? The whole block might have caught fire; it might have spread to Chicago, like when Mrs. O'what's-her-name's cow kicked over the lantern. And Jessie, I want to tell you something: it was that night I began to see that you're made of stronger stuff than I ever thought."

"Wow," Jakob said. "What did you do, Jessie?"

"I pulled her out of the living room and threw water on the fire," Jessie said. "And Kelly, I don't want you to get that way again."

"I won't," Kelly said, reaching for the wine bottle.

Jessie grabbed it and put it on the counter.

"Spoil sport," Kelly pouted.

"She's been dangerously sick, Kelly. We could have lost her," Jakob said.

"Seriously? Listen here, cousin, being sick is no time to run away from everybody. We're your people. Promise you won't do that again. Let's promise right now we'll all stick together, through thick and thin."

She extended her hand, which Jakob immediately

grasped. Jessie waited for a fraction of a second but laid her hand on top of theirs, and they gently pumped the air.

"Alright then," Kelly said softly.

Picking up her pizza and taking another bite, she chewed a bit, and then said, "Hey, listen Jessie, Roderick's also wondering what happened to you. We had a little dinner earlier, and..."

"Who did?"

"Rod and me."

"You did?"

"Yeah. I took him a gift bag with the same stuff as yours. And for Christmas Eve, we heated up the soup and had TV dinners with Swiss steak and mashed potatoes and green beans, pretty decent. And we toasted each other and listen guys, I'm telling you, that man is not in good shape. Looks bad, smells bad, talks crazy and..."

"Is he mad at me?"

"I don't think so. Why would he be?"

"Because of the cat dying."

"His cat died? Well, that's not your fault."

Jessie and Jakob both nodded that yes, it was her fault.

"I killed it—accidentally."

"Good grief," Kelly said. "Well whatever. He never

mentioned the cat, but he did say he still needs you."

"That's what I told you," Jakob said.

"That would be good," Jessie said, taking the meat pizza out. "That would be great if he still needs me."

"Has he ever talked to you guys about his wife?" Kelly asked.

"Yeah," Jessie said. "It was pretty weird this one time when he was talking as though she were there. He told her she should have mailed some letters. Her name is Genevieve."

"Was, you mean. He called her Vevie. Do you ever feel her ghost around, Jessie?"

Jessie shook her head, and Jakob said, "I think he does. You know that big painting of them over the fireplace? It fell down, and he wanted it out of there."

"It didn't fall," Jessie said. "He pulled it down—on himself—I saw it. I asked him if he was alright and he told me to go away but then let me fix him dinner. Weird."

"Huh. Well, he had me take it downstairs and face it to the wall. And then, one time he told me about a girlfriend he had in Vietnam."

"Yeah. I heard about her tonight. Her name was My Phuong. He said she was as beautiful as a lotus blossom.

Dude's got a lot of secrets," Kelly said, and they were silent in thought.

Jessie told Kelly about Fiona's fingers.

"Oh, geez, Jessie, that was awful. This one time I got my fingers smashed in the door. You could see..." Seeing their faces, she said, "Oh, never mind. Hey, why don't we go over to Rod's tomorrow? He's all alone. We should take him some holiday cheer. And you can make sure you still have a job, Jessie."

"I can't," Jakob said. "I have Christmas with my family at Martha's."

"I guess I'll go with you, " Jessie said.

"Great. He'll be happy. He's only a dot. "

"What does that mean?"

"Oh. Well, we were talking about your disappearance, and I said you must be with Doug because your circle is so small. Who else could you be with, besides me or Jakob? And then he asked me who was in my circle. And I said only you guys, and so I asked him who was in his. He said he'd burned all his bridges with his family and friends so he had no circle. He guessed he was only a dot."

22

"Now, for holy sakes, don't say anything about killing the cat, Jessie."

"Right. Okay."

Kelly pressed the doorbell again and waited. "One more time," she said, and knocked.

Jessie swallowed a gasp when he opened the door. He was wearing the same army green sweat suit he'd had on four days ago, smelled of beer and b.o. and his eyes were red with dark circles. Pieces of lint stuck in his hair, which sorely needed a trim, and he hadn't shaved for a while. He squinted, stared.

"Merry Christmas, Rod. Jessie and I couldn't stand the thought of you being all alone, so here we are."

"I'm not feeling too well."

"Yeah, you don't look so hot, kinda' gray around the gills. Whatsamatter?"

"Not sure. Something's hit me pretty hard this morning," he said. "Honestly, I've lost all track of time."

"Well, it's afternoon," Kelly said, pulling her phone out. "Two thirty-eight, to be exact. Have you eaten today?"

"I don't think so."

"You don't think so? Man, I never forget if I've eaten. How do you forget if you've eaten or not?" she put to Jessie.

"I see you found her," he said.

"I've been sick too," Jessie said.

"Well, good that you're better. Plenty of work to do around here."

"Right," Kelly said, and gave Jessie a told-you-so look. "So, Rod, you want us to entrez vous and get to celebrating? We brought games."

"And cake," Jessie said, holding up the holiday cake in its plastic showcase.

"I see that," he said, then sighed. "Okay. Let the celebration begin. Entrez vous."

———

"Whew, I'm glad he decided to take a shower," Kelly said, rummaging through Roderick's freezer.

241

"Yeah," Jessie said, rinsing dishes in the sink.

"Here's a couple Chicken Cordon Bleus, two breasts in each box. How's that sound?"

"Fine."

"And sweet baby peas. Ooh, and dinner rolls. Let's see what's in his pantry to go with it. Yum—pineapple chunks."

"The usual day-to-day stuff, maintenance, as it were—laundry, cleaning, sort the mail, that's helpful," Roderick was saying.

Wow, a shower and shave worked wonders. He actually seems happy right now. That's different.

"Oh, and before you leave, I need you to get down in the side of my chair and fish out some mail that slipped down in there the other day. Doesn't really matter—probably a couple Christmas cards from people who can't even pick up the phone to call me. Whatever."

They were in the front sitting room. "Look at that snow coming down. White Christmas, after all." They watched quietly together for a moment.

"Back to your work. You can do a thorough cleaning of the bathroom off the kitchen, remove the litter box for good. The cat died," he said, looking at Jessie.

"I heard."

"We found it dead the same morning you took off so fast," he went on, eyes locked on hers. "In the kitchen."

She nodded and sipped her spiced cider, eyes faltering downward.

Roderick let that hang in the air before he went on. "These cats were all Vevie's, not mine, and it's a mercy for that poor old thing to be out of its misery." She looked back at him and saw forgiveness and breathed easier.

"And then there are the more long-term tasks. The upstairs has hardly been touched since... for a long time. Also, in another week or two I'll be ready to transfer back downstairs, so maybe you can assemble your crew again for moving me back down."

"Yeah, she can do all that, can't you, Jessie? She's the best little housekeeper ever," Kelly gushed, then shut up when Jessie gave her a look.

"Uno!" Kelly shouted.

"Again?" Jessie groaned, playing her card.

Roderick played a Draw Four. "That'll fix her for awhile."

Chicken baking in the oven smelled good, and they

chatted while they played. Kelly started describing the wall-to-wall gallery of Jessie's paintings.

"Hard for me to picture," Roderick said.

"Yeah, it's intense. I crashed on her couch last night, and I could hardly sleep for feeling like they were going to attack me or fall down and bury me or something. But I mean it's good, it's amazing. Jessie, what's your favorite one?"

She felt put on the spot but managed to say Balloon Clown because it was her first and added that she thought her last one, Beyond the Gate, was her best.

"The tiger's the best. You should see this tiger, Rod."

"You have a passion for this. It's good to have a passion," Roderick said dispassionately.

"Thank you," Jessie said, pleasantly embarrassed.

"Jes-si-cah, you did not skip me again!"

Jessie laughed.

"This is the best Christmas ever," Kelly said. "Rod, did you have Christmas in Vietnam?"

"A couple times. No biggie. Good food for a change, but other brothers were out there having their heads blown off, so..."

Kelly urged him on with questions. "What's Agent

Orange?"

"Jellied gasoline," he called it, and described its horrendous effects.

He told the story of a vet buddy who had holed up somewhere in Washington state, ending his life during a standoff with authorities back in the '90s.

"But most of us have done okay. Successful careers, integrated back into society."

Hmm, you think you're doing okay? That's not what you said the other day, Jessie thought, keeping her eyes on her cards.

"Do you see any of them anymore, any of the soldiers you commanded?"

He shook his head. "I'm not in touch with anybody. My First Sergeant, Wayne, used to visit in January but he had to back out this time. Now we're incommunicado. Never expected that."

"Well," Kelly said. "Maybe that could be good. Help you put it all behind."

"Doesn't happen. 'Only the dead see the end of war.' Santayana. Uno. You can stuff it away, most of us have. Tried to live our lives separate from it, but it's impossible. How do you get rid of..." and he began to recall a scene of carnage. "But, God a'mighty, you ladies don't need to hear this. Nobody does."

"We can take it, Rod, if you need to get it out. You don't need to stuff it down with us, does he, Jessie?"

Jessie's head moved in a little circle, her eyes still on her cards.

"No, no, entirely unnecessary. It's Christmas. Let's give merry our best shot. And—I'm out," he said, throwing down his last card.

Kelly hooted and hollered, and Roderick laughed, and they moved on to dinner. Thoughts of Christmases past poked at Jessie's brain—*nothing different or special at our house*—and she felt a stab of pain right in the middle of this pleasure.

"Yoo-hoo, Jessie, we're trying to have a toast here, even though we're almost finished. C'mon, pick up your glass." Kelly sat there looking at them, her glass raised, and let out a little laugh. "Now I don't know what to say. Here's to—us?" And her phone rang.

She went in the hall to take the call, then reported, "Wow, that was Amanda from day care. Haven't heard from her in ages. She wants me to drop in for a drink and gift. Huh. Probably wants to borrow money, but I guess I'll go on over."

Jessie served the cake and Kelly gobbled hers and waved as she exited, glitter in her hair, bells a-jangling.

Awkwardness slithered in like a snake, Jessie and Roderick sitting at the table.

"How's Lauren?" Jessie asked. He didn't know. He asked if she wanted to take the rest of the week off or work tomorrow, either way was okay with him. *Hmm, I want the money—but I don't feel that good yet—but I want to get busy, things have been piling up—maybe that's what he wants me to do—but...*

"I'm not sure," she said, and then went into a coughing fit and had to go in the bathroom to recover.

He had his coat on when she came out. "You'd better lie low for a few more days. Why don't you start up again Monday? And I'll take you home, since your ride has left."

"I could clean up the kitchen first."

But he wouldn't hear of that and handed her a check for eight hundred dollars.

"What's this for? I've only worked three hours this week."

"I give paid holidays and sick leave—and a Christmas bonus."

"But so much money! At least let me put away the

food."

"Nope, let's go. I'm eager to drive. I'm supposed to wait another ten days, officially, but I'm ready."

The ride home was not fun. *Oh geez, all that groaning and the looks on his face. He is in a lot of pain. I don't think he's okay to drive at all. Oh dear, he took his foot off the brake too soon. Oh gosh, he barely missed that car when he swung left so fast. Thank heaven we made it without an accident!*

"Dad-blame it!" he said, parking for her to get out. "Again, I forgot to have you get that mail out of my chair. Well, shoot; maybe I can get it with my big mitts—but I'll probably forget it again by the time I get home. Remind me Monday, will you?"

"I'll try to remember," *but I probably won't*. "Thank you," she said, climbing out, "for the food and extra money and everything."

"Thank you," he said, staring through the windshield, "for saving my life."

23

Doug apologized for being so hard on her about shutting Fiona's fingers in the door. "I was stressed out and not thinking clearly. Not that it wasn't serious, but..."

"I'm afraid to have her. I might hurt her again. Is her hand okay?"

"She's fine, Jessica. Look, the truth is this could have happened with me. The other day she fell off the couch and hit the bridge of her nose on the coffee table, and it bled like crazy. Nobody was careless, it's just—accidents happen. But listen, you have to have a cell phone before you can have her again, okay?"

That is the last thing in the world I want. Yuk. But without hesitation she said, "Okay. Yes. I'll get one, but..."

"You can afford it?"

"Oh yeah—I have lots of money—but I'm still afraid. I want her, but I think I'll die if I hurt her again."

Doug nodded. "Pray, Jessica, for patience and wisdom; we'll be praying too. God will grant your requests, for they serve his good purposes. And we can start with short visits if you want, until you get your confidence back. It's obvious you're starting to love her, and you were doing fine with her before the accident. Kids need their mothers. Look how you turned out, hardly even having one."

That was so mean—even though it's true.

"So let me know when you get a phone. Give me a call. You have my number, right? And, wow," he said, looking around at her paintings as he made his exit. "They took me by surprise, so many of them."

Jessie felt great, swinging along the sidewalk in the brisk morning air, much better, still coughing but not as much. *A new week, a new year. I'll start deep cleaning upstairs today.* But she soon knew she wouldn't because when she unlocked Roderick's front door and stepped into the gray silence, she smelled beer and a depressed man asleep in his recliner. Tiptoeing past him into the kitchen, she gagged at a strong stench and was shocked at the filth. The dirty dishes from

Christmas dinner five days ago sat on the counter. Frozen entrée cartons overflowed the garbage. A roach nibbled intently on the residue of their happy holiday meal. She shuddered. *I don't know if this job is worth the money. I just want to get out of here.*

But she automatically put her coat on the washing machine, covered her nose and then—thought of the cat. *Jakob said they put it in the trash bin, but did anybody roll it to the curb? Usually I do it last thing on Mondays, but not last Monday.* She opened the door to the garage and had no doubt.

Roderick came into the kitchen.

"Is the dead cat in the garage?" she asked.

He stopped and looked at her.

"Can't you smell that?"

"Oh. I thought it was my life," he said under his breath, and went into the bathroom.

She stood like a statue, hearing him pee, her eyes on him when he came out.

"I guess it is the cat. Pick-up is tomorrow, isn't it? Be sure and put it out before you leave." He started on his way, then stopped in the doorway and said, "I spilled some beer in the living room last night, on the television. Please get to that when you can."

"While you go take a shower?"

He glared at her and walked out.

What has happened? Where is that nice, funny man from our Christmas dinner? He was sad at times, but not mean.

Ten minutes later, though, when the police came, he was in the shower. Jessie ignored the first ring, but they persisted, shouting, "Palatine Police. Open up, please."

"We had a report of a strong smell at this residence, maybe a dead animal?"

Jessie nodded. "A cat. It's in the garbage in the garage. But this is not my house. I only work here."

"Well, if you'll allow us, we'll check the cat situation and be on our way. Can you raise the garage door for us?"

The officers were gone by the time Roderick finished showering and dressing.

"They said it wouldn't hurt to bury it right away so more people won't call," Jessie told him. "And I don't know how you stand it. I hardly can. I might need to go home."

"Young lady, you don't need to be getting uppity with me."

Uppity? Maybe I am, but I have to do something because you're in bad shape. Very bad shape. I helped at Kelly's that night when she drank too much. I can help here.

253

"Jakob and I can probably bury it when he comes on his lunch break."

He walked over to the bay window and looked into the back yard. "I don't know how I keep going, with everybody against me," he said softly, not to Jessie. She heard him say "self-loathing" and how nobody would care if he "eliminated" himself. Oh, he knew help was available from V.A. services, if only he could reach out, get a telephone, for starters.

"I had the energy to go out and buy beer but not to get a telephone. How pathetic is that?" he asked, and then went out into the stinking garage and drove away.

Jakob laughed when she opened the front door with one of Roderick's handkerchiefs tied around her nose.

"Is this a hold-up?" he kidded, but then grabbed the kerchief she offered and put it to his face. "I smelled it outside, but it's so strong in here!"

"It's the cat."

"Precious? Oh my gosh, still in the garbage can?"

She nodded. "Will you help me bury it?"

The garage door thundered up, breaking the cold silence of the street. He carried the shovel, and she rolled the bin around the house and through the backyard gate. The wheels crunched across the icy crust of the snow to Chico's grave in the corner. In the gentle breeze, they took turns digging through the snow into the hard ground. A shallow oval now ready, Jakob tipped the bin on its side, reached in with the shovel, brought out the plastic bag with its putrid contents, and laid it to rest in the hole. Jessie covered it up and they stood, her shoulder against his arm, looking down at the site.

"She used to be alive and now she's not," Jessie said.

"Dust to dust," Jakob said.

"Like my baby brother, my sister, my father, my mother, my aunt," Jessie said.

Jakob pulled her to him. "I'll say a prayer."

I don't want to cry, but I think I'm going to... But Jakob's prayer made her smile instead.

"God, we give this cat back to you, this precious cat Precious, who came from dust and returns to this cold ground, a lamb of your own flock, loved at least by Genevieve, and love never dies. Thank you. Amen."

Ha! a cat as a lamb.

They ate their lunches in the front sitting room after spraying half a can of pine scent. "He hardly seems like the same person, sometimes," she told Jakob.

"Aren't we all that way? You, for example. Sometimes you're Jessie and sometimes Jessica. Jessica is the person you were when I met you, hardly talking or smiling, and Jessie is the person you're becoming by laughing and having some fun."

Jessie shrugged.

"Anyway, change of subject," Jakob said. "When are you going to get your phone? I'll get you one, Jessie, because I don't want to go through not being able to communicate with you again. I'll buy it, if you want."

"Yeah, it's time. I need one when Fiona's with me. I can pay for it myself, but I definitely need help knowing how to use it. I know nothing."

"Okay, well listen. There's this socially responsible phone company. We can sign you up online. They send you a phone as soon as you order, and they're not simply a phone company, they're a movement. They're green and they support all kinds of..."

"Okay. Sign me up. But back to Roderick McCoy. He's so different from when he played Uno with us on Christmas, and he gave me that bonus too, remember? Now he's all angry and drinking again. He said he spilled beer in the living room, but I think he threw a whole can of it at the TV. I worked in there for an hour, scrubbed on the carpet with three different cleaners to get rid of the smell."

"Jessie, you're a wonder. I want to kiss you, okay?"

Yes. Oh, yes, Jakob. Let's kiss!

"The physical therapist came," Jessie told Roderick when he came in.

"Well, confound it, I totally forgot. I went to get a phone," and he held up the bag in his hand.

"He said he'll come tomorrow at the same time. You should call him if that won't work. Here's his card."

Snatching the card, he said, "I think I'll be ready to move downstairs by the weekend. Can you and your helpers get the chair and flat screen down there by Friday?"

"I'll check with them."

He made himself a sandwich while she mopped the floor. *I want to tell him I'm getting a telephone too, but I can't make the words come out of my mouth. I get the feeling he wants to say something too, but can't.*

He took his plate and glass of milk to the living room. She kept mopping.

I feel like a robot. Why can't I talk to him?

257

The next day Roderick worked with the physical therapist while Jessie finished straightening the kitchen. She wiped the counter, hung up the dishcloth and dried her hands more thoroughly than usual. *Okay,* she sighed. *It's time.* She walked to the stairway and looked up for a long moment, then started up, hesitating when she reached the top. *This is like stepping on to another planet. I've walked around up here some, peeked in rooms, planned, but now, it feels mysterious, maybe magical. Oh gosh, it's like that time in Renee's room...*

Her mother had left Renee's room unlocked. She noticed rays of sun gleaming on the hallway floor through the crack of the opened door. Fearful but fascinated, she stepped in. This room was different from the rest of the house. In this room was life. Many pictures of a pretty blond teenager with a dazzling smile. In fancy dresses with boys in suits and their arm around her. Wearing a cheerleader outfit, a soccer uniform. Hugging a fluffy, white dog. Cheek to cheek with Jessie's mom. Lots of purple and lavender in the room, lots of glitter on wands and pom-poms and little dolls and animal knick knacks. Sports banners and posters of a scruffy rock band covered the walls. Trophies and other high school stuff filled a bookshelf.

She had her hand on the closet door when she heard her mother coming in and panicked. She should be painting at the kitchen table. She flew into her room and shut her door and sat on the edge of her bed, her heart and head throbbing harder with each footstep of her mother coming up the steps. Silence followed, and then her door flew open.

"You went in there, didn't you?"

She nodded.

"That room is off limits to you. Never again. Do you hear me?"

She nodded.

Now her heart was pounding the same way entering Vevie's room. Their wedding picture sat on the dresser along with perfume bottles on a silver tray with a mirror for a bottom and some fancy figurines of cats. More cat statues and photos of people from the olden days on the chest of drawers. The room was nicely decorated, the king-size bed covered by a quilted spread and matching drapes at the windows. Three large plants that Jessie imagined had once been beautiful stood dead and stark. A heavy hope chest at the foot of the bed held stacks of magazines, one named O, for some black woman named Oprah, apparently.

The closet was a jumbled mess. Her pulse back to normal, Jessie got to work, matching scattered shoes and placing them, for now, on a shelf under blouses and jackets. That's when she found a tin box, clunked it with a shoe. The box was pretty, olive green with pink flowers and dark green vines that she could feel when she ran her fingers over it. She opened it. Letters.

Vevie's letters! The ones he said she should have mailed. Light blue air mail stationery that folded up to make their own envelopes, written and signed by Vevie but not folded, not addressed except the top one, to First Lt. Roderick McCoy, CPO San Francisco.

I shouldn't. But I'm going to. She tiptoed to the top of the staircase and looked down. *Who would ever know?*

24

"Cousin, put knowing how to use a cell phone on your long list of things you have unbelievably not done," Kelly said. "Jakob, I'll work with Rod and you can work with Jessie."

"All I want to know is how to answer it and make calls," Jessie said.

"I only need a little help setting up contacts. That's it," Roderick said.

"But you can do so much more," Jakob tried to reason with him.

"Especially with yours, Rod," Kelly joined in.

"Right. I used all the bells and whistles when I ran around the world managing projects, but that was a few generations of cell phones ago. No longer interested, thank you."

Kelly sighed. "You two are pathetic. But Jakob, I think we might as well give up on them for now. We'll give 'em the basics, but you guys should know how to get your messages."

"Not me. If I don't answer when it rings, people can call back," Jessie insisted.

"Yeah, why not? That worked okay back in the day," Roderick agreed.

They sat around Roderick's kitchen table taking in the aroma of Kelly's baking: rolls from a pop can.

Phones started ringing—they both wanted classic rings—as the learners practiced. Jakob called Jessie. She pressed a button and said hello. "Hello," she said again, pressing another button.

Jakob pointed to the little green telephone icon. "That one. Think of green—go—talk."

"Oh," and she pressed and said hello again.

"Hello, Jessica," Jakob said into his phone. "How are you?"

She looked at him and said, "I'm fine. Can't you see that, sitting right here next to me?" and they laughed like lovers.

"No, no, no," Kelly said to Roderick. "You don't have

to hang up to add my number. Just go ahead and add. You won't get disconnected," she said, crossing to the kitchen and pulling the sweet rolls out of the oven.

They programmed and practiced while the rolls cooled and put down the phones when Kelly set the plate in the middle of the table.

"Here's our reward for hard work," and hands grabbed, pulling the soft pastries apart.

"Oh my," Roderick said, his mouth full of warm caramel and pecans.

"Yes. Good. But I have to get back to work," Jakob said, stuffing in the last big bite and making his exit with a muffled goodbye.

"Gotta go too. I'll take one of these babies for the road," and Kelly scooped a roll into a paper towel and was on her way.

"Thanks for moving me downstairs," Roderick called after them. He started another pot of coffee brewing, and Jessie started cleaning up.

"So, we have phones," Roderick said.

Jessie nodded.

"Are you glad to have one?"

She nodded again. "Yes, because of Fiona."

"I don't know who I'll call or who will call me," he said. "I've lost so many."

Such sadness in his voice, and he didn't even ask me who Fiona is. Yeah, he's a dot.

When the coffeemaker started gurgling, he yelled, "What's that noise? I think somebody's trying to break in."

"It's the coffeemaker."

"Good grief, man, settle down," he said to himself out loud. "Every morning...

Oh no, here he goes into one of his long talks about how bad everything is.

"...I wake up with that disoriented dread of facing another day. It would probably be better if I weren't driving because of being able to get beer, which throws me back into self-destructive behaviors. But I'm resolved not to let the drinking get away from me again. I can manage it, wait until evening and hold it to two or three a night. And I'll be more careful mixing the booze with the meds.

"I thought getting back down to my den would help because there's still too much Vevie on the main floor," he mused. "But it hasn't.

"I hate myself for making wrong and stupid decisions, and I make wrong and stupid decisions because I hate myself," he said as he walked out of the room.

Wow. If it weren't for his little times of being normal, I might not be able to stand it here. It seems too much like my mother, except she never said all the words. I've had enough of that kind of sadness.

Kelly had invited Jakob and Jessie to Aunt Barb's house for New Year's Eve, Roderick too. He had declined. And then she'd texted Jakob, "prtycncelld. 2 dprest." So he and Jessie were hanging out at her place, music on his phone, making out on the couch, lazy talk about her pictures and whatever.

"Friday night with Fiona can't come soon enough," Jessie said, her eyes dancing and her brain buzzing with ideas. "I got her these," and she showed Jakob the clear vinyl case of Baby's First Building Blocks. "And Tonya's working, so we'll go to Jewel to show her all the new things Fiona can do." She adjusted her position, Jakob's arm sliding off her shoulder.

"Um," Jakob said.

"Yes?"

"Could I come and meet her?"

"No. I have to get used to her again and get over being

afraid. Maybe in a couple weeks."

"Okay, but here's another question. When are you going to come and meet my family? You do know you're invited to New Year's dinner tomorrow, right?"

"Yes, and I've already said no, Jakob. Don't you remember? Besides, I've already met them."

"You know what I mean. Get to know them. Mom's always asking me when you're going to come. And Simon's crazy to see you. You're very popular with them."

You're only scaring me. "Give me time, Jakob. I need time."

"Yeah," Jakob said. "I understand."

"Thank you," she said, looking straight at him so he would know she meant it. It wasn't quite midnight, but they kissed anyway.

"Are you feeling better working at Roderick McCoy's again, since the cat smell is gone, and you've gotten back to point zero as far as cleaning?"

"I guess. Yeah. That guy's scary, though. I never know if he's going to be angry and rude or what. And he could fire me any time and then where would I be?"

"You'd be okay. Stop worrying so much."

"Stop judging my life," she said seriously, but they laughed a little, which led to another good kiss.

"Can I sleep over?"

"No."

"Oh Jessica. It's so cold out there," he groaned.

—❦—

On Friday morning, Jessie noticed that Roderick was back to sleeping in his bed. She also found the hydrator drawers stuffed with fresh vegetables and fruits. And she heard him counting off exercises on his own, without the PT guy. His walker had been folded up leaning against the wall for a while. *He's trying. That's good.*

She focused on Vevie's room now, each day like a happy game of solitaire, putting things in order. Making them pretty too. *Roderick's picking up the drapes and bedspread and that heavy cloth for the round table from the cleaner's today. They'll all be in place this afternoon. The finishing touches!* She had cleaned and shined the windows and window wells with vinegar water and spot-shampooed and vacuumed the carpet with rug freshener. He'd given no instructions nor even come upstairs since she'd started cleaning up there, and she'd discarded, organized, polished and sanitized, happily chewing her gum.

And read the letters. Mid-afternoons, she would fix a cup of hot chocolate and settle in Vevie's lovely flowered chair with the matching hassock and read. The first one started out, "I have decided to be more honest when I write instead of pretending everything is fine." In elegant handwriting, Vevie told Roderick she was leaving Jehovah's Witnesses because their beliefs contradicted serving in the military. A fellow from their Hall had chosen jail over serving—possibly killing—and many more were doing the same thing. "I can't live so hypocritically," she wrote. "When you come home, I hope we can find a church together."

In the second letter, she confessed to "...overspending the budget by quite a bit, decorating a beautiful home for your return, but I'll make it up in the months to come. These new credit cards are too convenient." Partly, she shopped out of loneliness, she said. She and her family were drifting apart since she'd left the church, and the same for her friends.

She got a cat. "Cutest little kitty you ever saw. I've named him Precious, and he sure is a help getting through lonely days and long nights." Often, she ended reminding Roderick of "the good news that God's heavenly Kingdom will soon end all wickedness and transform the earth into a paradise."

Vevie intrigued Jessie: her words, the luxurious aroma of her clothes, her jewelry, which Jessie tried on. She saw her as the bride in the wedding picture on the dresser and tried to imagine that young woman all alone, her husband half a world away. *I think I know why Vevie didn't send the letters. Too risky. He might not want her anymore if he knew the real her. I think that's why I couldn't be honest with Doug. And why I'm doing better with Jakob. Because he likes the real me.*

"Dah," Fiona said to Jessie, and surprised her by reaching for her—with a curious look—and slipping into her arms. *I was afraid she would cry when she saw me, or maybe not even recognize me after two whole weeks.* When she'd first called Doug on her new phone he had asked if she wanted Fiona to sleep over or just spend the evening. She'd opted for evening, a couple hours to get reacquainted. She carried her into the living room, Doug following, her little head turning this way and that, taking in the paintings, pointing and exclaiming, "Dah! Dah!"

"I didn't know she could point," Jessie said, truly amazed.

"Oh yeah. She's got lots of new tricks. Beware of putting your fingers in her mouth; two more teeth have come through—she can get you good. But sometimes you have to, to dig out little things she puts in there. Look out for that. And she understands the word no, so don't be afraid to tell her no."

"Okay. I'm going to be so careful, I promise."

"I know, Jessica," Doug said, but sat down on the floor with Fiona and stayed longer than normal.

Once he went on his way, Jessie examined Fiona's fingers. "Wow. Good as new. And Fiona, I'm so sorry."

Fiona raced away on all fours, garbling something, and pulled up on the hassock and walked around between pieces of furniture. When Jessie said, "Suppertime," Fiona dumbfounded her by saying some syllables as though repeating, and crawling towards the kitchen. She put her in her chair and set her sippy cup on the tray. Fiona took a long drink and then threw it on the floor.

"Oopsey," Jessie said, and gave it to her and she whacked it on the floor again with a gleeful squeal, throwing it so hard that it broke, milk splattering. Jessie laughed, despite the mess, but then thought to say, "No. No."

Fiona's face crinkled, and she cried a broken-hearted lament. "Oh," Jessie sympathized, hugging her. "It's okay, little girl."

Talking to the baby made sense now, and she told her, "There's this nice guy named Jakob. He's my good friend and he wants to meet you. Someday soon you can meet each other."

Fiona babbled in response. *Oh my gosh, that sounded like she said okay. Could she have? No way.*

"Little girl, you keep me laughing," she laughed. "And there's a little boy named Simon, Jakob's nephew. He's cute, but not as cute as you. And I work for this man named Roderick. He scares me sometimes, but he pays me lots of money, and it's fun cleaning his house."

When Doug came back, Fiona was wearing the velvet outfit.

"Her Christmas present," Jessie said.

"What a fancy Fiona," he said, kissing the baby. "Do you want to keep it here?" he said to Jessie.

"Just bring her dressed in it next week, okay? I want to show her to Tonya."

"Who's Tonya?"

"She works at the Jewel. She's my friend from high school."

"Good. Sounds good."

"Doug," she called after them when he and Fiona were going out the back door. He turned.

"Thank you."

25

───••───

A winter storm was whipping up Monday morning, but Jessie didn't care. She was a snow princess gliding the sidewalk in her new fleece-lined boots.

"Let's go shopping," Kelly had said over the weekend.

"For what?" Jessie had asked.

"Sometimes people go shopping just for fun. You probably didn't know that."

Actually, shopping was fun. That Chinese food was delicious, that surprised me. Fiona was fun on Friday night, thank heaven. And yesterday—with Jakob visiting his grandmother in Chicago, I loved having Sunday to myself, like it used to be. And I'm excited to start a new week on Harvard Drive. I'm going to try and be nicer to Roderick, more understanding.

She stopped at Zimmer Hardware, arriving at the house

with a couple bags of supplies sometime after nine o'clock. She sniffed at the smell of cold ashes and saw them in the fireplace in the living room. She could hear Roderick's shower going as she put the cleaning supplies away and straightened the kitchen, then ran up the stairs to behold her work and plan the next project.

Lovely, she smiled to herself, opening the drapes in Vevie's room and standing back to look through the clear windows into the gray swirls of snow. *I'll bring Jakob up here at lunchtime to see. And I'll tell him how well things went with Fiona, and he can tell me about his grandma.* Jakob wanted to talk by phone all the time, now that she had one, but she told him to call only when necessary and save their talking for face to face.

She leveled a picture and got a rag to wipe some lint off the mirror and studied the family pictures one more time, then switched on the light in Vevie's long neglected bathroom. That's where she would start now—after she read a letter or two.

Opening the closet door, she sensed before she saw that something was wrong. Garments had been hurled to the floor and shoes swept off the shelf, Vevie's scarves and sashes ripped off their hangars, strewn around. Doom seized Jessie's heart. And then she heard Roderick on the steps, the cane finding its place, his body heaving up. A shock ran up her arm as she shut the closet door at the same instant he appeared.

"Nice job you've done in here," he said, moving to the dressing table and holding up a bottle of Joy fragrance. "Here's five hundred dollars. Pour it down the sink and throw the bottle in the trash," he said. "And empty the closet, box it all up, clothes, jewelry. The cat knick-knacks too, and throw out the magazines. I want her out of here. I'm going right now to buy boxes from VVA. They'll pick it all up from the curb Thursday."

She blinked up at his saliva-spewing commands, and when he came near stepped back from his hot, stale, beer-scented anger. And then she thought of her own rage the night she hung her pictures. *I know why he's so angry. It's that awful sadness over not being able to change what's happened.* Emboldened with that realization, she opened the closet door and said, "Why did you do this?"

He considered her, weaving a little and balancing on his cane with both hands. He looked at the floor, then back at her. "I'll tell you why. I'll give you one incident out of a thousand whys." He limped past her and bent over with a groan to pull out a black crepe gown with a jeweled band under the bosom. He held it to his face and closed his eyes for a moment.

"She wore this to my retirement gala. We made a handsome couple, everybody said so. We were masters of putting up a good front. I paid tribute to her over the microphone and then, miracle of miracles, when we led off the dancing, I wanted her. I mean I was heating up, despite everything. So I thanked her. I said, with all the sincerity I could muster, 'Vevie, thank you for putting up with me for so long.' See, I had this half-teaspoon of hope watering in my mouth.

"She pulled back and looked me in the eye and with a beautiful smile for everyone watching she said, 'Stop trying, Roderick. It only makes it harder.'"

He looks like my mother, his expression—mad and sad.

"Multiply that a thousand times, like I said." Turning his back on her, he exited with, "I want her out of this house, all of her."

As soon as she heard him pull out of the garage, she went for the box of letters.

Gone.

The ashes in the fireplace.

"I can't work here anymore," Jessie whispered to Jakob over lunch on Friday.

"Uh-oh. What happened?"

"Let's go for a walk."

She talked on in the bright sunlight under the clear sky the same blue as Jakob's eyes. "I think he's worse than when I started, downstairs drinking all day long so how am I supposed to clean down there? And he's usually mad—weird and angry. I know he's sad about his life and all his mistakes, but he scares me."

"You have a right not to be scared. Do you want to pray?"

"No."

"Okay. But we could. It might help."

"It's weird how you bring God in so much when you're not that sure you believe."

"Aha. That's the most important time. We're the ones in the most danger, the devoted ones, so earnest and active, praying all the time, because belief is everything, it's our life, so if it goes, each day would be hell."

They walked in silence for a while, relative silence—a siren in the distance, a car driving by, the rustling of evergreen needles and their own movements.

"You're praying, aren't you?"

Jakob nodded.

"Okay, you might as well go ahead out loud."

"God, you know this hard situation with your child you love so much, Jessie. And then there's your child, Roderick McCoy, who you love the same. Please guide them to what is best and right. And guide me too, for I love your child Jessie very much. Jesus, you are right here with all of us, mysteriously. Help us to know it. Thank you. Amen."

Jessie blushed hot red from Jakob's declaration of love, but all she said was, "Thanks. I don't know if that will do any good, though."

Gosh, I am so jittery. I'm happy, but I'm not too sure about this. Even the butterflies making rounds in Jessie's stomach seemed to be saying, "Yeah. This could be bad." She and Jakob were waiting for the train, and she spied a teenager wearing platform boots and a puffy purple jacket playing with her long hair and looking at them like they were animals in a zoo. The girl looked away when she saw Jessie see her. It felt like high school.

"I can tell you're nervous," Jakob said. "Come over

here," and he took her hand and led her to the bronze sculpture of children playing by the huge fir tree, away from the bustling farmer's market, away from the chipper, cheery Saturday morning crowd destined for adventure in the city. Focusing on the circle of children statues, she imagined Fiona, in a few years. Her butterflies settled, and she leaned against Jakob, releasing for this moment worries about him judging her or trying to control her.

"Would you go on a date with me now?" he had asked after their sidewalk prayer yesterday.

"Okay," she had said. "Yes," nodding her head.

Jubilant, he had proposed taking the Metra to the aquarium.

"The train? It's so big and loud. Is it safe? Doesn't it have wrecks?"

Jakob had brayed his laughter at her and said, "Not much. They're safe. Comfortable. Energy efficient, carrying so many at once. C'mon, let's go tomorrow! Please?"

And here they were, gazing together at the sculpture, separate in their thoughts.

"I didn't get my check yesterday. He forgot, I guess. He wasn't in good shape, and I didn't want to ask him. But I've decided to quit."

"When?"

"I guess on Monday."

"You're stressing over it, aren't you?"

And then loud bells began dinging, and she jerked like she used to when her mother would bark her name from downstairs. She looked around to see if that girl with the purple jacket was watching.

Oblivious to the bells and the crowd movement toward the track, Jakob said, "Know what we could do, Jessie, if you want to... I could take you over there right now and get your check and you can quit. We'll catch the next train. Then you won't have to worry about it all day."

Light-hearted as those bronze children frozen in glee, Jessie perched behind Jakob on his scooter. *I'll move on to something else. I don't know what, but something. Another cleaning job, maybe. This is normal, quitting and getting a new job. I'm normal. And today I'm going to have this new experience in Chicago on this beautiful sunny day with this nice guy—who said he loves me.* She felt sorry for all the people walking along or driving by in their dull, little lives.

But when she rang Roderick's doorbell and he opened the door immediately—must have been passing by—a lump

281

came into her throat.

"What? Don't you have your key?"

"I'm not here to work. It's Saturday."

"Then what?"

"Um, you—I mean I—we forgot my check yesterday."

"Oh. Right. Come in."

He closed the door and went down the hallway.

"He's already been drinking," Jakob said.

Jessie nodded. "And it's like he could go off any minute. This is the usual lately."

He came back on his cane, none too steady, and handed her the check.

"Thank you."

Silence.

Jakob cleared his throat, his eyes on the floor. "Jessica has something to tell you." When she didn't speak, he turned to her. "Tell him, Jessie."

"I'm not going to work here anymore. I have to quit."

He looked hard at her. "I'll be right back." He headed down the hall again, turned left into his bedroom, reappeared a moment later, his left hand on his cane, his right arm hanging at his side.

"You're not quitting," they heard him say as he walked

282

toward them through the shadows. And then they saw the pistol clutched in his right hand.

26

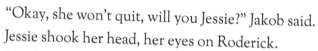

"Okay, she won't quit, will you Jessie?" Jakob said.

Jessie shook her head, her eyes on Roderick.

"And we're getting on a train next, so..." Jakob fumbled with the door.

"No. I need you here. I realize I need you here. Come downstairs with me." Roderick started toward the basement steps, then turned and gestured with his gun to the frozen couple. "Come now."

"Why?" Jessie said. "I'll keep working for you."

"Why should I trust you? You could be the enemy. Anyone trying to kill me is the enemy. Come. I need people with me. I'm lost. I'm dangerous. Come now."

They looked at each other.

"You don't have a choice," Roderick said. "I don't either.

This gun is in charge, I'm afraid. We're all going down to my den. Now. Don't make the gun fire."

"Roderick McCoy," Jakob whined. "This is our first date, for me to show her the wonders of Chicago, and her first time to ride the magnificent Metra. We'll come back tonight—or—or..."

"...or–or–you could come with us," Jessie stuttered.

"...or we could call you from time to time," Jakob said, desperation creeping into his tone.

"Call? Let me have your phones," Roderick said, hulking over them now, Jessie gasping as the pistol pointed haphazardly into Jakob's side.

"Give it to him," she said to Jakob, and he did.

"Yours too," Roderick said.

"I didn't bring mine."

He squinted at her

"I didn't."

Another squint. "Okay. Downstairs."

"But..." Jessie said, and he pushed her along and nudged Jakob with the pistol, marching them down the hallway.

"Roderick McCoy, what's happening? What are you trying to do?" Jakob yelled, descending the steps between him and Jessie.

"I don't know. I don't know who I am. I can't be left alone. I'm a suicide risk."

"We'll stay," Jessie said. "You don't need the gun to make us stay. Put it away."

"I can't take that chance," Roderick said, surveying the room. "First, we need to alter the environment so you are in my sight at all times."

Jessie edged close to Jakob's ear. "We should just do what he says for a while."

But Jakob couldn't handle it. He twirled a couple times and got in Roderick's face. "You can't do this! This is unexpected. We are supposed to be..."

Roderick grabbed him by his collar, jerking him off his feet and setting him back down. "Boy," he panted. "I don't even know where I am, don't you understand? It could be the battlefield, it could be the day my dog died, I could be in Timbuktu. Now stop your foolishness before you push me over the edge," and he threw him down on the couch.

Jessie went and sat beside Jakob. "I'll help him stay calm."

"Yeah. Calm," Roderick puffed. Once he'd caught his breath, he told them what to do, and they did it, pulling his recliner back to the end of the room near the stairway, still facing the TV on the backyard wall. Then he had them angle the heavy, leather couch toward the screen on one side of his chair, the matching love seat on the other side, and the coffee table in the middle.

"Okay, now sit down and take your coats off. I don't want to hurt you kids. We've got a battle to fight here, and my job is to protect you, but my job is also to win the battle. Don't forget: I own this place.

"Now, anyone want a beer?"

They sat there looking at him, and he told Jessie to bring him one.

"I don't think you should be drinking," she said.

"Insubordination will not be tolerated," he thundered.

When she handed it to him, he thanked her and said he would have gotten it himself if he weren't on lookout.

"I have to pee," Jakob said, and Roderick told him to go ahead.

When he came out Roderick said, "My turn," and kept the door cracked.

Their backs were to him. "Let's go!" Jakob said, grabbing Jessie's hand.

"I am still armed and vigilant," Roderick's voice came, and they fell back into the cushions.

When they whispered, he separated them, Jakob on the long couch, Jessie on the shorter one, across from each other.

This is ridiculous. What can we do? There must be something to do.

"So are we hostages?" Jakob asked.

"I guess so," Roderick considered. "You know, it's not as though there's a strategy here. My brain's bouncing all over the place," He fondled his pistol, then looked up and stared, as though surprised to see them.

"Let's watch a movie," he said. "I've seen it a dozen times, I guess. Maybe it will help you youngsters get the message that peace isn't the end of war."

Jakob munched pretzels until the violence depicted on the screen stopped his hand halfway to his mouth. He set the bag on the coffee table, eyes riveted on the movie. At the end, the Vietnam vet shot himself.

After a long silence, Jakob said, "Please give us your weapon, Roderick McCoy. We'll help you."

Roderick stood up, motioning them to the staircase. "Right now, we need rations, and we need to expand operations, so let's advance."

Jessie looked hard at Jakob. *Maybe we can attack him on*

the stairs. I think Jakob's thinking the same thing. But with Roderick and his firearm behind them, that didn't happen.

They made sandwiches and got apples and carried them back down with milk and orange juice and a bag of chips. Jessie had suggested they eat at the kitchen table, but Roderick rejected that idea because they might try to signal someone through the window. *He read my mind. It probably would never have worked, but maybe...*

"I should give my parents a call so they won't worry. They'll be wondering where I am," Jakob said between bites.

No they won't; they're in Haiti on that church trip. But yeah, I see...

"And we should let Kelly know we might not make it tonight," Jessie lied.

"Permission denied. Another beer, please."

Roderick rambled on one topic and another, his words slurred and sloppy. "My parents were mighty proud of me—almost made that hell worth it, sometimes. Mom died not long after I got back. Forty-six years old. Cancer. Dad called me Captain, saluted me all the time, took me to his Legion Hall, down there on Roosevelt, showing me off.

"I heard Muhammad Ali: I had no quarrel with the Viet

Cong. They'd never called me nigger either. But opportunity shined like polished brass—money, college, being somebody on his way up. Thought I'd stay active, but Nam finished off that idea. Did me good, though."

"What good?" Jakob asked.

"Huh?"

"What good did fighting in Vietnam do you?"

"Did I say that? I don't know what I meant."

Then, abruptly, he said to Jakob, "What about you, son? Give us a little personal history."

"Me?"

"Yeah, you, soldier."

"I don't know, Roderick McCoy. I graduated from Palatine High School. I finished my B.S. at U of I Chicago but needed a break. Right now, I'm a one stream sorter for recycling at Groot Industries, but I have greater ambitions, once I..."

His phone rang in Roderick's pocket. He pulled it out and looked at it. "Kelly." He turned it off and put it back in his pocket. "There. That takes care of that. You were saying?"

Jakob leapt up. "I was saying nothing important! What in the world is going on here? Do you want us to move in with you? Are you going to use that gun? For all we know, it isn't even loaded."

"Jakob," Jessie cautioned.

"I'm afraid it is, son," and he pulled the magazine out and showed them the shiny cartridges. "Now behave yourselves, will you?"

Jessie woke up in the night to the sound of Roderick using the bathroom. The TV and lights were still on, and she saw the muzzle of the gun sticking up over the arm of his chair. Her heart surged. She jumped up to grab it, but too slow, and he knocked her backwards onto the couch, throwing her a steely gaze.

Ow, that really hurts. He is really out of it, dangerous. She massaged her chest where he'd hit her.

Jakob sat up and rubbed his eyes, oblivious to what had just happened. "We're hungry, I think," he said.

"Upstairs," Roderick ordered with one more warning look at Jessie.

He looks tired and mean and scared all at once.

They baked frozen lasagna and ate it in the kitchen. A full moon beamed through the bay window so brightly they didn't turn the light on but lit Kelly's tiny Christmas candle, still in the middle of the table.

Jessie took a hot-but-not-too-hot bite into her mouth and held it there, eyes closed. *Oh, this is so good. I feel so thankful right now, and safe. Which makes no sense.*

"Do you have any wine?" she asked. *I shouldn't ask; he sure doesn't need it, but I do.*

"Maybe in the pantry."

She found a bottle of Sweet Red and the three of them ate and drank around the table for an hour.

Roderick went on and on about the war, words slurred, sometimes indecipherable. "Hemming blew it all to hell," he mused at one point. "I've thought many times about something the manual says, memorized it: 'Most morale problems can be overcome by the exercise of good leadership and the proper indoctrination and orientation of troops prior to operations.' Ha! That doesn't go for a black captain commanding a redneck know-it-all who hates his guts. A bad seed, a bad apple. If only he'd been like the rest of my men, brave, decent and–oh, screw it. Who wants to hear these sorry stories from forty years ago?"

Right–except it's more interesting than not talking at all–and I guess it helps us understand you better too

"And you?" he said, to Jessie. "Born and raised in

Palatine?"

Surprised and chewing, she nodded, then sipped. She took another swallow, then another bite.

"You are a woman of few words, aren't you?" he snorted. "What about your family?" he urged, but she only shrugged.

"She had a rough childhood," Jakob put in.

"I did not. You act like something big and terrible happened to me in my childhood, but nothing happened."

"That's what's big and terrible," Jakob said. "That nothing happened. Childhood is supposed to be full, not empty."

"My childhood was not empty! Don't call it empty."

"I'm such a fool," Jakob muttered.

Then, in the quiet moonlight, Jessie began to speak.

"My mother didn't want me, that's all. I mean I guess she didn't. She must not have. Was she mean to me? No, not so much as—as—worn out. Hardly alive, sometimes. I mean she walked around and went to work and all that, but she wasn't—interested in anything."

Jessie continued staring into the little Christmas candle, talking, not moving. "Her other daughter was killed on a motorcycle when she was sixteen. I think that killed my mother, inside. That must be what happened." She picked up her wine glass and sipped, the men's eyes fixed on her face."But my mother didn't talk about Renee, and she didn't want me asking questions. I didn't know what happened to Renee until my Aunt Barb told me. Aunt Barb also told me," Jessie said, sipping again, setting the glass down, crossing her arms on the table and settling, "that my mother had tried to give me to her, to Aunt Barb, when I was first born. Aunt Barb said she would have taken me if she hadn't had big problems with her own family. I wish my mother would have talked to me more. Or left me some letters like..."

"...like Vevie did," she almost said. She glanced up at Roderick and saw him looking at her funny and looked down again. "But it's all okay. I got to paint. And then Doug came, so I have Fiona. And now I have you, Jakob. And that's good." He reached over and took her hand. "Most of the time it's good," she added. He nodded and smiled, the very picture of a happy fool.

"You two take good care of each other. You have something special," Roderick said, picking up his gun. "Now we're going to go back down and get some shut-eye."

"Not until I clean up this kitchen," Jessie said, pushing her chair back.

"Well, then, I'd better adjust my position to avoid an attack from the rear," Roderick said, shifting to the other side of the table, his back to the window, watching her work while Jakob laid his head on his arms, apologizing for not helping. Twenty minutes later Roderick nudged him awake and marched them back downstairs.

But the next day at noon, after a morning of televangelists and news shows and brunch upstairs, the delicious aroma of bacon and eggs and freshly brewed coffee still hanging in the air, Jessie saw new energy in Jakob. He'd only picked at his food after Roderick, drunk and drowsy from pills, had run his mouth the whole time he cooked, incoherent stories about "the Nam" and his "gook lover" and "gonads stuffed in mouths as a warning" and other atrocities. When Roderick ordered them back down the stairs after he and Jessie had washed the dishes, Jakob said, "No."

27

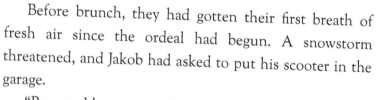

Before brunch, they had gotten their first breath of fresh air since the ordeal had begun. A snowstorm threatened, and Jakob had asked to put his scooter in the garage.

"Reasonable request. Okay, troops, let's move out," Roderick said, opening the back door. "And don't forget I'm armed," and he pressed the button to move the heavy door up in its tracks and ushered them past his SUV.

"Could we go for a walk?" Jessie asked, standing next to him while Jakob got the scooter. Roderick ignored her. A woman walked by and looked at them, then waved.

"Wave," Roderick ordered, and they did.

And then, while they were eating, Kelly had come, ringing the bell, then knocking and banging and yelling,

"Rod, are you in there? I can't find Jessie again, or Jakob. Where in the world is everybody? For God's sake, open up if you're in there."

Roderick pressed the barrel of the gun to his lips. No one moved. Kelly left.

And when he ordered them to trudge back down, Jakob refused.

"No. I'm not going, Roderick McCoy! I'm done playing along with this travesty," he screeched, rocking way back and way forward.

Before all his words were out, Roderick was at him. Jessie threw her tiny self between, screaming stop, but Roderick's pistol swiped down the side of Jakob's face, leaving a red stripe.

"Don't you mess with me, boy, don't you mess with me," Roderick yelled. "I could kill you. I wouldn't want to, but you could make me."

Shell-shocked, their heaves pulsed into the kitchen air. Jessie patted Jakob's back. "It's okay," she said, as if to Fiona.

Roderick said "okay" too, again and again, hanging over, hands on his thighs, still grasping his pistol. "Oh, God, okay," he said, gulping air. "Okay," and yet another "Okay," as he tried to catch his breath and settle himself. He

297

straightened up and ordered, "To the latrine for first aid," motioning for them to go down the hallway.

"He doesn't know who he is," Jessie said as they walked, her arm around Jakob's waist, his blood dripping on her hair.

"At ease on the stool there," Roderick told Jakob, who sat down on the toilet. "Peroxide," he said to Jessie, gesturing toward the medicine cabinet. He held a clean towel under Jakob's chin. "Pour it down the wound."

"Ouchy-ouchy-ouchy."

Roderick examined closely. "Not too deep, you'll live. Best to leave it open to the air. Sorry, son, but no more sudden moves, okay?"

They heard the faint sound of a siren.

"That woman saw you at the front door with your weapon and called the police," Jakob said.

The siren came closer and closer.

"To the den," Roderick commanded, and down they went.

The siren turned onto Harvard Drive, but the blast whooshed by and faded to nothing.

Jakob spoke out from his couch. "It's going on twenty-eight hours since we stopped on our way to boarding the

Metra for the aquarium, and our life has been hanging in the balance since then, with diatribes and bullying from your tortured soul. Now what are..."

"Stop–talking–stop–rocking," Roderick said. "And troops, stop the counter tactics, or I might have to get my duct tape and secure mouths and hands."

Sunday afternoon. Jakob prayed and dozed. Jessie straightened the room. Roderick watched retro TV, the remote in one hand, the pistol in the other.

Yawning and stretching, Jakob said, "I've been thinking, Roderick McCoy. When you take hostages, you're supposed to have demands. What are your demands?"

"I'm trying to watch a movie here."

Jakob jumped up and grabbed the remote and powered off. "You can't just do this. What is it you want? Let's negotiate terms."

"Yes, let's negotiate terms," Jessie said. *But yikes, what does that mean? Will it push him over the edge?* She stopped dusting and came to the circle. They sat for a minute, and then she said, "What do you want, Roderick?"

"Beer," he said, in serious thought.

Jessie got him a can and one for herself. Jakob said,

"Okay, me too." She got him one and they sat popping open and drinking. *Yuk. This tastes awful, but maybe it will help me relax. Even the boredom is stressful.*

"Death," Roderick announced. "That's my demand. Fact is, I'd have shot myself Christmas Day but for you and your crazy cousin. I was loading my weapon when you rang the bell."

"What?" Jessie said, leaning forward.

He nodded. "That's the closest I've come, so far." He was dazed and exhausted, with the manner of a suspect finally confessing, telling the story. "I couldn't tell if it was the demons or the gods in charge. I didn't care."

Wow, that is exactly how he looked when he opened the door, like someone who couldn't keep going and didn't care about anything and didn't quite even know where they were. Wow.

"When you rang the bell, I startled and dropped the box of shells, and then walked down the hall like a robot and opened the door—to life."

"You surrendered, Roderick McCoy. Do it again. We're here for you," Jakob said.

Roderick's head bowed, swung back and forth. "My list of reasons to live are pretty well crossed off: Family—nope. Friends—gone. Honor—lost. God—don't think so. And the list of reasons to die gets longer and longer. Nightmares, ghosts, addiction, self-hatred, terror in my gut," and he clasped himself around the middle, his face scrunched, perspiration dripping off.

He lurched up and went over to the shelves and grabbed his Silver Star. "See this? It's shicken chit," he slurred, and threw it across the room, then swept everything off the shelves, glass from picture frames shattering, awards and souvenirs flying like frightened birds, and he leaned on the shelves, shoulders heaving.

Jessie and Jakob stared. Roderick wiped his face with his sleeve.

"Why do you say it's chicken shit?" Jakob asked. "A Silver Star is a high honor."

"Not this one," he said. "I had my suspicions. Pure chaos reigned in that jungle, and then I got hit. By the end of it, I was unconscious. Later, Wayne and a couple others wrote up eyewitness accounts to nominate me. I told them I didn't think I'd done Silver Star duty, but they turned them in, and I got it at a ceremony in the field." He shook his head and took a deep breath, walked over and plopped hard into his recliner.

"And then, at our last reunion—Christ, it's been fifteen

years—Wayne had too much to drink, started shooting his mouth off over in the corner, spouting something like, 'Maybe not technically, but hell, who cares about technicalities in Nam? Everybody thought Captain deserved the star—except for that s.o.b. Hemming.'

"It got quiet in there, and my beer brain comprehended what he'd said. And then we had it out. I said I hated the damn star. Well, they all put in their two cents saying why I deserved it. Hemming had plans to shoot me in the back and plead friendly fire, they said. Told me I should have gotten rid of him. 'Tolerance was your mistake, Captain,' somebody said.

"The way I see it, I got this prestigious award because my men liked me," he croaked. "The phoniness sickens me every day."

"But I read the citation, Roderick," Jessie put in. "It says you ran around under enemy fire encouraging your men until you got hit. It says your side won the battle because of you."

"Yeah. That's what it says. But I told you—pure chaos."

There was enough silence to sail away in. Then Jakob said, "There are a lot of people worse off than you. Think of the soldiers of today with their TBIs and robotic limbs and broken marriages and the..."

"I think of them, all the time. They're another reason on my list of why to die."

"That's very sad stuff, but listen," Jessie said. "You don't need us to die."

Tears in his eyes, Roderick made a helpless gesture with his gun and drained his can.

They dozed for a while and then tried to cheer Roderick up with a game or some popcorn. He was undeterred from listing his woes.

"Who would want to go on after the sham of a life I've lived? Adultery. Murder. Deceit of the highest order. Wounding a young man for no good reason," he said, looking at Jakob.

"I forgive you, Roderick McCoy."

"Not good enough—though I appreciate the gesture," he said with a loud burp.

"I'll take your forgiveness, Jakob," Jessie said.

"For what?"

"Sometimes..." Jessie started, then stopped.

"What, Jessie?" Jakob said.

"I don't know. Sometimes I feel like I did something wrong by being in the world, by being born. I'll be walking down the street and feel like I snuck in illegally and might get stopped and kicked out, I don't know why."

"And you think you need forgiveness?" Jakob asked.

She shrugged. "Yeah, kind of."

"Well, I don't think you do, except in the sense we all do. Essentially, you've described the human condition. But we have God's love and forgiveness, grace unending. And Roderick McCoy, I beg you to accept God's grace too. You know, sin is separating ourselves from God, despairing of God's mercy. That's what you're doing."

"Is it now? Well, that's a tight little package. God abandons us to a hellish world, and then, when we don't fall on our knees and grovel for mercy, that's a sin too. Pretty hopeless."

"But you're missing the main point. Hopelessness is unnecessary," Jakob said.

"Whatever. I'm not ready to jump over that cliff, that leap of faith chasm. My only hope is in this firearm," he said, holding it up.

"We could have a salad," Jessie said into the refrigerator, "except the lettuce is brown, the spinach is slimy, and the tomatoes have black spots. Hmm, maybe soup and grilled cheese."

"Bread's moldy," Jakob said.

"Euh. So's the cheese," Jessie said, throwing it in the trash.

"Maybe we should go grocery shopping. We'd behave, wouldn't we, Jessie? You could keep your gun in your pocket, just in case," he appealed to Roderick, who paid no attention.

They heard the snowplows on the street, the revolving yellow lights reflecting through the house as they sank down in the kitchen chairs to tomato soup and peanut butter and crackers. At eight o'clock on this snowy night around this unlikely table, hunger and fatigue kept mouths eating rather than talking. A comfortable familiarity fell over the trio slurping and crunching together in the most basic act of staying alive. Bowls empty and the last cracker gone, they sat there still, Jakob weaving a bit on his chair, Jessie staring into the candlelight, Roderick staring out the window.

Finally she broke the spell. "Now what?"

"Now what what?"

"What do we do next? Back downstairs or play cards or wash dishes or what?"

"Downstairs, I guess," Roderick said with a small sigh. "The day is over. Time's almost up."

They filed down and found their places and formed the circle, dark and heavy. America's Funniest Home Videos brought neither snicker nor smile. Roderick switched to a documentary on climate change until it got Jakob sputtering alarming statistics.

"Stop talking, Jakob. We don't care," Jessie said.

He began to cry and rock.

"Oh, for God's sake," Roderick snarled, turning the TV off.

Jakob said, "I should be digging out my fire hydrant. I adopted a fire hydrant. What if there's a fire tonight, right there, right in the house by my fire hydrant?" he whimpered. "And I should be at work in the morning."

Roderick said, "You can probably go to work in the morning."

After a second, Jessie asked, "He can? What do you mean by that?"

"I don't know. I'm not sure which one said it."

"Which what?" Jakob asked.

"Which one of me," Roderick said.

"There's only one of you! One good man. One beloved

306

child of God named Roderick McCoy."

"Jessie, please get me a beer," he said.

"All gone."

Gosh, I even want to get him one, kind of. He called me by my name.

She heard Roderick through the night—nightmares, strangled profanities. He cursed a jammed rifle, cried over a dead soldier yelling, "Oh, God, Bobby, don't die on me. No. No!" Jakob stirred at that but didn't wake. She lay staring into the dark, more intrigued than worried. *Maybe we could have escaped a time or two—or been shot to death. I wonder what's coming next,* and she drifted off in the wee hours of the morning.

"Oof," Jakob said, stubbing his toe coming back from the bathroom, and Roderick let out a yell that shook the room and brought Jessie to her feet from a dead sleep

"Oh! You scared me so bad," she said, bending over holding her stomach.

Roderick moved to the edge of his chair, his breath coming in little gasps. He turned on the floor lamp, his face glossy with cold sweat, his eyes wild. "I can't—take—much more..." and he rushed to the bathroom and threw up in the toilet, his breath held so long on some retches that Jakob turned around to see if he was still breathing. Jessie watched him slurp water from the sink and run a wet hand over his face, then stagger back to his chair.

"Look, why don't you give up, Roderick? You can go back to the V.A. and get help again," Jessie said.

"Right," Jakob yawned, and then said, like a robocaller, "You have a lot to live for."

Roderick's head tilted back, his eyes closed.

"You really do. You say you have no friends, but we're your friends. We baked you cookies and brought them to the hospital. Kelly and I spent Christmas with you. You said we saved your life."

"Your affections are sadly misplaced. I don't deserve..."

"But it's not about deserving, Roderick McCoy!" Jakob said. "It's about the grace and love of God. We love you because God first loved us."

Jessie said, "All I know is that there's this power that helps us keep going when it's hard, when terrible things happen."

"God is the power," Jakob said.

"Okay," Jessie said. "And Jesus loves us," seeing in her mind's eye her painting Let the Children Come Unto Me.

"I think Jesus loves you and cares about you, Roderick."

Wan and wasted, Roderick said, "Children, you all don't get it, do you? I want to die. I am a lost soul," he gasped. "I can't..." Sweating, breathing hard, he cocked the pistol and pressed the barrel to his temple.

Jessie squawked and made a leaping dive to grab it. The pistol discharged.

28

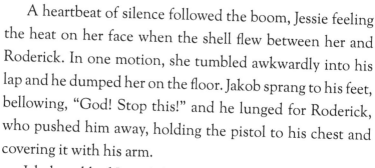

A heartbeat of silence followed the boom, Jessie feeling the heat on her face when the shell flew between her and Roderick. In one motion, she tumbled awkwardly into his lap and he dumped her on the floor. Jakob sprang to his feet, bellowing, "God! Stop this!" and he lunged for Roderick, who pushed him away, holding the pistol to his chest and covering it with his arm.

Jakob grabbed Jessie's hand and pulled her up, and they ran up the stairs. When they got to the top, they sat down in each other's embrace, breathing heavily. No sound from below.

After a minute, Jessie said, "We can't leave him, not with that gun. We just need to wait this out with him."

Jakob nodded.

"Let's go!" Jessie said, jumping up. "He could do it any second."

They ran back down the stairs and settled on their couches. And began to wait.

Oh! this is boring and senseless and we smell bad! "We need showers," Jessie blurted.

"I should be at work," Jakob quickly put in. "They'll call me in a little while to see where I am."

"You can go," Roderick said. "Go."

"Not with you cradling that pistol like it's your favorite toy," Jakob said.

Roderick shrugged. "I got nothing else," he went on, slowly shaking his head. "With the twisted, phony life I've been living all these years..."

Jakob interrupted. "Instead of all this woe is me, let's tell each other what we're going to do after this." He closed his eyes.

He's praying.

Opening his eyes, Jakob said, "I'll go first. I'd benefact nonprofits for eco-change with the inheritance coming to me from my grandmother. And something about God, about my faith. Try to keep having it, I guess."

Silence.

"Jessie?" Jakob said.

I hear the begging in his voice, but dear Jesus, I am too tired for this. I can't think. I can't feel. I can't. Help, somebody help. A quark of the same kind of energy that kept her hanging her pictures brought her to her feet. Unsteady, she plopped back down but rose again and headed for the bathroom.

"I'll be back." Shutting the door, she slumped on the toilet. Her muscles settled into her fatigue. She let a few tears come. "Okay, Jesus, God, whoever," she whispered, then stood up, and commanded herself, *Go, Jessie. Go back out there now. It's okay.*

Settling back on the couch, she started out. "Okay. If I survive—well—I have a grandmother too, named Raven, in Kalamazoo. I'd probably try and visit her. Maybe Tommy knows where she is. He's my brother. I might try to get to know him. He lives in Moline, I think, or East Moline." She took a big breath. "And I'd finish painting The Glowing Night." She looked at Jakob. "It's the painting kit Jakob gave me for Christmas. Your turn, Roderick."

"I don't know how to play this game, this future game."

Jakob growled slightly and rocked slightly and started looking around the room. "What are those boxes stacked against the wall by the stairway?"

"It's stuff Roderick ordered," Jessie answered.

"How come you haven't opened them, Roderick McCoy? Too depressed?"

"I suppose."

"Want to?"

"Whatever."

Jessie and Jakob forced themselves up and brought the stacks over to his recliner.

Roderick pulled a Vietnam Vet license plate holder out of the first box. "That'll look good on your Tahoe," Jakob said.

Next a pair of GI sunglasses, then a Rugged Ridge parka from LL Bean.

"Oh, you really need this, Roderick—a clean, new Army cap. You can get rid of that ratty old thing you wear every day," Jessie said.

"Roderick McCoy, do you see what's going on here? This stuff is for living," Jakob said.

Jessie nodded, keeping her eyes on Roderick's face. *Please, please Roderick. Want to live. I know it's hard, but come on, try. We'll help you.*

No response.

"I see one more package," she sighed, and walked over,

kneeling to pick it up, then, "Oh my gosh!"

"What?"

"I think the bullet from when the gun went off went through the back of this picture."

It was the formal portrait of Roderick and Vevie from over the fireplace.

Jakob went over to look. "Yeah, wow. Here's the shell, stuck in the wall."

"Let's see the picture," Roderick said.

They carried it over.

Roderick shook his head in wonder. "What a clean hole! In the back," he muttered. "Turn it around," and they did. "Through the heart. Good God."

"Don't get carried away with this," Jakob said. "It's just freaky—that it got your wife—a picture of your wife, that is—through the heart–from the back. That's all it is, Roderick McCoy. Freaky."

"Ah, but the irony. How many times did I shoot that woman in the back, starting with unfaithfulness, her a new bride, all alone..."

"But she did the same thing," Jessie said, and then flushed a splotchy pink.

Roderick studied her. "You read those letters."

She nodded, maintaining eye contact. "See, I don't think you need to feel that guilty, since she had someone too, when you were in Vietnam."

Roderick sighed. "So what? It's done and over, forty-five years of lying and pretending, hating, resenting. Too late, too much to bear—even to comprehend sometimes, much less live with.

"Did you read her letter asking for a divorce?" he asked Jessie.

Her eyes widened. "No. I didn't get through all of them before you burned them."

Jakob stopped rocking. "Wait, what did you say? She asked you for a divorce?"

"She asked in a letter—which she never mailed."

"You mean you could have ended your marriage way back then instead of..."

"Ruining each other's lives? Affirmative," and all three of them were still.

"And through all the mess, she never brought up divorce again—after that letter—which I did not see until she was gone—nor did I ever bring up divorce.

"Oh, God," he struggled on. "So little spoken. She asked about the war a time or two, but I only wanted to move on, forget..." He closed his eyes. "We built a wall between us with all we didn't say, added a brick or two of small talk and silence every day." Staring down, he folded over himself, head on his arms, gun pointing at the floor. They leaned in to hear his words. "If only I'd known she needed forgiveness as much as I did," he wept.

He blew his nose. "Go home. I apologize," he said, wiping his eyes. "This has not been me holding you but some pathetic addict that's taken me over, maybe the pathetic warrior I tried to be. God help me, I'm not stable. I want you out of here," he said, wincing as he stretched in his chair to get Jakob's phone out of his pocket. "Here," and Jakob took it.

"We'll go as soon as you hand over your weapon, Roderick McCoy," Jakob said.

Roderick shook his head.

"We're not leaving you alone with it," Jessie said.

"You better retreat before I change my mind."

The chime of the doorbell cut through the air.

"I'm ordering you to go. Don't be fools."

Jessie held her hand out to him. "Give us the gun and we'll go."

"A man has a constitutional right to bear arms," he

mumbled, and he closed his eyes as if against pain, and his lips moved silently as if in prayer, and the doorbell rang a second time.

"Give it!" Jessie repeated.

"I can't, I can't," Roderick rasped.

Jessie grabbed his face with both her tiny hands and looked into his frightened eyes. "Yes you can, Roderick."

And he could. He did. With quivering hand, he held the pistol out, bowing his head, swallowing a sob.

Jakob grasped the gun and breathed, "Oh, thank God,"

Jessie wrapped her arms around Roderick.

The person at the door started pounding.

"Captain, I plead innocent on that charge. I busted my butt to get word to you that I was coming after all. See, Jackie had that accident, broke her leg, but she's done great and insisted I come and..."

Roderick was staring, Jessie and Jacob next to him, but they couldn't see outside.

"Oh my gosh!" Jessie whispered to Jakob. "It must be Wayne, his army buddy, the one who said he wasn't coming."

The voice went on. "I called your phone, but it said out

of service. I didn't have an email for you. You're not on Facebook, so I tried snail mail. You didn't get my Christmas card with the note either, huh?"

"Oh," Roderick said. "I think it's down inside my chair."

"Swell. Sounds like the forces aligned against us being in contact. Well anyway, when I found out they were having the Nam vets convention in Chicago, I said to Jackie, 'Okay, baby, I'm going, and I hope against hope Captain is still on Harvard Drive.' And thank God, man, here you are."

"More or less," Roderick said.

"You okay, man? You lookin' rough. Smellin' pretty ripe too."

"Rough. Yeah. I need help. I—I'm..." And he crumpled, and his friend put his arm around his shoulders, and both of them stumbled a bit as Roderick leaned into him, small, old, tired.

"Okay, okay. I'm here, Captain. I'm here now."

Roderick covered his eyes with his hand, shook his head. "You're a goddamned angel from God if there ever was one. And I'm in shock, man I can't take it in, hardly, that you're here. My head's messed up something terrible. I can't..." His sentence broke off.

"Well hey now, since I've traveled halfway across the country to see your sorry self, maybe I could come in."

Roderick straightened up, moved back. "Come in, come in. Good God, get in here, man."

He stepped in and saw Jessie and Jakob. "Oh, you're not alone. Who are these, your staff?"

Roderick looked at them each. "These are my friends," he said. "This is Jessie. She takes care of my house. Jakob, here, is her boyfriend."

"Any friends of yours are friends of mine, man. I'm Wayne, one of his soldiers from Nam." He smiled a sunshine smile and shook hands with them. "Good to know you've got your people, captain."

"Right," Roderick said, his eyes connecting with them again.

Wayne looked at Jakob. "How'd you hurt your face, son? That looks nasty."

Jakob said, "There was an accident."

"Yeah. Bad," Roderick said, under his breath.

They stood in the foyer, still and silent.

Wayne broke the freeze, looking from one face to the next. "Something's happened here," he said.

Jakob let out one of his whinny laughs.

"Jakob!" Jessie said.

"What? I think it's funny for him to say something's happened here," he laughed, "when so much has happened."

Jessie shrugged. "I guess," and she smiled, looked at Roderick and said, "Now that he's here, we can probably go?"

"Whoawhoawhoa," Wayne said. "If this is sentinel shift change, young lady, I need a status report. What the hell have you three been up to? Roderick? Somebody"

Jessie shrugged again. Jakob focused on the floor, rocking gently. Roderick leaned back on the door and took a breath that started out small and built up and up, and then he blew it all out with a whoosh tainted with bad breath and three-day whiskers. "Okay, Wayne, here's the story of the last few days. It's a bad one, man. Insane. I cracked. I almost..." His voice broke off.

But three minutes later the story was told, Wayne's face tight with concentration, his eyes alight with incredulity.

"Good God, man, that is bad. But not worse, not worse, thank God, thank God almighty," his head weaving.

He looked at Jessie and Jakob. "Hostages, huh?"

"Sort of. Maybe," Jakob said.

Wayne looked back at Roderick. "This is a mess, man."

Roderick nodded. "I did a stint in psychiatric care in November, at the V.A."

"I don't know what to do with this," Jakob said, and took the handgun out of his coat pocket.

"Turn it in to the Palatine PD. Tell them I asked you to because I'm suicidal. And go ahead and press charges if you want."

"Against you?" Jessie said.

"Right, Roderick McCoy. Against you? After all we've been through together?"

"I'll take care of the weapon," Wayne said, and took the gun from Jakob, popping out the round with a whistle and one more quiet, "Thank God."

"So now we'll go, okay? Is it okay, Wayne?" Jessie asked.

"What about it, Captain? I'm new here."

"Yes, for sure. Get on out of here. And I'm sorry. I don't know what else to say right now, but that sure is the truth. I am so sorry."

"That's okay," Jakob said. "All's well that ends well."

"Yeah. It wasn't that bad," Jessie said.

"You two are crazy," Roderick said, his eyes misting up again. "Stay in touch, okay?"

They nodded and went through the garage and got the scooter and went out into the world for the first time in two and a half days, squinting into the brightness, shivering into the cold. They paused on the sidewalk to look in the window of the sitting room at the two old friends easing down to the sofa. Roderick leaned on his knees and held his head in his hands. Wayne patted him on the back.

"They're okay. Let's go," Jessie said.

29

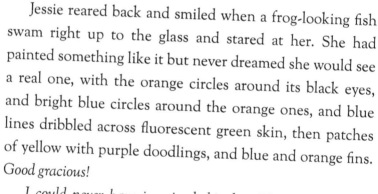

Jessie reared back and smiled when a frog-looking fish swam right up to the glass and stared at her. She had painted something like it but never dreamed she would see a real one, with the orange circles around its black eyes, and bright blue circles around the orange ones, and blue lines dribbled across fluorescent green skin, then patches of yellow with purple doodlings, and blue and orange fins. *Good gracious!*

I could never have imagined this day. The Metra is okay. Stretching my leg so far to climb up that first step was hard, and it's a good thing Jakob was there to force open those heavy sliding doors and hold them or I think they might have crushed me. Everything moving by us—oh wait, we were the ones moving—was like watching a movie. Actually, it seemed like a movie when the conductor walked down the aisle calling out, "Tickets. Tickets, please." And the skyscrapers! How they were there all of a sudden when we came around that curve. And then walking right next to them! She had bent her head backwards as far as she could, to see the tops. Lake Michigan amazed her. As far as she knew, it was the ocean. The whole day—holding hands, the veggie panini, the girl playing her saxophone right on the street—was as fresh and right as anything Jessie had ever known.

Walking to Shedd Aquarium in the crowd of noisy, happy people had been both fun and stressful for her and Jakob. She'd snapped at him when he'd criticized her gum chewing one time too many. Then he'd gotten antsy when she didn't want to leave the sea dragons, unreal mini-horse fairies drifting around, blessing the water with their leafy limbs.

"Jakob, you need to leave me alone," she'd warned on his third attempt to move her along. He'd started whining and calling her Jessica but had handled it, promising to come back and get her, then moving ahead on his own. She had jittered though, standing there by herself, nervous he might not find her again.

I had to do that though, she thought now, with a sigh, on

the train going home. *I had to take the risk. And he handled it pretty well. It worked out*, and she sighed again in the relative privacy of a corner seat, their backs to everyone. She sat by the window, all the sights coming at her. Jakob smiled a goofy smile and head butted her. A sweet fatigue took over her body as she leaned against this nice man, this friend. *I think Fiona feels like this when she leans on me.*

"Where were we a week ago?" Jakob broke in to her thoughts.

"Roderick's," she said. "Hostages."

"Yeah."

They thought about that for a while.

"Maybe we could visit him soon."

"Yeah, Wayne said we could go with him."

"How long is Wayne staying?"

"Until Roderick comes home from the V.A. and he can help him settle in. In the meantime, he's paying his bills, driving his car, taking care of his house."

"You're doing that."

Jessie let out a rueful chuckle. "Yeah, Wayne's a slob too. The good news is Roderick said I should keep cleaning and doing roach patrol. And guess what? Wayne's trying to talk him into moving to California."

"Aha. That might be a good idea for Roderick McCoy."

"Yeah, because he'd have Wayne, and now he has Lauren back after he found her Christmas card in his chair."

She told Jakob about last night with Fiona, and now she savored the time again. The sweet, soft fullness of the child in her arms. Her funniness playing peek-a-boo with variations on the game, and her baby giggles that grew and grew, defining joy. *I thought my heart would burst wide open with happiness when we went to the Jewel so Tonya could see her in her Christmas outfit. And then Tonya coming over to hang out, bringing that bottle of wine and talking and talking, and listening too, Fiona asleep on the couch between us. Wow. My apartment is becoming a home.*

Tonya had said she wanted a new job, a new apartment, a new boyfriend. "You know what, Jessie? What I want is a whole new life. Let's take off for Colorado, want to?"

"How about New Mexico? That's where my family comes from."

They had laughed the idea away, and Jessie had thought, *Wow. That would be way beyond the gate.*

"This is where they have horse races," Jakob said, the train pulling into Arlington Park. She craned her neck to look at the long white grandstand as they slid away, then said, "I'm a lot like Roderick."

Jakob hooted. "I don't see how."

"Because not so long ago I was all alone, no friends, no family. Now I have Fiona and you and Kelly and Tonya and him—Roderick—and Wayne too, because we talk and laugh while I work. Even Doug." She began to weep.

Jakob put his arm around her and drew her to him. She cried and cried, snuffling into his coat.

"Because you're happy?" he asked, his chin on her head.

She nodded. "But I still wish I knew my whole story, why my mother didn't want me or love me or whatever. All that."

"Yeah," Jakob said, squeezing her.

The train chugged to a halt in Palatine. *Good thing for this handle*, Jessie thought, grasping it and climbing down the corrugated steel steps to swing herself down to the asphalt. They walked to Jakob's scooter. *I see people looking at us, but I don't care.*

While they put on their helmets, Jakob said, "Okay, how about going out for supper with my parents? They got home from Haiti yesterday. You're invited, you know," he said.

"Boy, I'm worn out, I don't think so—but tell them I said thanks. I just want you to scoot me home. "

"Sure, okay."

When they said goodbye at her door, he tried again. "How about dinner with my family tomorrow after worship? I could pick you up," he said, his eyes on the ground. "You wouldn't believe what a good cook my dad is. He's baking fish tomorrow, Icelandic style. It's the best thing you've ever tasted, and Simon will..."

Jessie could hear the hope in his voice. *Look at me, Jakob. Look at me, see me.* And he did.

His shoulders fell at the expression on her face, but he looked into her eyes and cupped her face in his hands and they kissed. Their lips still touching, he apologized for rushing her, and she accepted his apology, and the kiss continued.

Fiona was turning one in February. Jessie was frazzled over whether or not to go to her party. Guests would be Alicia and her little boy and Doug's parents.

"I know I should, and I think I can," she told Jakob and Kelly. "But I don't want to. I'll be so nervous maybe I shouldn't. But it's for Fiona, and those people are going to be her people all her life—I better get used to it, I guess. But..."

"Jessie, may I go with you?" Jakob asked.

She shook her head, not looking at him, not wanting to see his disappointment and frustration.

"I've got it!" Kelly said. "We'll have our own party for her. You, me, and Jakob."

"No," Jessie said, looking at the floor, then quickly up. "But thanks, Kelly. Thanks, Jakob."

———

She and Jakob visited Roderick at the V.A.

"If it weren't for you two, I wouldn't be here," Roderick told her and Jakob. "Wayne would have found my corpse and..." clearing his throat, "I'd have had no chance to reconcile with Lauren."

With more life than they'd ever seen in him, Roderick told of the tough work he was doing. "Here's what we do for flashbacks: when the aura starts—a smell or a sound or a pain can kick it off—I check for a trigger and then bring myself out of there, out of the jungle or wherever. Maybe I go to a star, then to the earth—'You're on the earth, Roderick'—and keep coming back—in the U.S., in Palatine, in this place, this room, looking at this table, until I'm back

330

to this moment," and his eyes rested on them. "And adjust my breathing all along the way, don't let that hyperventilating start up."

Oh, geez, I remember that scary time when I first started cleaning his house, when he fell down the stairs and hit Lauren so hard he knocked her down. "You're doing great, Roderick," she said.

"And I'm learning how to open up. These younger vets are something else; they're really helping me. It's tough getting the stuff out, even with each other, but it's do-able because we've been the same place," he told Jessie and Jakob. "There's no way to get across to anyone else the bond we have. Different battles but the same insanity, the same thousand-yard stare," he stared, then came back, looked at them, looked down, cleared his throat again.

"Your forgiveness," he started, looking out the window. "I don't know where I'd be without that. It's too late for forgiveness with some of the people I've hurt, but grace, as you say, Jakob—grace coming from—from some place, from some good thing beyond us—well, how does it go? 'saved a wretch like me'"

331

30

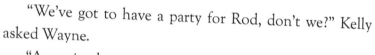

"We've got to have a party for Rod, don't we?" Kelly asked Wayne.

"A coming home party? Hmm, let me think..."

"He might not like that," Jessie said, folding dishtowels. "You know, he still gets real low sometimes. He hardly said a word on our last visit."

"Yeah, he's still struggling," Wayne said. "Always will, probably, but transitioning back home will have its challenges, and if he's in a funk..."

"...he'll need a party!" Kelly said.

"Not everybody's like you, Kelly," Jakob put in.

"Oh, you got that right, bro," Kelly said with a bright smile and proud tone. "Hey, I know! We'll plan the party—surprise, of course—and if he's seriously blue, we'll dial it back. You can let us know while you're driving him here, Wayne, and if it's ix-nay we won't yell when he walks in the door or wear the hats or blow the horns, we'll..."

Wayne's laughter cut her off. "No hats, no horns, and no surprise. That's not a good idea. Maybe something later, a day or two in, a quiet meal like this lunch we're having, minus brown bags and carry-in."

"Yeah!" Kelly said, clapping her hands. "With all his favorite foods and wine and music, and then a game of good old Uno."

"No wine, Kelly. Roderick McCoy has alcoholic tendencies. Maybe you should be in psychiatric care too," Jakob said.

Roderick told Jessie to keep doing what she was doing with the house but step it up.

Yes! Yay!

"Think in terms of showing it, with people walking through all the time. Finish off the two upstairs bedrooms and work in the basement too.

I'll have this job for a long time, she exulted. *But wait... what did he say?*

"Are you going to sell it?"

"Possibly."

Hmm. A little cloud floated over her sun. *But even if I lose this job, these days are the best of my life so far. I love the walking,* and she laughed to herself about slipping on icy patches in her boots. *I feel safe in my boots. I love how the snow sparkles in the darkness. That coyote following me on Palatine Road the other morning scared me at first, but then when it crossed the street with its slowness and disappeared, I realized it didn't even know I was there. That helped me stop worrying so much.*

Job routines as usual: organizing, sanitizing, beautifying. The work continued to satisfy her desire—her need—for order and sense, and she enjoyed conversations with Wayne, lunch with Jakob and occasional appearances by Kelly.

One day, Wayne told her she had turned Roderick's house into a home.

"You think so? That's one of the nicest things anybody's ever said to me."

"It's a different place from last January," he said. "And thank heaven for that. Whew!"

Another day she and Wayne and Jakob had eaten lunch and after Jakob left, the two of them sat at the table finishing up.

"He's on the autism spectrum, right?" Wayne asked.

Jessie nodded.

"How long have you been seeing each other?"

"Um, we first saw each other at the recycling center right after I started working here. It was around Halloween. He started coming here, and we kept getting to know each other. Our first time to go someplace together was supposed to be the day Roderick took us hostage."

"Oh. Only a couple weeks ago."

Jessie nodded.

"So you're a new couple."

Jessie considered. "I guess, but I've never talked to anyone as much as Jakob, and I'm his first girlfriend. Sometimes I feel like we're an old couple."

Wayne smiled and she smiled back.

"Had you had other boyfriends?"

"No, but I was married."

"Married? That surprises me."

"It surprised me too. And now I'm divorced."

"That's a good bit of action for one so young."

Jessie nodded. "And like Kelly says, I don't look the part—to have boyfriends, I guess she means because I'm not beautiful at all."

335

"Hey-hey now, you look fine," Wayne said. "And physical beauty might get things started but doesn't have anything to do with genuine love. Look at the movie stars for proof."

Jessie crumpled her wax paper around her apple core, stood up and headed for the kitchen.

"And if what you and Jakob have proves to be genuine, that's all that matters," Wayne said, and sat looking out the window, then continued. "If you are blessed with love like mine and Jackie's you can go the distance, forty-two years for us so far."

"Forty-two years! With Jakob?"

Wayne laughed. "Slow down now. Take it one day at a time. You don't need to imagine decades."

"Yeah," she said, wiping up the table. "I like Jakob. I like him a lot. I think he's great at living his life with his condition." She paused. "I need to get busy upstairs, but..." and she sat down. "When we have a good time together, I feel—I know this sounds silly, but I feel tall. But when we don't understand what the other one means and he starts losing it, I feel like—" groping for words—"this," and she held up an old, shapeless rubber band lying on the table.

"Ha, I get it," Wayne chuckled. "Jakob stretches you.

Yeah, he's high maintenance, all right."

Jessie nodded. "Well, that's enough about that right now. I'm going to clean."

On weekends she saw Jakob and Fiona, not at the same time. The baby was the easier of the two, toddling along chubbily, usually happy and funny and pretty easy to handle when she fussed. Food, sleep, diaper change, playing, cuddling and soothing. *It's getting easier—and more fun. I wonder, did my mother ever rock me, feel my tiny toes, smooth my cheeks? I don't know. I doubt it.* Her gratitude for learning how to mother and the joy it brought absorbed her yearnings for what she never had.

On Friday, the day before Fiona's party, Jessie sat at the kitchen table sorting a box of winter wear from the front closet while Wayne put groceries away. *Roderick telling me he trusts my judgment on what to get rid of sure makes things easier. Wow, we have come a long way. But I'd better check with him on this crazy hat; might be something special.*

"Do you have any weekend plans, Miss Jessica?" Wayne inquired.

337

"Jakob and Kelly are coming over for pizza tonight. Jakob wants to teach us a game on his computer, but Kelly wants to play Dominoes, real ones. They're already arguing over that. Then tomorrow..." She paused to focus on where to put a pair of gloves. "I don't know about tomorrow. Doug—that's my ex-husband—is having a birthday party for Fiona—that's my little girl, she's turning one and—um—I'm having a hard time deciding to go or not."

"Who will be there?"

"Alicia, his girlfriend and Lucas, her son, and his parents, the grandparents."

"Ah. You'd be a party of one. Might feel a little awkward, huh?"

"As usual."

"Well, here's my sage advice, whether you want it or not: do whatever you want to. Either way is fine."

That wasn't much help. I don't want to go, and I don't want to miss it. Like life. That thought made her smile, and she decided. *I'll go. For Fiona. For myself.*

———

She climbed the steps to Doug's apartment hating the knots and rumblings in her stomach but had no thoughts of turning back. Doug welcomed her into the small living room lined with people gaping at her. Fiona squealed and slid off her grandfather's lap, scrambling over to Jessie on all fours. She was happily amazed but felt too awkward to lean over and pick her up, so the baby held on to her knees, reaching up and starting to fuss until Doug picked her up and placed her in Jessie's arms. *Oh gosh. Now I'll drop her or something.*

She didn't know what to say to Doug's parents, stammering single syllables in answer to their courteous questions. She wanted to disappear into a crack like a roach when Alicia's whirling dervish of a boy tripped over her feet and fell, going into a sustained scream. The worst moment was when Doug brought the presents out, and she realized she hadn't brought one. *Oh my gosh, I've been so worried about even coming I forgot all about that. I should say, nice and loud, "I forgot, but I'll be getting her something," and then Doug would say, "Don't worry about it."* But she couldn't say anything, haunted by the ghost of mother failure. Fiona ripped the butterfly gift wrap off a little musical, plastic table with cute, age-appropriate activities, instantly pressing and turning the gadgets. Jessie saw the tag: from Daddy and Mommy Alicia

Doug sat Fiona in her high chair and Alicia presented

the cake she had baked: a butterfly decorated with brilliant colored icing. Fiona's mouth made a rosebud and her eyes got so big everyone laughed at her delight. *That's better than my best painting.* When Alicia invited her to cut the cake, Jessie shook her head and tried to smile. And then they let Fiona demolish a cupcake, smearing gold icing all over her face. *How stupid. What a mess. I don't get why everybody thinks it's so funny*

When everything seemed to be over, she didn't know how to leave. She had to pee but couldn't summon the courage to ask where the bathroom was. Her head throbbed. *I've got to get out of here—isn't it over?—when are they going to leave?—maybe they're staying for supper or overnight—I should say goodbye but I don't know how—I'm too tired—would it be okay just to go?*

She was about to get up and walk out somehow or other when the grandparents said they guessed they needed to hit the road. She grabbed her coat as they were putting on theirs and imitated their goodbyes and thank yous. They kissed Fiona and she tried to, but the sticky, weary child pulled away from her, whimpering into her father's neck.

She surged out of the apartment and down the steps and through the outside door like a swimmer breaking the surface of the water for air. Trotting, she was so far down the sidewalk when the grandmother called out asking if she wanted a ride, it was easy to pretend she didn't hear.

Gosh, that was awful—at least I survived my first birthday party—I hope I get home before I wet my pants—it was all worth it for that second when my daughter crawled across the floor and wanted me.

31

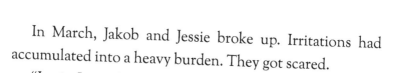

In March, Jakob and Jessie broke up. Irritations had accumulated into a heavy burden. They got scared.

"Jessie, Jessie, Jessica!" Jakob had yelled at her one night, holding his hands over his ears. "Don't say that again. I can't stand hearing you say you're not ready. You're never ready. Not ready to be with my family. Not ready for me to know Fiona. Not ready to introduce me to Tonya. You're not ready for anything."

"You sound like a ten-year-old."

"How would you know? When did you ever know a ten-year-old?" he spewed at her.

"Why?" Kelly demanded when Jessie told her. "I mean it, cousin. You two make a perfect odd couple. Seriously, why?"

"What a silly thing to say, Kelly, that we're perfect for each other. We broke up for obvious reasons. You know how he won't stop talking sometimes. I guess he can't. I guess he feels like he'll blow up if he can't get every thought in his head out. It might be the earth dying that gets him started, or God, or somebody looking at him wrong. And gosh, at those times he's like a puppy that wants to jump all over me and yip and bark. I'm afraid of dogs."

"I'm confused," Jakob told Roderick. "I was trying to be nice when I told her how well I thought she was doing on coming out into the world, how much progress she was making, seizing the day, et cetera, and she says, 'Shut up, please.' And why did she say 'please' when she was mad?"

"Women," Roderick said.

"Last week from the train," Jessie told Tonya, "he saw somebody throw trash out of their car window and freaked out, giving litter facts the rest of the day."

Jakob complained to Kelly, "This may be inappropriate coming from an atypical, but she can go for hours without talking and doesn't look me in the eyes a lot."

"Well, your eyes are a lot higher than hers," Kelly said.

One time when they were walking, Jessie told Jakob he was reminding her of Doug. "Give me a break, Jessie. When you say that, I think you don't like me and don't trust me. You divorced him, you know."

"Sorry," she tossed over her shoulder, walking a little faster to get away from him, thoughts jumbling in her head. *I should have stopped and looked up at him and said, "I'm sorry, Jakob. You're not like Doug. It's just that I get scared when I think people want me to be somebody I can't." I'll bring it up again and tell him that.* But she never did.

In the turbulence of the relationship, Jakob lost his job.

"For being autistic," he told Jessica.

"No, really," she said. "Why exactly?"

"Okay," he said, shoving his half-eaten lunch aside. "For talking to people at the recycling center too much—offering too much information—giving too much assistance."

Yeah. I remember you coming up behind me and helping shove cardboard through the slot that first time we ever saw each other. That was scary. But I'm not going to say anything about it. Not right now.

"It's all documented. I was transferred twice and had three warnings, and I tried to tighten up each time. I thought I was..." He stopped, staring at the table.

"It infuriates me, Jessie. I have the intelligence and knowledge to be running the place—I'm serious—but because of my..." He spit out the words, rocking a bit. '...pervasive developmental disorder not otherwise specified' I'm getting a negative work history and..." He broke off.

She held her hand out. He took it and said, "I'm tired, I'm sad, I'm worried."

I don't know what to say. I get it so much, how hard it is being out in the world. But he and I are different kinds of different.

"I know how hard it is, Jakob," she said.

But I don't, really. I'm learning so much and getting more comfortable a lot of the time, but it seems like it will always be harder for him. Oh, gosh.

The breakup came in Walgreen's on the first spring-like day, the kind that usually makes people feel in love, with its fresh, warm breeze and dreamy blue sky piled high with puffy clouds. It was over gum.

They'd been to the Clayson House and Museum, Jakob proudly showing her around because he'd been a docent there. *He's overdoing on details. I bet people got bored.*

Then they rode over to the drug store and went their separate ways to shop. Jessie was checking out, reaching down for a couple packs of Eclipse Sugarless when she heard Jakob yell, four people back, "No-o-o. Do-o-on't." She and everyone else turned to look at him, but he had eyes only for her.

"TMJ! Gum deterioration! Possible fish ingestion! Resist temptation, Jessica."

He pushed through people to be at her side, putting his arm across her shoulder and bending over to look in her face.

"Stop," she hissed. "Get away."

That brought him back, and he slunk to the end of the line.

She was three blocks down the street, carrying her purchases and the fancy helmet he'd gotten her—black with fuchsia butterflies—when he caught up.

"I'm sorry," he yelled, riding slowly along on his scooter beside her.

"Don't break up with me, Jessica," he bellowed. "You know I'm troubled, and I'm stressed out, and that helmet cost over two hundred dollars!"

She crashed it onto the pavement with a loud crack.

Roderick topped the stairs to his den and paused in his bedroom doorway. "Weird how we forget how to breathe as we grow up," he said.

Jessie looked up from making his bed. "Huh?"

"My breathing exercises. As I just now practiced, concentrating on inhaling and exhaling the right way, it struck me how there are breathing classes all over the place in modern society to help us cope. In yoga, in spiritual meditation, for PTSD. If you're depressed, if you're angry, if you're worried—learn how to breathe right. We are rats racing around not breathing right."

Oh my gosh, that's so true. I'm short of breath right now, stressed out over Jakob—oh, and forgetting to pay my electric bill—and always worried I might hurt Fiona. I can't even feel where the bottom of my stomach is. This is what high school was like every day—oh, but no point in thinking about that. Silently, she drew in a long, deep breath, Ah-h-h. There's the bottom of my stomach. That feels so good.

She sailed a sheet up in the air, and Roderick caught the opposite corner. "I'll show you how to make a bed like a soldier. Here, watch this—it's a hospital corner. Tuck the bottom of the sheet tight underneath the mattress, no wrinkles, then pull it straight out here at the corner, fold it over to form a forty-five degree angle, bring it straight down, and swoop the whole matter under the mattress, like this, for a square corner. Tighten-smooth, tighten-smooth, that's the process. Now you do this corner."

"That's it," he said as she lifted the mattress for the final tuck.

"That's a great way," she said. "Thanks for teaching me."

They finished quickly, one on one side and one on the other. Roderick took a quarter out of his pocket and threw it in the air. It landed in the middle of the bed and took a good hop. Jessie laughed.

"Tight," he smiled.

They stood there.

She reached down and smoothed a wrinkle where there wasn't one.

They stood there.

Unclench your stomach muscles.

"The house looks good—Jessie."

She looked up at him across the bed and nodded.

"It lists tomorrow, and we're in good shape, thanks to you. You are some kind of cleaning machine." He sat down on the edge of the bed, turned toward her. "We've been through a lot together, haven't we? In a short time."

She nodded again, slipped her sneakers off and settled

on the bed hugging her knees, the way Tonya had done on her couch the other night.

He kept looking at her, and then asked, "Do you feel safe here now?"

"Oh yeah, especially since there aren't any guns or alcohol in the house. And not so many pills. You've gone off some of your pills."

"Right. Wayne helped me clean up and look ahead—Wayne and grace."

"Grace who?"

"Of God. Jakob's good friend. She's helping too."

"Oh. Yeah," Jessie said. *Am I sitting on a bed with Roderick McCoy? Are we talking like normal people? It feels strange. Okay, though. Good. It's good. Take a breath, unclench your stomach muscles.*

"I miss Wayne, that old fool," Roderick said with a grin and slow turn of the head.

"I miss him too," Jessie said.

"I miss Jakob, "Roderick said.

"The old fool," Jessie said.

Roderick laughed, and she smiled.

"Do you think you two are finished for good?"

"I don't know. It's a lot easier without him, but..." She

paused. "But it's harder, too. Getting up in the morning is hard. I feel sad even before I think of him." *It's like sadness is spreading through my body. Hmm, it's like that peach I had, with a spot in it, and it got a little rottener every day until I finally threw it out.*

They sat in silence for a minute.

"Yelling at me in the drug store was the worst."

"Yeah, that was bad. He felt terrible, you know. He came and talked to me wondering what he could do, remember?"

She nodded. "And you told him to lay low. That was good advice, Roderick. I need to be without him right now."

"Timing is everything," Roderick said. "Hold to what you need."

Jessie looked at him, nodded, breathed, and relaxed her stomach muscles again.

She saw him buzz by on Plum Grove one day when she was coming out of the Jewel. Her eyes burned but she walked home trying not to feel, like in the old days. She put the groceries away and got her painting stuff out. She was almost done with The Glowing Night. It wasn't going to be one of her best. Too much patching where teardrops had fallen.

Kelly told her Jakob was praying a lot that they could get back together.

"Him and his prayers," Jessie said.

Starting down the steps to her apartment after an extra-long day of packing at Roderick's, Jessie saw the blue envelope stuck in her storm door. She'd never seen Jakob's handwriting, but she knew it was from him. She walked through the apartment and laid it on the couch, then changed into her pajamas, ate a dish of coleslaw, and drank the last glass of Pinot Grigio from the bottle Tonya had brought. She lay down on her bed and stared at the ceiling, her thoughts racing so fast they were nothing but a blur. After a while she went into the living room and sat down next to the letter. She looked at it and tried to bring Jakob's face into focus. She picked it up. *Jesus, help me with this.* She started to rip it open, but stopped and went to the kitchen and got her paring knife out of the drawer to open it neatly. She went back and sat down and slipped the letter out and held it, smelled it, smoothed it, unfolded it. And she read.

Dear Jessie,
You are the best female friend I've ever had. You have a beautiful soul. You are

honest and keep giving me chances, and if my chances ended in the drug store that horrible day (I HOPE NOT), I understand. I feel like I'm too much and yet not enough for most people, especially women, and boy was I ever too much that day. I'M SORRY.

But back to you. I want to thank you in case we don't get back together (I HOPE WE DO) for being the best girlfriend I've ever had. (I guess you get that joke since you're the only one so far.) You're wonderful at listening and at not judging except when it's helpful. You are laughing more and more, and I love laughing together. And making out, let's not forget about that.

Now here's the hard part. If you don't want to try again, I accept that and bless you on your way. I will not bother you. Just someday—when you're ready— please let me know, one way or the other.

I'm pretty sure I really do love you, Jakob

She sighed and wanted to smile but didn't have the energy. *Okay. Whenever the time is right, I'm ready to let him know.*

And then, early one morning she headed into Zimmer's on her way to Roderick's and saw him, his back, at the cash register. She ducked out, looking for a place to hide, but then changed her mind and swung the door wide open, and there he was.

"Jessie," he said, bouncing a bit. "I wish..."

"Me too," she said.

32

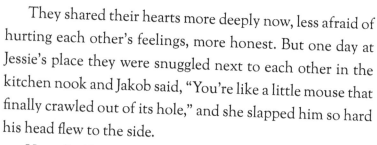

They shared their hearts more deeply now, less afraid of hurting each other's feelings, more honest. But one day at Jessie's place they were snuggled next to each other in the kitchen nook and Jakob said, "You're like a little mouse that finally crawled out of its hole," and she slapped him so hard his head flew to the side.

He pulled her to him. "Good for you, Jessie."

She pushed him away. "Stop saying things like that!"

Jakob rubbed his cheek and said, "But I'm trying to encourage you, and I'm proud of you. Hey, I even let you hit me. I don't get it. I am getting frustrated, Jessica!"

She sat with her arms folded over her chest, looking at him. *He's warning me, I hear it. He's going to blow. But I've got to say everything.*

"I don't want you to be proud of me."

"I don't know what you want! I'm confused," he whined, his pitch going up. "I'm stressing," he let out, and headed for the door.

She watched him disappear, the storm door swishing shut behind him. *I want to let him go, but I don't. I want to cry. I want to yell but don't know what to yell. I feel frozen.* And then she jumped up and raced outside. He was climbing on his scooter.

"Hey!" she yelled, "If we want us to be together, I think you better come back in here."

Hesitation. He looked at the sky.

The beat of her heart hurt. She turned and went back and sat down in the living room chair. *I'll hear him either start his engine or open the back door.* She closed her eyes and tried to catch her breath.

The back door opened.

<hr>

"I don't know why your encouragement makes me mad." *Be careful. Don't mention Doug.* "I think it's because I'm trying to figure out how to be in the world—to be or not—out there—with people so much—doing so much that's new—all these new places."

Jakob started to speak. Jessie put her hand up. He made the zipping-his-lip motion.

She thought some more. "When you think you're encouraging me, you're actually pushing me when I'm still deciding, every day, how much I can handle."

He tried to respond, and she put her hand up again.

"And when you say you're proud of me, it's like you think you own me or like I'm your child." She went and sat on the opposite end of the couch and looked at him, her eyes huge through her lenses. "You can talk now."

"Patronizing. You think I'm patronizing you. I understand that. I'll try not to do it. I'll never say I'm proud of you again, even if I am. I won't let those words come out of my mouth.

"And I'm sorry if I'm pressuring you, Jessie, but I—I wish you could know how wonderful it is for me having a girlfriend—after wanting one for so long—a girl who doesn't think I'm weird and..."

"Oh, I think you're weird."

"I mean you're not afraid of me. You don't make fun of me."

She nodded.

He nodded back.

They breathed a big sigh at the same time.

"Just by having a girlfriend, I'm so much stronger, and I don't think that will ever go away, do you understand? I don't mean any old girlfriend would do. I mean you." He looked down and took a deep breath. "But if I have to do without you, I'll be okay."

"Like you said in the note," she said.

"Yeah."

"I guess I don't want to do without you either, Jakob. It's just that..."

"I know. It won't be easy."

"Yeah."

The silence was alive.

I could sit like this forever. Something good is happening, something I don't understand. And we're not doing it, it's happening to us. It reminds me of my painting of Hansel and Gretel and the angel watching over them. Jakob would think it's God, the Holy Spirit. I don't know, but it's something good and powerful.

Jakob spoke. "Here's one of the worst days in my life, in first grade," he said, like he was giving her a gift. "Mrs. Franconi changed the seats around. She told me ahead of time, talked with my parents, had me stay after school and help her rearrange. But the next morning I stressed out big time anyway and went over by the windows and started flapping and then started clapping." He closed his eyes tight. "After that, these two kids would flap and clap at me every chance they got. I started understanding what was going on, so..." He covered his face with his hands and stammered, "That's how I felt in the drug store after my outburst, like I was back in first grade, flapping and clapping and..." He had to catch his breath. "...and I was so sorry—because I hurt the one I love the best," he whispered.

Jessie moved next to him, grasped his wrists and gently, firmly pulled his hands down. They became lovers.

<hr />

"I see a triceratops—with a baby triceratops—eating a prehistoric tree," Jakob said, languid from the sun and the breeze. He and Jessie lay on their backs on a blanket in the park with Fiona, looking up into the pillowy mountains of clouds rolling by.

"I see—I see—clouds," Jessie said, and Jakob hee-hawed. Fiona joined in the joke, clapping her hands, and they all laughed harder.

Jessie sighed. "I'm going to have to start looking for a job pretty soon."

"The deal went through on Roderick McCoy's house?"

"Yes. Lauren's coming in a couple weeks to help, and then drive to California with him."

"That's good."

Jessie nodded.

"Are you scared to look for a job?"

"Not too," she said. "A little. Okay, yeah. I am. But how you did your job hunt helps me, how you stayed at it, even when it was so hard. And it paid off."

"I'll say. Groot's smart to put me somewhere I can use my brain and make sure they meet all the regulations."

"You should be thankful they're giving you another chance."

"I am—but they're being smart too. Oh, but hey, guess what I heard? The retirement center on Plum Grove is hiring custodians. They have a roach infestation."

Jessie sat up. "Really?"

"Yup," Jakob said, and closed his eyes.

Fiona crawled into her arms, tired as a little squirrel at dusk. Nestling in, she was soon asleep, Jakob too. Jessie lay back and cuddled the toddler to her chest. The clouds had drifted away, and she gazed into the clear blue sky, recognizing contentment and giving thanks. Fiona fussed and Jessie patted her back to sleep, whispering, "I promise you'll have it better than I have, little girl. You already know more than I do about living out in the world, probably. And I promise I'll tell you what happened before you were ever born, so you won't have to spend your whole life wondering." Fiona looked up, gave her mother a sleepy smile, and settled back in.

ACKNOWLEDGEMENTS

Like the writing of any book, or any other creative, artistic project, writing this book took me beyond my gate, and I would not have accomplished it without the support of many people.

Thanks, first of all, to Sara Boggs Rowell, cover design, and Rich Erwin, interior design/formatting. Fortunately, we came out unscathed on the other side of "It can be tricky doing business with friends." Our friendship was only strengthened by working together on *Beyond the Gate*. These two made the production process fun and stress-free. What a gift to employ their talents and attain the look I had in mind.

Next, thanks to my readers. Priscilla Fossum and Judy Aebischer have seen several versions of this book, and I am deeply indebted to them for their patient, thoughtful feedback through all of those manifestations. Additional readers at various stages offered important—even crucial—input, and i appreciate their feedback too, immensely, so thanks to Marilyn Stauffer, Robbie Buller, Sue Byler-Ortman, Pete Dybdahl, Dinah and John Brock, and Diane Tune Smith along with Candy Spasojevich and other sisters and daughters who read the beginning concepts and character formation of Jessie and her story. Their interest and encouragement helped me persist. Sue Byler-Ortman and Marcia Shumate-Schultz's proofreading is highly valued and greatly appreciated as well.

Professional editors Beth Bruno and John Matthew Fox improved the story with their suggestions and advice. Rachelle Gardner, agent with Books & Such, offered advice through an online course and feedback on the manuscript. Her agency's website and blog are excellent resources. Judith Shepard of The Permanent Press energized me with her positive response to the manuscript, describing BTG as "a sweet and unusual love story." At writing conferences, Meg Reid of Hub City Press and Marc Jolley of Mercer University Press critiqued sections with practical suggestions and kind affirmation of the writing.

Fellow writer Bob Rogers, author of *First Dark, A Buffalo Soldier's Story*, generously sat with me in a Charlotte restaurant for a couple hours talking about his experience as an African-American army captain in the Vietnam War, enriching my narrative and enabling me to develop Roderick McCoy more authentically. Jim Dukes, veteran of combat in the Middle East, also shared his most intimate struggles, and his kind input informed the portrayal of the PTSD Roderick faced.

Officers in the Richland County South Carolina Sheriff's Department graciously allowed me to pick their brains regarding ballistics to make the shooting scene and aftermath plausible—if amazing.

I am grateful to the Village of Palatine, established 1866, for their website and E-newsletter which helped me add detail to the setting. I walked around the village feeling like Jessie was at my side as I plotted her tiny world. Nice folks in the Environmental Health Division didn't hang up on me when I said I was gathering information for a novel; this was way back when I thought maybe Jakob was employed by the city as a restaurant inspector. Regarding the role of Fremd High School, I want to emphasize that the portrayal of that fine place, from which several of my dear ones have graduated, is not to characterize the school in a negative way but simply to tell how it was for Jessie. I daresay there are few high schools without troubled kids who bully.

And, again, I acknowledge my sister Robin for her support and encouragement of this book in its earliest stages. As mentioned in the dedication, we shared the wonderful mutuality of writing stories. We went to the Iowa Summer Writing Festival together in 2000, where she was a proud dropout, skipping the Sunday morning session "to get away from the pretentiousness that's getting to my insecurities." Anyway, as Jessie was becoming a person in my mind, I imagined her living in Palatine in Robin's apartment building. Over many years, quite a few family members besides Robin have lived in Palatine and still do. I hope and trust they will appreciate how I've treated their town.

Finally, thank you dear readers of *Sunday by Sunday* and of my blog *Reflections on Any Given Day*, for your interest and comments and compliments and encouragement along this pathway to publication. Many of you have told me how much you enjoyed Rose and her people in *S by S*. Now, I sure hope you enjoy Jessie and her people in *BTG*!

PREQUEL AND SEQUEL

Regarding the prequel and sequel to *Beyond the Gate*

WARNING: This section best read after reading the book—unless you're the type who likes to start with the last page. In other words, this is a spoiler alert.

During the writing of *Beyond the Gate*, a prequel and sequel began developing in my mind. BTG is, of course, Jessie's story. The prequel would be the story of Nan, her mother, and the sequel the story of Fiona, her daughter. I don't ever plan to write them, but, to satisfy my curiosity–and perhaps yours–I'll flesh out some of the thoughts I've had.

PREQUEL: *Nan's Story*

Nancy George died at the age of 59 but meaningful life had ended 20 years earlier when her 16 year old daughter Renee was killed in a motorcycle crash.

- Raven, mother of Nan and Barb—Pueblo, raised in New Mexico, she is obsessed by her indigenous American heritage and enraged to her core by the exploitation of her people. She forces traditions and activism on her daughters to the point of their rejecting the cause and heritage altogether, especially because her priorities resulted in neglecting them on a daily basis
- Gerald, their father—Cheerful and funny, beloved by his daughters despite his struggles with mental illness and long absences from family because of his work as a cultural anthropologist, he disappears altogether when Nan and Barb are 10 and 12. The daughters suspect their mother of killing him, though they don't voice these suspicions to each other until years later when they've estranged themselves from their mother.
- Barbara, sister (Jessie's Aunt Barb)—The sisters were often at odds growing up, largely because their mother pitted them against each other. They reconciled as adults when they wound up both living in Palatine and were close until 1) Barb engages in a special relationship with Nan's

husband claiming it's platonic, 2) Renee dies, 3) Nan's husband deserts her, 4) Barb's husband takes his own life, and 5) Jessie is born. After all that, they are estranged again.

- Bruce, husband— A good-hearted, free-spirited cowboy who met Nan in a Santa Fe diner, married her three weeks later, and pledged to settle into family life. He worked manual jobs, loved reading the encyclopedia, loved his children, and struggled with addictions.

- Tommy, son—Six years older than Renee, Tommy bonded with his father more than he did with Nan and tended to side with Bruce against her. He left Palatine for good upon high school graduation and rarely came back.

- Renee, daughter—She was the bright spot in her mother's life, Nancy's first relationship that seemed healthy and felt good. As she grew up, she served as the antidote to the hurt and confusion Nan had known in relationships thus far.

Renee stretches their bond in her adolescent years, but they are still close. On the day of the fatal accident, they bicker fiercely. They are yelling and slamming doors as

Renee leaves the house and gets on the motorcycle with her boyfriend in defiance of her mother's orders.

Nan's grief is a monster she cannot tame. Bruce leaves for good. Devoutly Roman Catholic, she finds comfort from a priest who finds comfort in her as well, and she becomes pregnant by him. He leaves town, and she gives birth to Jessie, allowing the impression that Bruce is the father. The book ends with Nan, emotionally and spiritually dead, staring at her baby who resembles the short, odd-looking priest she has come to revile.

SEQUEL: *Fiona's Story*

Fiona lives primarily with her father Doug and stepmother Alicia and six step-siblings. The children are homeschooled, but Fiona rebels strongly against this at age 14 and enrolls at Fremd High School, her mother's alma mater, where she's a pop.

She often spends time with her mother Jessie who works at a nursing care center and stepfather Jakob, an official with the Illinois Environmental Protection Agency. She doesn't ever want to go out in public with them, though, embarrassed by their unusual affect, with Jakob neurologically atypical and Jessie socially backwards. Nevertheless, they have good times in the household, including with her mother's cousin Kelly, and she turns to them when she gets pregnant at 18. At this juncture, her maternal grandfather, the priest who fathered Jessie, enters the scene. He becomes part of this family and reveals himself as the friend who had sent Jessie paint-by-number kits through her growing up years.

Fiona becomes especially close to her great grandmother Raven, claiming her own heritage as an indigenous American and joining Raven in her crusade for Native rights and reparations. She and Raven move to New Mexico. After a string of lovers, Fiona marries a distant cousin of the Pueblo tribe. Both sets of parents visit her and her husband and their three children. She and her stepfather Jakob become closely aligned in all-out efforts to save the earth, particularly focused on the drastic effects of climate change on marginalized peoples. Jakob and others try to dissuade Fiona from violent radicalism in the cause, but their efforts are in vain and they cannot save her from herself.

CRISTY FOSSUM moved to Comer, Georgia after a few years living with nearby Jubilee Partners, a Christian service community. In this north Georgia village transformed by refugee/immigrants settling here after being welcomed by Jubilee, she enjoys many friendships, pursues her writing enterprises, and volunteers with El Refugio Ministry in Lumpkin, visiting people who are detained at Stewart Detention Center. Holy Cross Lutheran (ELCA) in Athens is her home church. She travels frequently (did before COVID-19 and will again, someday!) to visit two daughters and their families. She earned a B.S. in English at Wartburg College and the University of Illinois at Chicago and an M.S. in special education at the University of Tennessee. Her main career was serving people with special needs. She also served as Director of Public Relations at Lutheran Theological Southern Seminary. Previous self-publications include a trilogy of church fiction based in the Revised Common Lectionary, *Sunday by Sunday*. More at cristyfossum.com